# RANSOM'S

# REDEMPTION

**by**

**Rhavensfyre**

RANSOM'S REDEMPTION

# ACKNOWLEDGEMENTS

To all of our wonderful readers, of course,
and to our hard-working Beta Readers;
Marion, Myra, Dava, Gail and Tammy.
Thank you for all you do.

# Chapter One

For what seemed like the seventh time that night, Ransom Greathouse asked herself what she was doing hanging out at a dive bar. "Wasting my time away," she muttered under her breath. Her muttering caught the attention of the bartender who headed her way with a lazy smile that seemed to offer more than just a fresh drink. A curt shake of her head dismissed the woman before something embarrassing happened, and Ransom went back to slowly stripping the label off her lukewarm beer and pretending she was enjoying herself.

The smoky bar didn't hold any interest to her, so why was she still there? The answer came easier than she liked, mostly because it was so damn cliché it was painful. She was there because that was what single sailors and soldiers did prior to deployment. They went out to a bar, got drunk, and if they were lucky, picked up a willing partner to spend their last few hours in the States with. Her buddies back at the unit wanted her to go out with them but she had begged out...not wanting to explain that she wasn't really interested in ogling young men in tight jeans at the local cowboy bar.

Instead, she had headed across town to a little bar she had heard about, one better suited to her taste for the ladies and holding a very small likelihood anyone she knew would find her. Despite the fall of don't ask/don't tell, Ransom still wasn't comfortable with the idea of coming out, not with some of the uptight assholes that were still in charge of her reserve unit, and certainly not now while she was trying to transition from enlisted to officer. It was bad timing, being reactivated now. She had just finished her Bachelor's and was waiting for her package to go through, but there was no way she would hear a thing until they were well into their deployment.

Disgusted, Ransom forgot herself and took a sip of warm beer that was flatter than plain water and tasted twice as bad. "Screw it," she said, pushing the bottle away from her. It really wasn't any of their business what she did when she was off duty.

Ransom got tired of staring at her reflection in the mirror and turned around, hooking her elbows on the edge of the bar and leaning back against the hard, round edge. The bar was starting to fill up, with a few women running solo like herself, but there were more couples hiding in the corners or clinging to the few tables surrounding the dimly lit dance floor. Her gaze kept falling on the couples, on the way they touched, the secret smiles lost to subtle kisses and somewhat less subtle caresses no amount of shadows could hide.

"Jesus." She was feeling the lack of companionship more deeply than usual tonight and her melancholy mood was proving hard to shake. She was here all alone, hanging out in a dark corner and nursing a beer she wasn't really interested in, looking at the same old tired Friday night crowd that populated every gay bar in every city that was big enough to have one. Shaking her head at the morose observation, Ransom asked herself if it wouldn't be better to just go home and spend her weekend in quiet solitude before they headed out at the requisite oh-dark-thirty on Monday morning.

She had just peeled herself away from the bar when a slim, slightly older woman walked in, timing her entry with the jingle of Ransom's keys. She was well dressed and had a look about her that told Ransom she had never been in a place like this before. In other words, fresh meat for the local trolls who immediately honed in on the dark haired beauty. The air practically crackled with interest as several heads turned to watch the woman wander farther into the dark interior, shadowed forms stiffening up and standing straighter, reminding Ransom of her father's hounds. Dogs going on point at the scent of something worth chasing.

Ransom changed her mind about leaving. Stuffing her keys back into her jeans pocket, she found herself a small table within view of the unknown woman and settled in to observe. The woman was obviously upset. Unsure of herself in that unique way that people who are uncomfortable with themselves are…a combination of fear and determination that signaled a change happening in their lives. A change that made them realize their skin no longer fit them properly, and they needed to find a way to shed it.

A barmaid cleared the half-empty glasses and empty beer bottles from her table and asked her what she'd like to drink. She couldn't justify sitting at a table without something in front of her so she ordered a cognac and dropped a twenty on her tray.

Ransom took a sip of the hard liquor and grimaced at the unexpected burn. She had forgotten to specify top shelf. Still, the motion gave her the opportunity to continue observing the other woman without being obvious. Ransom wasn't a slave to high fashion, but she wasn't ignorant of it either. Her mother was quite fond of designer things, just like her father was fond of good cognac. *Interesting how much of your parents you bring into adulthood with you,* she thought, then smirked...*and how much you leave behind.* Daddy didn't approve of her choice to join the military, and Mommy hated that she was never going to see her only child produce all those grandbabies she always wanted. Ransom took a bigger sip of her drink, using the hollow burn growing in her gut to exorcise those memories and return her attention to the woman who had changed her mind about leaving.

She oozed with a level of sophistication that only served to highlight how alien her presence was in the seedy bar. It wasn't just her clothes and shoes, it was the elegant way she held her neck and the curve of her spine. Supple, yet hinting at a core of iron that told Ransom the woman was politely used to getting her way. The business chic designer outfit stood out in a sea of denim and flannel like a bit of precious gold pulled from a miner's pan, it drew your eye straight to her. Everything else, everyone else might as well have been dull bits of dirt and grit floating in river muck.

Ransom sucked in her breath, caught by the graceful movements of slender fingers when the woman accepted her drink with a tip of her head, as if she was a queen accepting homage from her subjects. She pulled it off well. That haughty exterior had kept some of the less aggressive patrons from approaching her directly, but Ransom wasn't fooled. She could tell by the small, barely noticeable tremor in her hands and the stiff set to her shoulders that the other woman was scared to death and not willing to give in to her fears. Ransom pinched her lower lip between her fingers, considering what that meant. She looked down at the woman's hands. She was too far away to determine if the telltale indent from a wedding ring marked her bare ring finger or not. Ransom flipped her gaze back up at the woman's face.

So, it was one of two things then, experimenting or discovering.

*Discovering*, Ransom decided, finding none of the false bravado of the casual experimenter. She knew the type too well, straight women who convince themselves that it wasn't cheating if it was with another woman, then use alcohol as an excuse for their bad behavior. In the morning, they would return to their mundane lives with a promise to never drink like that again. Regret could be washed away with a morning chaser and perhaps a trip to the gym to sweat away the desire. A phone call or follow up would be met with dreaded silence and stuttered excuses that only made you feel like a heel and wonder if it wouldn't be better to just become celibate. Ransom made it a rule to avoid those types like the plague.

No, this one wasn't experimenting, but she was using alcohol to find some kind of liquid courage.

Ransom frowned. Despite the short amount of time, the woman had already consumed an impressive amount of alcohol, courtesy of a few of the butchier women who didn't bother hiding their intent. Ransom found her sense of chivalry rising, offended by the obvious predatory nature of some of the women sending those drinks...indelicate souls who trolled the bars for one-night stands, falling into the macho image of the "player" that she abhorred in men or women. When one particularly obnoxious barfly clumped over to the other woman with all the finesse of a bull in a china shop and took the seat across from her without asking, Ransom held her breath. She waited for the woman to give her a glaring send off, but she was too far gone into her liquor by then and the other woman obviously knew it.

Ransom was surprised at the level of outrage that sparked red and hot in her blood when the newcomer attempted to wrap her arm around the inebriated woman and leaned in close, whispering something in her ear that made her blush. The idea of the crass, vulgar barfly taking such an elegant woman home with her for the simple base need of a quick fuck felt so wrong, she couldn't wait any longer. Launching herself from her chair, she walked up to the bar with quick, sure strides and ordered another cognac, then grabbed the bartender's hand before her twenty disappeared.

"Make sure its top shelf this time." The bartender froze for a second, then nodded before heading for the good stuff. "And give me a water with ice," Ransom added, smiling just enough to take the sting out of her order.

Winding her way through the crowd to the dark haired woman's table, she had to suppress a low growl as the slab-sided butch leaned in and tried to kiss the intoxicated woman. Slapping the two glasses down on the small table with a solid thunk, she was rewarded with a beady eyed glare meant to scare her away, much like a vulture hovering over its prey. Well, Ransom wasn't too keen on vultures, so she just stared back, letting her eyes grow cold and hard as stone. It was a look that anyone in her unit knew meant trouble, usually for them, and she had reduced more than one overly large attitude to apologetic compliance with just a look and a word.

"Excuse me," Ransom spoke softly. Her smooth, clear voice could be heard easily above the clattering din of the music playing in the background, "But I believe you are inappropriately handling my date."

The denim and leather clad woman stood, proving herself taller and heavier than Ransom once she reached her full height. Ransom almost laughed at her attempt to loom. Sure she was bigger, but Ransom had a feeling a good chunk of that height difference was the heavy biker boots. Ransom ran slimmer, but due to genetics and a lot of training, she was more the sinewy sort that camouflaged her strength, a fact the other woman might soon find out if she continued her puffed up attitude.

"Is that so?" she asked, her gravelly voice carrying the foul odor of cheap whiskey and even cheaper cigarettes on her breath. Ransom scowled at the combination. There was never an excuse to drink cheap whiskey unless your sole intent was to get pissed...and smell bad to everyone else around you.

"It is," Ransom answered easily. Her disarming smile should have set off alarms in the other woman's head, but Ransom figured it would have to get through the sheer density of the other woman's skull first. Then, she would realize that Ransom, although smaller and lighter, was standing in front of her without a lick of fear in her eyes, her body calm and relaxed...waiting. It was the loose limbed posture of a true hunter, not the pale imitation of bravado that was standing before her.

Ransom had learned a long time ago that how you presented yourself went a long way towards garnering respect from her fellow sailors. If her body and eyes told them she could kick their ass if she chose, then they would believe it. It simplified things greatly, and it didn't hurt that she actually had the training to do what she promised, even if she chose not to. The tableau between them was unusual in its lack of motion, drawing the attention of the other bar patrons. Ransom could feel a collective breath being held, waiting to exhale in anticipation of a fight. The moment passed, and the tension in the room dissipated instantly when the other woman lowered her eyes, acquiescing the win to Ransom before walking away with a huff. Ransom didn't even care that she acted like it was her idea, the pale haired woman staring at her with an amusing "what the hell just happened" look was safe from a pitiful night of grunting and rough handling.

Ransom sat down and slid the ice water over to the other woman.

"Here, drink this. You need to hydrate."

"What is it?"

"Just water," Ransom said, reaching over and moving her drink off to the side. The last thing she needed was more alcohol.

She took the water and sipped it, then her body took over. Within seconds she had consumed the entire glass. "Thank you."

Up close, the woman was even more gorgeous. Even in the dim lighting she could tell that her skin was ivory smooth, begging for her caress. Ransom found herself staring at the soft hair floating around her head like a halo, chocolate brown with red gold highlights that gathered the light and made the smoky room feel like a purposeful backdrop. Dark, almost obsidian, eyes glittered back at her. Sharp, intelligent eyes that, despite shining a little too brightly, held an air of sorrow only time and experience could bring about. That was what she truly found fascinating. The woman seemed so damned interesting, it made her want to know more about her. Why she was here tonight, what made her want to drown her sorrows in bad whisky and worse company, all the questions she would gladly spend hours finding answers to. She raised her glass in salute to the woman sitting across from her and drank in honor to her beauty.

Then she introduced herself.

\*\*\*

Ransom startled awake and almost fell off the couch. She scrubbed her scalp through wildly tangled hair and stretched, taking a moment to reorient herself. She ran her tongue over her teeth and licked her lips, trying to remove the thick layer of fuzz that seemed stuck to the roof of her mouth.

The sound of someone moaning in pain reached her, reminding her of the reason she was sleeping on the couch. Someone else was occupying her bed. Rolling off the couch and gaining vertical status presented itself with its own challenges, she hadn't gotten much sleep last night and her body was complaining about giving up her bed.

"Still better than a cot," she mumbled, rolling her neck until it popped, then stumbled into the kitchen to start up the coffee maker. Another moan brought her attention back to her guest. She would need coffee, too, and Ransom realized she hadn't a clue how she liked it. *Tylenol wouldn't hurt either,* she thought, and detoured for the bathroom.

Before heading back to her hijacked bedroom, Ransom ran some water over the worst of her bedhead and brushed her teeth. *No need to scare the poor woman first thing in the morning.*

"Good morning, Sunshine," Ransom announced, grinning at the woman curled up beneath the covers. "I brought you coffee, I hope black is okay."

That statement brought her visitor up out of the covers, eyes brightening at the mention of caffeine.

Shaking the bottle of Tylenol resulted in a free hand shooting out from under the blankets to accept the offered capsules.

"Thank you," she murmured, sitting up enough to take the pills with a swallow of coffee.

"You're very welcome." Ransom sat down on the edge of the bed. "I didn't know how you liked your coffee."

"It's fine," she said, a slight tremor in her voice. She rubbed her temples for a moment before opening her eyes again. "Um, I...you?"

"Ah, yes." Ransom cleared her throat. She knew that look. "How much of last night do you remember?"

"Not much," the other woman admitted, then looked down at the tangled bed sheets around her, "Did we?"

Ransom shook her head. "No. You were very drunk. I tried to get you home, but you refused and insisted on accompanying me. I put you to bed, and I camped out on the couch."

"Why would you do that?"

"You weren't safe there. I didn't think you wanted to wake up finding out you did something you'd regret." Ransom was not the type to take advantage of a woman too drunk to know what she was doing. "I'm Ransom, by the way."

"Victoria."

"I know," Ransom smirked.

Victoria blushed, pink crawling up her neck and tinting pale cheekbones a lovely rose color. Ransom looked away and coughed. She hadn't meant to embarrass her, not like that. "I'm sorry. That was mean."

"No, I deserve that. I drank way more than I ought to have last night."

Victoria took another sip of her coffee, her expression turning thoughtful. "Ransom? That's an odd name."

*Not what I was expecting,* Ransom thought. "Yeah, my dad was a big fan of old spaghetti westerns. He had his heart set on a boy, and I guess he wasn't willing to give up the name when I showed up instead."

"I think it's a great name. It suits you."

"Thank you. I uh, suspect you'll want to be getting home soon?" She was surprised at how hard it was to ask that.

"Um, could I get a shower first?" Victoria asked, then squeaked when she started to throw off the covers. They went back up, her fists tangled in the sheets and pressed against her throat. Ransom jumped up, a ready apology already on her lips.

"Yeah, sorry about that. You kind of got naked last night until I could convince you that sleep was more important," she informed her, trying to ignore the memory of Victoria's naked body laid out on her bed, inviting her to join her. Victoria's cheeks colored even darker, a bright pink glow against the stark bed sheets.

"Bathroom is over there." Ransom pointed. "I laid out some clothes for you to wear. There is also some new toiletries I keep for visitors. I'll be in the kitchen when you're ready to come out." She retreated from the bedroom, closing the door behind her to give Victoria some privacy.

***

Ransom had a lot to think about while her guest cleaned up. Last night, Victoria had made it clear she was going to go home with someone, anyone...and Ransom couldn't get her to tell her why she was so adamant about it. She also couldn't figure out why the thought of Victoria going home with anyone else was so damn unacceptable. She could have walked out or walked away at any time. She could have put Victoria in a cab and hoped she didn't turn back around and head back to the bar. There was a lot of things she could have done, but didn't, including sleeping with Victoria last night.

Victoria hadn't made it easy for her, either. The minute the door was closed, and they were alone together, she had crawled onto Ransom's lap, demanding a kiss and taking it from her forcefully. Ransom could feel her arousal ignite, hot and pulsing against her stomach, sending her past reason long enough for both of them to lose their clothes, tossed on the floor in a crumpled mess in their rush to discover each other.

"Christ," Ransom whispered, her mouth going dry at just the memory. She pulled out a bottle of water from the fridge and finished half of it before pressing the cold bottle against her forehead.

On Monday, she would leave and do her duty to her country and to the ideas of freedom it held. This weekend she wanted to take everything she could—as eagerly and selfishly as she could. Her body thrummed with that need, demanding her attention and making her weak when she needed to be strong.

She spun on her heel at a small sound behind her. Victoria stood in the doorway of the kitchen. She was wearing Ransom's bathrobe, her face freshly scrubbed and glowing, without a drop of makeup to hide her natural beauty. Her hair was damp, pulled away from her face and revealing high cheekbones that led Ransom's eyes straight towards a pair of plump lips that she swore she could still taste.

"Oh, God, you look so good," Ransom groaned, backing up until her back was pressed against the counter. She understood now why war brought so many people together. The need to connect with another human being, to feel their life pulsing beneath your fingertips, knowing that you have someone safe at home while you head into danger...it was a powerful force that demanded its own sacrifice. Hunger flared inside her, deep and low in her belly, her pulse pounded in response to the intensity of her need and echoed between her thighs.

Victoria walked up to her, slowly bringing her hands up to run tentative fingers through her hair. Ransom closed her eyes, memorizing the feel of it and shivering into the delicate touch.

"Victoria, stop." Regret stabbed through her, gripping her heart in a vice like grip. "I can't."

"Why not?" Victoria asked, nibbling along Ransom's jawline and making it hard for her to think, to remember why this was a bad idea.

"Last night..." she said, the words strangled and hoarse before losing both her voice and her breath when Victoria captured her lip with her teeth. She lost her balance and fell into Ransom's arms, her breasts pressing against Ransom with only the thin fabric of the robe between them. Ransom clenched her teeth together, trying to keep her wits about her, but all she could think about was how easy it would be to untie the belt around Victoria's waist and explore what lay beneath. She took a deep breath and gently grasped Victoria's hands, pulling her arms away from her and giving her some much needed breathing room.

"Wait, wait. Last night...you have to tell me. Why were you so upset?" Ransom asked. That was one of the reasons for her sleepless night. After leaving Victoria alone in her bed, backing away at the last minute before she violated her own rules...she had sat on the couch and listened to the unmistakable sound of a woman crying and trying to hide it.

Victoria gazed up at her with an intensity that made her want to take back her question. Her pupils were blown, a sure sign of her own excitement, and those dark depths glittered with the same hunger and passion riding Ransom's soul. "I have to know, because those tears tell me you might not be ready for this. I don't want to come between anyone."

"You are quite the chivalrous one, aren't you?" Victoria asked, her inviting smile somehow making her all the more a fool for it.

"Yeah, a veritable knight in shining armor," Ransom responded bitterly, almost wishing she was a different sort of person. That person wouldn't be talking right now, they would be heading for the bedroom, with no concern past the need coursing through her body.

"No, there isn't anyone to worry about," Victoria said.

"Then why the tears?" Ransom asked, confusion etching her brow.

"I...It's been so long since I felt anything for anyone. I thought, if I went out, it wouldn't matter who I found...I just needed to feel something. When we kissed, I felt alive again. It was overwhelming. I hadn't even realized what I had been missing, until that moment." Victoria stopped then, shyly looking away from Ransom, "I know that sounds silly, but..."

"No, it doesn't," Ransom answered, she understood that feeling quite well. "Wait a minute. I thought you were too drunk to remember all of that. You practically threatened to go home with anyone if I didn't take you with me."

Victoria laughed then, an almost devious sound if it hadn't been colored by something a bit naughtier. "Ah, as to that. I wasn't quite that drunk, but you seemed to need a little encouragement to take me home. I had noticed you the minute I walked in, trying so hard to not be like the others."

Ransom's shock must have registered on her face, because Victoria laughed again, this time the gentle sound washed over her skin like a caress. "You are such a gentlewoman. I wholeheartedly regret overplaying my hand last night, but it did prove one thing...I didn't choose badly. Besides, I think I like this better. Nothing between us, and no excuses for our behavior." Victoria reached down and undid her robes tie, letting the soft fabric fall open between them.

Ransom swallowed, hard. Her eyes traveled down, taking in the thin vertical line of naked flesh peeking out from beneath the open robe. The slight swell and curve of Victoria's breasts teased her, taking her breath away before even letting her vision slip along the length of flat stomach. "You know, I should be angry," Ransom said.

"Should I apologize?" Victoria asked, stepping away from her and holding out her hand for Ransom to take. The movement left no room for Ransom's imagination, the robe shifting and exposing more of Victoria's body for her inspection. "Or should we make up for lost time?"

Ransom shook her head, it didn't matter. She took Victoria's hand and let her take the lead, returning to the bedroom she had so chivalrously left to her last night. Surprisingly, Victoria's bold behavior ended when they reached the bed. She turned away from her, suddenly shy even though she hadn't given up ownership of Ransom's hand. It was perfect.

Ransom stepped up close behind the shorter woman, nuzzling her lips against Victoria's neckline before reaching up and sliding the robe from her shoulder. Her lips followed the line of exposed skin while her other hand found the soft skin of Victoria's flat stomach. Victoria relaxed into her, leaning back with a soft sigh that encouraged her to find a reason to recreate that delectable sound. Ransom let her hands wander, mapping out the planes and swells of Victoria's body with her fingertips until she reached the curve of her breast. Caressing that uniquely feminine attribute of soft swell against firm body, Ransom moaned in delight. She cupped the slight weight, running the pad of her thumb across the firm nipple.

Victoria cried out when Ransom's circling fingertips found the soft curls resting at the apex of her thighs. The open robe had teased her, offering her just a sliver of a view that made it all the more enticing, but that hadn't prepared her for how it felt to slide her fingers along that soft nest of hair, nor for the rush of arousal that arched her spine when her fingertips grazed along bare lips that had so obviously been freshly shaved.

"Christ, Victoria, that's hot," Ransom moaned, slipping her fingers between silken folds that were already slick and wet in anticipation. Victoria's hips jerked in response to the intimate touch. Ransom held her close, stroking along the wet folds carefully, avoiding the sensitive bundle of nerves as much as possible. Victoria rocked in her arms, swaying in time to her internal orchestra as Ransom played her body. Victoria's clit swelled and hardened beneath her touch, and Ransom found joy in teasing her until she moaned and thrust against her hand. She grasped at Ransom's forearm, digging into her skin with blunt nails as she struggled to stay upright. Ransom's other hand was busy at her breast, pinching and rolling the swollen nipple in time with the firm strokes along Victoria's clit. Ransom pressed her lips along the side of Victoria's neck, sucking at the sensitive skin there before nipping gently. A low keening noise reverberated through Victoria's throat, and she came gasping and shuddering within Ransom's embrace.

"Ransom...Ah, God."

Victoria's gasped words scorched across Ransom's brain, sending her own arousal into overload mode.

"Ransom, please? I need to lie down before I fall."

"Of course, but this has got to go." Ransom slid the robe the rest of the way down her shoulders. Victoria shrugged out of the offending fabric and slid onto the bed, turning on her side and looking up at Ransom. She didn't have to ask, the look on her face told her everything she needed to know. Ransom pulled her shirt up over her head, completely aware that Victoria was watching every move, noting every line and curve on her body as she stripped in front of her. Ransom watched in silence as Victoria's expression changed, the speculative look in her eyes becoming hazy and heavy lidded as her gaze focused on what Ransom was doing. When Ransom ran her fingers along the waist band of her boxers, Victoria wet her lips with her tongue. When she drew the cotton fabric down over her hips, Victoria drew in a deep breath and held it. When she stepped forward, leaving the boxers behind her on the floor, Victoria sat up and met her at the edge of the bed.

Victoria drew her close, pressing full lips against her abdomen before rolling her eyes up along her body until they locked gazes. She ran her hands along Ransom's flanks, massaging along the muscles there until she reached her breasts. Victoria's palms grazed across her nipples and she threw her head back, arching into the overly delicate touch. Ransom shivered when she felt hot breath skim across her skin, close enough to her overheated sex to send tendrils of electricity racing up her spine. She felt muscles clench deep inside her when Victoria suddenly changed ploys, running her nails lightly along the side of her breasts and trailing back down along her stomach and inner thighs. Victoria grinned up at her.

"Got your attention, do I?" Victoria accentuated her question with another swipe along her inner thighs, avoiding the spots that screamed for her touch. She smiled up at her, oh so sweetly, then blew gently across her swollen lips. Ransom had never been so sensitized to needing someone's touch. Just the promise of Victoria's lips and tongue between her thighs was enough to make her want to come. The promise became a reality when she felt Victoria's tongue slip between her lips. She shifted, spreading her legs a bit for balance and in turn, giving Victoria better access to her. She threaded her fingers through the thick brunette hair and lost herself to the feel and sight of Victoria going down on her.

"Christ woman, I'm not going to last like this." Ransom wasn't lying, the familiar tightening prior to release coiled deep within her, keyed to the touch of Victoria's tongue curling along her swollen clit. When Victoria latched onto her clit with her lips, sucking the hard bundle of nerves into her mouth, Ransom cried out at the sudden and intense orgasm that rolled over and through her.

They tumbled onto the bed together, both breathing hard and trying to recover. Ransom moved first, pushing Victoria's legs apart with her thigh while claiming her lips again. She wasn't surprised to find Victoria still ready for her. She ran eager fingers along the slick folds, circling her core gently before stilling her movements.

"I want to...can I?" Hoarse, still breathless from her orgasm a few moments ago, she failed to make any sense.

"Yesss," Victoria growled, bucking her hips against her. She was pulled down for another kiss, surprised at the ferocity of Victoria's tongue as it dueled with her own. Ransom moaned as her fingers slipped deeper inside Victoria's core. She was tight, the slick muscles grasping at her as she pushed in and out, matching her rhythm to Victoria's hips. She was delighted to find out that Victoria wasn't shy about asking for what she wanted, what she needed from a lover. When she asked for more, Ransom gladly obliged her. When she threw her head back and begged for her to go faster and harder, that she was close to coming, Ransom reared back so she could watch her face as ecstasy took her. The webbing on her fingers ached as she matched Victoria stroke for stroke, thrust for thrust, until strong muscles clamped down on her and trapped her there. She stared in awe as the woman in her arms shamelessly rode her orgasm, claiming her right to the wanton abandon Ransom was a witness to.

"You are so beautiful," she whispered, kissing Victoria's brow gently.

The next morning, Ransom rolled over in the bed and stared at the alarm clock sitting on the table. It was already set for 0400 Monday morning. The red lettering stared back at her, daring her to count the time between now and when she would have to leave. It was just before dawn, and that meant she had less than twenty-four hours left. A warm hand stroked along her bicep. Her movement must have awoken Victoria. That she was still here was a source of both happiness and sorrow. They had spent the entire day together, then returned home to continue what they had started that morning. Their passion hadn't subsided after that first encounter, and Ransom found herself at a loss. She hadn't been able to tell Victoria she was leaving on Monday.

"When are you leaving?" Victoria's voice, soft and blurry with sleep, interrupted her thoughts.

"What?" Ransom sat straight up in bed.

"When are you leaving?" Victoria propped herself up on her elbow. She took Ransom's hand and squeezed it. "I saw the sea bags. I know what they mean. I saw it often enough when my father was in the Navy."

"Monday," Ransom answered glumly.

"Well then, we still have today. Let's make it count." Victoria caressed Ransom's jaw, turning her face towards her. "Kiss me. Kiss me until the sun comes up, and only then, maybe...we'll stop and find some breakfast."

Ransom couldn't resist the offer. *Sometimes feeding the body isn't as important as feeding the soul,* she thought, greedily taking every bit of passion Victoria was offering her.

# Chapter Two

*Three years later.*

"Victoria, we need to talk."

Victoria Carrillo looked up to find Samuel Johnson, the practice's owner and her close friend, standing in her doorway. He looked upset and agitated, which was highly unusual for the usually calm and self-controlled older man.

"This can't continue any longer."

"Whatever are you talking about, Samuel?"

"We found these this morning. No delivery notice, nothing to show where they came from, yet here they are. Why didn't you tell me this was still going on?"

A plain manila envelope landed on Victoria's desk with an angry smack, spilling the offending photos out onto her desk. Victoria hesitated before reaching out, rubbing her palms together before spreading the photos out, using a single fingertip to move them about the surface of her desk. Touching the slick surface of the 8 x 10's made her feel dirty, violated by the intrusion into her privacy. She scrubbed her hands again, hard enough to generate heat, but that did nothing to rid herself of the sensation.

"I thought it would stop if I ignored it," Victoria admitted, shaking herself to get rid of the creeping feeling running down her spine. Samuel was right, this was escalating seriously. First it was just the odd phone call that hung up when she answered, and then there were the bouquets of flowers from some unknown "admirer" who left rambling and downright alarming promises on the enclosed card.

The phone rang, interrupting their conversation.

"Hold on, let me get this." Victoria practically lunged for her phone.

"No. We need to talk about this now." Samuel took the phone from her and slammed it back down in its cradle. An irritated frown warned her not to pick the phone back up while he leaned out the office door.

"Bridget, please hold all of Ms. Carrillo's phone calls." The hold light on her phone blinked out a second later.

"This whole thing is getting out of hand," Victoria grumbled under her breath, clenching her hands hard enough to leave marks on her palms. This asshole would not keep her from seeing her clients.

"I couldn't agree with you more, Victoria." Samuel stepped back into Victoria's office, closing the door behind him before sitting down. "The question is, what do we do about it?"

Samuel spread the photos out, forcing her to look at them again. This new development was more than disturbing, photographs sent to her with no explanation, just a plain manila envelope sent to her home, and now to her office. For all intents and purposes, the photo's themselves were innocuous. They reminded her of surveillance shots, the kind you would get from a PI. There was only one problem. She was the sole subject of the black and white glossies. The photographer, whoever he was, had captured her leaving her house, going shopping, and even coming out of the gym.

She stopped at one particular shot and inhaled sharply. A spike of fear ran through her as she realized that not only did this person know where she lived and worked, but they also had an overly familiar knowledge of her routines and driving patterns. She was in her running gear, jogging along the trail that cut through the wooded park near her house. It was a secluded area, and the route was one she enjoyed because it was green and quiet and not filled with dozens of women pushing their strollers along with total disregard for anyone else. The spot was secluded and far from any parking areas. Whoever took the shot had to have hiked it in to catch her there.

Her head shot up at the next one, looking to her friend and colleague for reassurance.

"What the hell, Samuel?" The last shot was from this morning. She was wearing the shoes she had bought just last weekend. This morning was the first time she had laced them on, planning on breaking them in on the longer trail run.

Victoria glanced at her watch. *Four hours.* Only four hours had passed since she ran across that particular bridge before turning around and heading back to her car. Four hours since she had been there, all alone in a secluded wooded area. With her iPhone strapped to her arm, she had been lost in the music and the sound of her heart pounding in her chest. That rapid beat returned, brought on by a surge of fear induced adrenaline that left a bitter metallic taste in her mouth. She had been a victim waiting to happen, and all because she was too stubborn to see how dangerous this game had become. She flopped back in her chair and tilted her head back, both hands pressed against her temples. "Fuck."

"You need to get away from here until we can find this bastard," Samuel said. Now that Victoria was finally taking this situation seriously he felt comfortable pushing his own agenda—keeping her safe.

The woman was so damn stubborn. Her courage was one of the things he admired about her, but this was altogether different. Having a stalker was no joke, and this one was particularly disturbing.

Neither of them knew who her stalker could be, but Victoria had dealt with a lot of bad people in the past. Working inside the system like she had during her time with DSS, she had dealt with people who had no business being parents, who thought it was okay to beat their spouses...or worse, then expect to waltz right back into their family's lives after a stint in prison.

She was too smart, too savvy for the average Joe who thought they could hide their intentions from the woman whose job it was to sign papers advocating for them. Essentially, telling the world that they were now safe and sane enough to be around their loved ones. It was inevitable that she had pissed off more than one chronic abuser when they heard the one word they hated the most. No.

"I have clients, Samuel, I can't just abandon them."

"Exactly. I have to think about our client's safety, too. I'm serious, Victoria. I don't want you coming back in after today."

"What are you saying? You want me to leave the practice?" Victoria started to freak out. What would she do without her work? As sad as it sounded, her job was her life. She loved helping people and Samuel treated her as one of the family. This was home to her.

"No, not that...but I do want you safe," Samuel said, shaking his head at Victoria's assumption.

"This is really unfair. I feel like I've lost control of my life, and now this? The police department is overworked and despite my contacts, the lack of any real threat or suspect makes the prospect of catching this bastard a daunting one at best."

"I know, Victoria. We can only hope that he will tire of this game and simply slink back into whatever slimy wormhole he crawled out of and find another person to terrorize," Samuel spoke earnestly. He felt terrible about the whole thing, but he would feel worse if he woke up one morning to find Victoria's face plastered all over the news, another victim given twenty-four hours of posthumous fame. "That's why you need to disappear. Without a target I'm hoping they'll get bored and give up."

"Where?" Victoria asked, dreading the answer. She knew just as well as Samuel that wherever he was putting her, it could be a while before she returned to work.

"I have just the place in mind. It's the last place anyone will ever think to look."

*** 

*I wonder if she liked my pictures? Ecstatic, lost in her music, her cheeks rosy-red against the cool morning air, a smile on her lips. Now she knows even her morning runs are mine.*

# Chapter Three

First thing the next morning, Samuel was at Victoria's doorstep, waiting for her to come out.

It took two tries on the doorbell before she opened the door. With each passing moment, he started imagining the worst. He gave up the doorbell and started banging on the door.

"Stop, stop. I hear you." Victoria's voice was barely audible through the solid door.

"Jeez, Victoria...you look like shit. I was about to knock down the door."

"That's silly," Victoria said, opening the door wide enough to let him through. A small pile of bags sat in the foyer, waiting to take her on this reluctant journey.

"Coffee?"

"No time. We need to get going and I don't need you worrying about what appliances you didn't turn off. I'll just get these things put in the trunk and we'll head out. It's a bit of a drive and I'd like to beat rush hour traffic." Samuel rushed out with the first load of bags, moving as efficiently as possible while trying not to look as harried as he felt. Victoria had been a pain in the ass all afternoon, fighting him tooth and nail about everything. It eventually came down to you are going or else...and she finally calmed down enough to discuss her clients. They managed to reschedule or move her clients to one or another of the other counselors, and he, himself, took the few that she was particularly concerned about. He was going to be pulling a few long days in order to absorb her clients, but he was happy to do it.

As soon as she was gone, he had a few favors to call in. Someone was going to be very surprised if they showed up at Victoria's house while she was gone.

"If I have to light a match under the entire police department to catch this prick, I will." That vow had barely passed his lips when he felt a strange prickling sensation crawling across his shoulders. He slammed the trunk door and scanned the area.

In the pre-dawn shadows, the place was a ghost town. No one else was up and moving around yet except for a lone jogger heading towards the park, but he dismissed them. Earbuds in and focused on the road ahead of them, they were oblivious to everything else around them. *That would be Victoria on a normal morning, out there running...all alone like that.*

With the photographs from yesterday still fresh in his mind, he narrowed his eyes and scanned the area. Unable to shake the feeling he was being watched, he squinted against the morning glare that turned every single windshield into a multicolor mirror image of the trees lining the cobblestone street. The sun was coming up, and it was time for them to go. After one last long look, he jogged back to the house and went looking for Victoria.

Victoria was still peeved about being woken up so early, and because of that, the first half of the drive was pretty quiet, at least when it came to actual conversation.

That didn't mean she wasn't having one heck of a chat inside her head, one that kept landing back on the same question over and over again until the words finally forced themselves out into the open.

"Is this all really necessary?" Victoria asked, wincing at how peevish she sounded.

She had spent a good part of the evening trying to figure out what to pack, then gave up after a while and found herself a good bottle of wine to ruin. It made sense at the time. She couldn't pack it, it was too good to waste, and she didn't have as much of a problem falling asleep as she thought she would have.

Waking up was a bigger problem. She was hungover and grumpy and ready to balk at Samuel's insistence they leave right away. His only saving grace had been the steaming hot redeye waiting for her in the car, courtesy of Jitterbugs, her favorite coffee shop.

*Another thing I'm going to leave behind,* she thought, *along with a nice house, my clients...my favorite restaurants, oh, and civilization.*

Samuel smiled past his neatly trimmed beard and adjusted the rear-view mirror for the umpteenth time. "Yes."

That was it. Just one curt, tense word. It was too much. Victoria snorted at the overprotective man.

"Really, Samuel. I swear. If we pass a State Trooper we're going to get pulled over for suspicious behavior. I'm getting whiplash from watching you check behind us."

"Just being careful. Don't worry, we're almost there."

"Almost where? You still haven't told me where we're going."

"Right there." Samuel pointed.

Victoria almost missed the sign before they passed it. Even replete as it was with a variety of logo's decorating the wooden sign that announced every socially aware organization operating within the city limits of the quaint little town of Johnsonville, Population, 2,457.

"Christ, Samuel...could you have found anything smaller?"

Visions of anything decent to eat...or drink, or do for that matter, flew out the window along with the hopes of anything resembling real life happening. Boredom loomed high on her new list of activities—unless she wanted to take up knitting.

"Hey, don't knock the place until you try it."

"Easy for you to say, you're not going to be stuck here for God knows how long."

"Actually, I can say. I grew up here."

That was a surprise. Victoria raised an eyebrow at him and smirked. "I didn't know that you came from a little Podunk town."

"Yes, as you so succinctly put it, I grew up in a little Podunk town. Or, to be more exact, a farm just outside of a very small Podunk town." Samuel snorted, laughing at his own joke. The farm was bigger than the town, and it wasn't exactly a farm...it was more like an estate.

"I thought you didn't have any family."

"I do, actually. I just don't talk about them much. My brother took over the family farm when I left for college."

"Is that who you want to send me off to?" Victoria sniffed. She didn't think much of Samuel's plan. What the heck could a country yokel do to protect her? Images of creepy cabins in the woods flashed in her mind, courtesy of too many late nights sitting up and watching cheesy but overly bloody B grade horror movies.

"No. I've got someone there, acting as a caretaker. She's the one I have in mind."

"Where's your brother? Did he finally get disillusioned and leave?" Victoria smirked.

"No, he never left," Samuel paused, swallowing hard against the remembered pain. "It's ironic, you know. He was always such a worrywart. He didn't understand the lure of city life and thought I was mad wanting to leave our little piece of heaven. He was always afraid something would happen to me in the city, what with all the crime and the crazies, as he put it. Sometimes I wonder if he was right, especially when stuff like this happens," he said, tapping the folder full of photographs and other evidence he had brought with him.

"I'm sorry, Samuel. I didn't know," Victoria said, trying very hard not to go into counselor mode. Empathy was a fact of life in her field, so was professional detachment—that Samuel was a friend and a colleague made it harder.

*I thought I knew Samuel, but there's a lot I don't know about his life.* That realization was sobering. She reached out and touched Samuel's hand.

"We're friends, Samuel. You know I'm here if you ever need to talk."

"I could say the same, Victoria," Samuel admonished gently.

Self-care was beaten into them from the get-go. You can't take care of others if you don't take care of yourself. That was rule number one. That she kept this problem from him for so long still made him angry. "Anyway, back to the farm. I obviously can't keep it up, so I hired someone to stay there and make sure no one trespasses or tears up the house. She's an old friend of the family, a veteran—and she owes me a favor. No one will suspect or expect you to go there."

They were almost there. Rubbing his temple with his fingertips, he took a moment to consider what and how much he should tell Victoria. He took a deep breath, choosing his next words wisely, Victoria had to know what she was heading into but she also had to trust his judgment in sending her away.

"Before we arrive, I think I need to warn you. Lynn isn't the easiest person to get along with. Her last deployment was rough; some things went down that she still doesn't talk about. I know she was injured along with a couple of her buddies and it hit her hard. She got out of the service after that and moved back to the farm. It's quiet there, and she needed some time to get over her injuries."

"Are you telling me she's broken?" Victoria asked. "What are you sending me into, Samuel? How well do you even know this woman?"

"I know her. She used to work for me, for one...but more importantly, she's from Johnsonville. I've known Lynn her entire life, watched her grow up even." Samuel pulled to a stop and turned, looking directly into Victoria's eyes before continuing. "I know Lynn, Victoria, she's capable and trustworthy, and I know she will protect you."

*She just hasn't been the same since she came back from the war.* Her father hadn't wanted her to enlist, but he couldn't stop her, she was hell bent on making her own way, and that meant having enough money of her own to go to school and real-world experiences to take her away from Johnsonville.

Her decision had horrible consequences. He knew deep down inside that her visible wounds were the least of what she had brought back with her and he had tried to do everything he could to help her. Part of that help was letting her stay at the farm while she healed, but now she insisted on staying isolated up there and he didn't think that was healthy at all.

He was still in the position to hear things, and none of it was good. She made little attempt at staying in touch with her friends or interacting with their hometown community.

The only time anybody saw her was for the occasional supply run into the grocery store or the rare meal at the diner, always alone and always silently unapproachable.

She would eat and leave—that was it.

"But, what am I going to do?" Victoria's thoughts were practically visible. She was used to working sixty hours a week; she would go stir crazy with nothing to occupy her time. Unfortunately for her, this was the last thing that he was worried about right now.

"Stay safe, Victoria. That is all I want or need you to do." Samuel wasn't a stupid man. He knew Victoria too well to think she had given in all the way, not just yet, even if she knew he was right. Despite himself, his gaze kept dropping down to the damning envelope. Those photos represented a real danger that Victoria had to be feeling all the way down to her core. "It won't be for long, I'm sure. The police are involved, and we will get this taken care of. Before you know it, you'll be back to work, I'm sure of it."

"Fine." Victoria sighed. "But I still don't like it."

***

*Where are you Victoria? The front door swung open, and the hooded figure ducked farther into the rapidly shrinking shadows. Anticipation twisted into full blown rage. What's he doing here? Where is he taking her? Samuel Johnson bundled Victoria into his car, then jogged back around to the driver's side. Victoria rolled down her window and said something, a question from the way her voice changed at the end. Samuel's baritone was even more*

36

*muffled, lost in the engines hum before pulling away from the curb. So close. Not close enough to touch, but close enough to catch a whiff of Victoria's perfume on the breeze. Looking left and right, the hooded figure stepped out into the street, raised their head and sniffed the air like a dog trailing a scent.*

# Chapter Four

"Shit."

Samuel's curse brought Victoria's head up instantly.

"What's going on?" She yawned, then sat straight up when she got a look at what was waiting for them outside.

Victoria's jaw dropped. The rental car was blocked by a woman sitting atop an ATV, a rifle tucked into the crook of her arm rather than the flat-black scabbard mounted on the handlebars. She wasn't pointing the gun at them but the threat was fairly obvious.

"Good God, what have you gotten me into?" Victoria couldn't take her eyes off of the woman. Blue jeans, black shirt, a black ball cap and just enough curves to give away her gender. *Definitely a woman,* she thought. *A very pissed off, long legged, blonde haired woman at that, even if I can't see her face.*

"Ah, Yes, I probably should have called and told her to expect us." He shut off the engine and took off his seat belt with slow careful movements. "Don't worry, I'll go out and explain. Stay here."

"But..."

"Don't worry. I forgot to tell her about the rental car, that's all. Just give me a few minutes."

Frustrated, angry, and more than a little disturbed, Victoria stayed put while Samuel did something she thought was incredibly stupid and downright dangerous. Got out of the car.

Samuel stood there for a moment before walking around to the front of the car. The tall blonde watched him for a second, then slid her rifle into the scabbard and dismounted, the movement smooth and quick and ending in a small puff of dust blowing up around a pair of equally dusty boots. They shook hands, and suddenly all of the tension in the air just disappeared. Victoria relaxed perceptively, taking her cue from Samuel.

*This must be Lynn, the woman he was talking about.*

More curious now than scared, Victoria took a closer look at the woman. She had been spot on about the long legs, those blue jeans were almost sinful, the way they hugged her hips. The rest of her wasn't bad either, slim waist, sleekly muscled...she looked like a runner. A simple pony tail pulled her hair away from her face, but that damned hat kept most of her face in shadow.

*Come on, take off the hat, let me see your face.*

Victoria shook her head. What the hell was she doing checking out a perfect stranger? *Scratch that*, she thought to herself, *what was she doing checking out this very dangerous looking stranger? You know, the woman with such a nice tan, long blonde hair, and legs that went on forever? You should be trying to hear what they're saying, not checking out a woman who's probably 15 years your junior.*

\*\*\*

"What the hell, Samuel, are you trying to get shot?" Ransom growled, her upper lip twitching from holding back a smirk. She wasn't really upset. She just couldn't resist, especially since the great and powerful Samuel Johnson still looked green around the gills. He really should have told her he was coming, especially in a car she wouldn't recognize.

"No, Dear. I'm sorry. It was kind of an emergency."

"What kind of emergency?"

"Something you're already familiar with. A woman with a stalker. It's been escalating, enough that I don't feel it's safe for her to stay in the city. I couldn't think of any place better than the farm."

*Of course not, because you knew I wouldn't come to you.* Now she was angry. "I don't like having my hand forced, Samuel."

"Please, just look at these first before you say no. Tell me I'm overreacting and I'll turn right back around and go home." Samuel handed her the envelope.

"Huh." Ransom thumbed through the photos. Her curiosity continued to climb as he continued to explain, her piqued interest competing directly with her intense need for privacy. "What about the police?"

"The police can't really do anything without physical contact and we have no idea who this person is."

"How closely do these photos match her daily routine?"

"Very. The last two showed up yesterday morning, only hours after they were taken, but that's not the worst of it." Samuel glanced over at the car, making sure

Victoria was still in the passenger seat before continuing. "When I showed up this morning to pick her up, I found this on the front porch." He turned his body so no one but Ransom could see what he pulled out of his pocket.

"She didn't see this?" Ransom's expression sharpened.

"No, I didn't want to make the drive down any more uncomfortable than it already was."

She took the rose Samuel was hiding from his passenger and examined it. A single rose so darkly colored it appeared black, the velveteen petals still fresh and not a single blemish anywhere. That wasn't even the most remarkable thing about the gift. Whoever left it had paid special attention to the thorns. They hadn't removed them like lovers often do. They had painstakingly painted the tip of each one with bright red fingernail polish. A half-dozen pricked thorns.

"Christ, Samuel...I can't believe no one's been able to trace this guy."

"You know how it is." Samuel shrugged.

She'd been there before. There was no such thing as pro-active justice. Give the police a bruised and battered body and they were on it in a flash. Trying to keep someone from getting bruised and battered fell under the auspices of potential danger, intangible and full of what if's and when's...not a priority for an overworked and underfunded department struggling to keep up with the ever expanding violence modern society offered.

"Too well." Ransom shuddered delicately. "I take it since you came all the way out here, you want me to watch over her."

"Yes. Just until we can catch this guy," Samuel said. "There's only one problem."

"Oh?" she asked, going on point instantly. Samuel looked guilty about something. He never looked guilty about anything unless he was pulling a swift one, which meant he was about to hand her free tickets to a major shit show and try to convince her it was a chocolate tasting convention.

"Yeah. As in, she doesn't want to be here. She's stubborn as hell and she's not exactly happy with me right now. If I hadn't found these photos, she'd still be ignoring this guy, coming in to work like nothing was happening, putting herself and her clients at risk."

Ransom stilled. He was leaving something out, something important that he was trying to avoid telling her. "Coming in to work? Samuel, who is this woman?"

Samuel hesitated before answering. "Uh, her name is Victoria Carrillo. She's a good friend of mine."

"And?" Ransom wasn't about to let him off that easy. He had more to say.

"And, she's a fellow counselor of mine."

Ransom exploded. "Fuck it all, Sam! Now I know why you came here like this. No phone call, no warning..."

"It's not like that. I promise. Victoria is a friend, she's in danger and I need someone I can trust to keep her safe. I haven't asked you for anything since you came back, but I am asking it now."

"Really, you're going to hold me to this because you gave me a place to stay? That's not like you, Samuel."

Samuel scratched his beard, a nervous habit he had picked up years ago to stall when he didn't know what to say. "You're right. I'm sorry. I shouldn't have said that."

"No, you shouldn't have," Ransom fumed.

"Please, it's just until we can figure out who this creep is." He reached out to touch her arm, just for reassurance, then remembered she didn't like to be touched. *Not since she came back.*

"Fine, I'll watch her. But I mean it, if this is some ploy of yours to bring in some freaking babysitter to watch over me!" The rest of the threat lay between them, unspoken. She would do it for him, but she wasn't happy.

"Understood. Thank you." Samuel exhaled, relieved that the worst was over. She would do this, for him...and that meant a lot. Just then, the car door slammed behind them. Ransom jumped, spinning towards the noise as neatly as a ballet dancer. Her left hand slipped behind her back, then dropped just as quickly, but not before he got a glimpse of flat black.

*Damn, she's fast,* Samuel thought, recognizing the awkward bulge of a concealed handgun tucked into the small of her back. *And still wound way too tight. Am I making a mistake, asking her to do this? I wish she'd accept my help. She still needs counseling no matter how much she denies it. Or at least someone to talk to.*

\*\*\*

Victoria was getting tired of waiting. It was getting stuffy in the car and she hated not knowing what those two were saying. At one point they had both turned and looked at her, then turned away again. The sensation of losing more control of her life grew with every passing minute.

"This is ridiculous," she muttered, resting her fingers on the door handle. She had half a mind to just step out and introduce herself. After all, they were talking about her, shouldn't she be a part of the conversation?

Then the woman, what was her name? Lynn? Threw her hands up and stalked away before turning back on Samuel. She was livid, Victoria could tell by the way she stood, and she was yelling at him.

"...freaking babysitter...!"

That was it, just two words made it to her ears, but it was enough to make her decision for her. She jumped out of the passenger seat and slammed the door behind her.

"Listen here, I don't need to be babysat by anyone!" Victoria spat her words out. It didn't help her anger that the woman, her eyes hidden in shadow by the brim of her hat, stood silently by as she continued her tirade. When she finished, the woman smiled, no smirked, at her with lips that twitched against held back laughter.

She stepped forward and held out her hand politely, pulling off her cap with a flourish. "It's nice to meet you, Victoria. I'm..."

"Ransom?" Until she took off the hat, Victoria hadn't recognized her but now? Same sandy-blonde hair, a little lighter now and much longer than the short military cut she remembered, but that smile? The last time she had seen that smile was over three years ago, and it was still as fresh in her mind today as it was the day they met.

"What?" Ransom physically stepped back and Samuel was quick to fill the space between them. Too quick.

"Victoria, this is Lynn, the one I told you about." Keeping one eye on Ransom, he frantically searched his memories. Did he slip up and mention Ransom's name at some point? He couldn't remember.

"Dammit, Samuel...that's not part of the agreement and you know it. Why did you give her my real name? Because she's a colleague?"

"No, I didn't, you've got to believe me."

Stunned and more than a little confused, Victoria stood speechless while they argued. It was Ransom, the woman had confirmed it herself...so why was she acting like she didn't know her?

Ransom hopped back on her ATV. "Somehow I'm not quite believing that, Samuel, but we made an agreement." She kicked the ATV alive and cast an angry glance in Victoria's direction. "I'll see you up at the house, but don't worry. I can assure you that I am not YOUR babysitter."

***

*Where the hell is she? She should have been back home by now.*

*I will wait for a little longer.*

# Chapter Five

"What just happened?" Victoria asked, still shaken after seeing Ransom.

"I was just going to ask you that same question. I know I didn't tell you her name." Samuel opened the passenger door and gestured for her to get in. If he knew Ransom, she'd be waiting for them at the main house. Taking their time would give her a cooling off period.

"Why would that matter?"

"Ah. That's a long story. I'm more interested in how you know Ransom by name."

"You first, Samuel."

"Okay." Samuel started the rental car and turned on the A/C before turning to face Victoria. "You know I take special cases at times, people who might otherwise get lost in the cracks?"

"Yes. It's how we met."

"Then you know that some of the cases I take are not pretty, especially ones involving DSS or the justice system. It's not unusual for a soon to be ex-spouse to go a smidge too far when it comes to keeping their family. Sometimes a heavy hand turns homicidal when they lose control of their tiny little world. That's where Lynn...ah, Ransom came in handy. She made sure at risk clients were safe so they could make it to court without getting the snot beat out of them, or worse, disappearing altogether. As a female, she was safe, unassuming in appearance but utterly effective if it came to hands on protection." Samuel's smile held a touch of sadness. "I could never fathom how some people think a wedding ring gives you the right to do anything you want to someone else. But as to the name? Ransom is unusual enough to be remembered. It was safer for everyone involved if she wasn't noticed so she made it a rule to only use her middle name."

"Everything makes a lot more sense to me now. The rental car, the whole secret agent man act, no wonder you seem like an old pro at this."

"Pretty much." Samuel shrugged. It was his way to give back to the community, and it made him feel good doing it. "Hey, what can I say? Maybe if I had been blessed with 20/20 vision I'd be one of those secret agents instead of a lonely counselor."

"Samuel! You're selling yourself short." Victoria chuckled and slapped his shoulder. It felt good to laugh, even if it was at her friend and not with him. "I'm still not happy that you made me leave my cell and computer behind."

"IP addresses can be hacked; phones can be traced. Either can lead the stalker straight to you." He had rented a car, left his own vehicle in a rental lot and bought Victoria a pre-paid cell phone with cash, and then insisted on driving her to the farm. It was the best he could do to prevent someone from following him or tracing Victoria's location. "I think that's enough for now. It's your turn to share. How do you know Ransom?"

"I met her three years ago." Victoria leaned back in her seat and stared up at the car's ceiling. She didn't want to go into the details of how she met Ransom, not with Samuel. It was too personal and special—even after all these years.

"She must have made some impact," he said.

"You could say that. It was right before I joined you at your practice, after that last case," Victoria admitted. *The case that convinced me that I needed to step back and do something else with my life.*

Samuel did the math in his head. Ransom's reserve unit had been activated about that time. He wouldn't see her for over a year after that, and when he found her again...she wasn't the same woman he used to know. "That must have been right before she left. I take it something happened between you two?"

Victoria nodded. The minute she closed her eyes she saw Ransom. Not the hard woman looking at her with the eyes of a stranger she met today, but the intense, vibrant woman wanting to taste everything life had to offer before being shipped off the next day for God knew where. "I don't know if I'm comfortable talking about this with you."

"I won't ask for details." Samuel scratched at his beard, thinking. "But this could be a good thing."

"How? She doesn't look particularly happy that you brought me here." Victoria kept her eyes on the driveway in front of them. Ransom was up there, somewhere, waiting for them to show up and she was sitting here, nursing hurt feelings. *The woman acted like she didn't know me, what's up with that? I thought there was something there, and even if there wasn't...that weekend was pretty memorable. At least to me.*

Samuel chuckled. "Very astute observation, counselor. She's not. I have to assume she didn't know what you did for a living, uh...before, and now? She doesn't trust people like us."

"Like us?"

"Yes, you know. Shrinks...counselor's, to her they are all the same. Trying to fix something she won't admit might be broken. She thinks I brought you out here to 'babysit' her. That's what you heard earlier."

"Why would she need babysitting?"

"She doesn't." Samuel rubbed his forehead. Technically, Ransom wasn't a client. He wouldn't be violating any rules about privileged information, but he doubted Ransom would appreciate the hair splitting. "Maybe this was a mistake. I didn't expect her to react this way to meeting you. Maybe she's right and subconsciously I thought it would be good for her if I sent you her way. Two birds with one stone and all that." Samuel scrubbed his face, trying to wipe away the worry lines creasing his forehead. "She does need someone to talk to about what happened to her while she was deployed. Maybe I'm too close to her. I can't help her. I can't stay impartial."

Samuel took a deep breath and exhaled. "Put your seatbelt on, Victoria. I made a mistake. We'll have to find another way."

He was about to shift the car into reverse and back up when Victoria stopped him. He looked down at her hand, covering his on the shifter, then up at her face.

50

"No, we've come this far. I'm not sure you're entirely right about what's going on but I can say one thing, you're not entirely wrong." She had never seen Samuel this upset before. It was pretty clear that Ransom meant more to him than just an employee. He cared about her, deeply. "You said something happened to her while she was deployed? Do you know what it was?"

"No. She won't talk about it. All I know is she came back with some pretty extensive injuries. By the time I found her, those were pretty much healed, but that's not what I was concerned about. She couldn't sleep, had horrible nightmares almost every night, classic PTSD. I suggested coming out here to get away from the noise, to try and give her a break from the city. I thought that without all the overstimulation, she would be able to relax, and honestly, I was worried about something happening to her. I figured when she was ready, I'd be there for her. I didn't expect a couple of months to turn into a couple of years. She's become quite the recluse."

Victoria listened quietly, adding her own knowledge to what Samuel was telling her. She was in the rare position of glimpsing a before and after snapshot of what war can do to a human being. So was Samuel. No wonder it bothered him so horribly. No one wants to watch a friend fall apart, not when you know there is something terribly wrong and not if you can help them.

"You do know if I agree to stay, we will be doing exactly what she accused you of trying to do? Babysitting the babysitter. She might not appreciate that too much if she finds out," Victoria spoke gently. She had to make sure Samuel knew just how much was at stake here.

"You don't have to be the babysitter. Just let her protect you." He didn't need Victoria to play counselor to have an effect on Ransom. He knew Victoria pretty well, and it wouldn't take her long to get bored out here in such an isolated place. If anyone could convince Ransom to leave the farm for more than an hour every week, it would be her. The two women matched each other well, both were tenacious and more than a little stubborn.

"Oh, Samuel. I wish I could. But, I can't."

"Why not?"

"Because..." Victoria bit her lip against the unexpected pain in her heart. She looked away, knowing that she couldn't hide what she was feeling from him. He would see it in her eyes. "Because, Samuel. I spent an entire weekend with that woman, and yes, it was years ago, but..."

"But?" Samuel asked, automatically responding just like he was supposed to. Repeat, encourage and wait for the person to keep talking.

Victoria almost laughed. She would have done much the same if the tables were turned. "You didn't fail Ransom. You gave her a safe place to hide away while she healed, and that's a good thing. You recognized that she was having problems, and you stayed close enough for her to know she was loved, but you gave her enough space that she didn't feel the need to run away. I don't know what strange fate brought us together all those years ago, only to meet again now...all I know is that the woman up there? She looked directly at me and there wasn't a single ounce of recognition on her face. I thought it was all an act, but now I'm not too sure."

"Tell me what you want to do."

"Take me up to the house, and we'll see how this play's out," Victoria said, ignoring the little voice in her head telling her this was a bad idea.

*Samuel wants to know what I want to do. I honestly don't know. Am I going up there to be what he wants? The counselor in need that has a chance to help someone in pain. Or, am I the foolish woman who needs to know if she's that forgettable?*

***

*Is this where she slept last night?*

*The pillow still carries her imprint, the covers disheveled, hastily thrown into a partial semblance of being made. Being inside her bedroom was so exhilarating. It is almost too much, but it has to be done.*

*Tsk, tsk...so messy. I wonder what she dreamed to toss and turn so. Was she having nightmares of me?*

*The high pitched sound of a car horn soured the sweet taste of forbidden desire with metallic fear and ruined my perfect moment. Assholes. The vulgarity sounded foreign on my tongue, as alien as the fear that leaped into my throat. I need to be beyond fear. It is beneath me, a base metal spoon meant to feed the masses, not me.*

*Still, I've been gone too long. Just do what I'm here to do and go, before someone notices I'm not where I'm supposed to be.*

*It had taken hours to make it just perfect, each thorn painstakingly painted blood red. It belongs here where Victoria rests her head each night.*

*This time she won't miss it. She needs to see my presents to appreciate them.*

# Chapter Six

"Holy cow, Samuel. I thought you said you grew up on a farm. This?" She gestured at the huge colonial dominating the rolling hills around them. "This is a freaking estate."

"Yeah, well. I..." Samuel was saved from explaining about just how extensive the family "farm" was when Ransom popped out of the barn and headed straight for them.

Victoria stilled. The house, the buildings, even Samuel was forgotten while she watched Ransom approach. *What is it about her I can't forget?* Three years was a long time. Maybe she was asking too much of Ransom. Why would she expect her to remember their weekend together just because she did? Every thought she had was suspect, every assumption she made, all because she wanted Ransom to acknowledge her. Why? Because she felt like a fool.

She had sent letters to Ransom, addressed to her unit...trying to keep the connection alive that they had shared for what? One weekend. Ransom had never replied, not once. After a while she stopped writing, but it had never stopped bothering her.

*Oh, hell.* In retrospect she wondered what Ransom actually thought of her. Perhaps the offer to write was just a way to end an awkward moment, and she never expected Victoria to follow through.

"Are you okay?"

Victoria nodded and smiled pleasantly before answering. Her doubts were her own, she wasn't about to share them with the woman responsible for them. "Yes, I'm sorry. I'm just a little overwhelmed by all this. I really had images of a rustic cabin hidden deep in the backwoods."

"Sounds creepy." Ransom's clear green eyes surveyed her with mild interest. The sun seemed to seek out the golden strands of her hair; dust motes dancing in the air around her created a halo effect that almost made her seem angelic looking. The effect was ruined by the woman's stance; she stood in a deceptively relaxed posture that promised the ability to casually move into instant violence. Those eyes never stopped moving, taking in the surrounding landscape before sliding past Victoria again. Ransom made eye contact with her only fleetingly before she scanned their surroundings again.

"I need to do a few things before coming in. It's your place Samuel, would you like to do the honors and show our guest around while I take care of them?" Ransom needed to have one last moment of solace before Victoria invaded her sanctuary completely.

"Actually, I need to head out as soon as possible. With her stalker still at large I need to get the rental car back before nightfall." Samuel smiled not so innocently at the two women before walking back to the car. "Oh, and Victoria? I cancelled your mail already and opened up a P.O. Box. I'll forward your mail to Ransom."

If he didn't leave now and let them work things out, she would figure out a way to delay him. It was better to just cut and run, so to speak, and let them have at it.

Victoria's presence was exactly what Ransom needed to push her back into the land of the living. *I hope.* No one should live with ghosts like that day in and day out, reminding you that you survived when others didn't.

He opened the car door and ducked in before either of them could find something to prevent him from going. "Ladies, stay safe. I will call later."

Samuel turned the rental car around and waved on his way out, leaving the two women, one light and one dark, standing there with identical looks on their faces. He had to chuckle, it was the first time either of them had been left speechless in front of him.

"The bastard," Ransom growled. "Okay, do you want to go into the house or come with me?"

"Can I help with anything?" Victoria asked, trying to be polite.

"I doubt it," Ransom muttered.

"I was just trying to be polite, Ms. Greathouse I didn't ask for this anymore than you did."

"Don't call me that," Ransom snapped.

"So what am I supposed to call you? Lynn? Isn't that what Samuel said you preferred to go by when you're working?" Victoria regretted her snarky response immediately. "Jesus, I'm sorry, that was uncalled for."

"No, you're right, you didn't ask for this. We will have to make the best of this. Just call me Ransom. I'm not big on formalities and you aren't a regular assignment."

She was used to being called Ransom, or Petty Officer Greathouse, or even just Greathouse to her buddies, but she really preferred being just Ransom. It was simple and unassuming; two things she was trying to keep her life right now.

There was something about her voice, a certain unexpressed sadness that held Victoria's next question. *Why wasn't she a regular assignment?*

"Ransom it is then." Almost on a whim, Victoria held out her hand as if greeting her for the first time. "I think we got off to a bad start. Should we try this again?"

"Yes, a fresh start sounds awesome." A genuine smile flashed across Ransom's face, chasing away the shadows and transforming her into something eminently desirable.

That brilliant smile couldn't be denied, or ignored. Somewhere, buried beneath all that bravado and self-enforced isolation was the carefree and spirited Ransom that Victoria remembered.

"Let's get your stuff up to the house, I'll do my rounds after you get settled in," Ransom said, changing the subject abruptly. She stooped down and picked up Victoria's bags and headed for the house.

"Ransom?" Victoria called out. Her feet felt glued to the driveway. Her heart pounded, but still it dared her to ask.

Ransom stopped walking. "Yes?"

The cool, proficient protector was back, Victoria could see it in her eyes. As quick as the moment happened it passed, leaving nothing behind to even indicate it had transpired at all. Victoria took a deep breath and exhaled her impatience. What was she going to do, ask the woman straight on...hey, do you remember that night at the bar?

"Um, nothing. It's not important."

Ransom took Victoria's bags up to the second-floor bedroom that would be hers for the duration of her stay while Victoria stayed below to snoop around in the kitchen. She had been too nervous to eat lunch and now she was starving. She wasn't a big breakfast person, so the last real meal she had eaten was dinner the night before.

"Ransom, you don't have anything to eat." She was appalled at the state of Ransom's kitchen; the empty refrigerator was a vacant wasteland of bright white light illuminating a sad collection of questionable condiments and a jar of jelly. The cabinets weren't any better, a few shelves of canned soup and some peanut butter.

"Yes, I do." Victoria didn't know what was worse that Ransom believed what she just said, or that she was completely unaware of how little she had in the way of food.

"I absolutely refuse to live on peanut butter and jelly sandwiches. We are just going to have to go grocery shopping."

"I'm sorry, what?" Ransom's face slipped into a look of horror as she realized what Victoria was asking her to do.

"You heard me just fine," Victoria said, glancing at the time. "I am quite sure that this small town has a grocery store but I doubt it has any reason to stay open very late. I'd suggest we go now before it gets dark outside."

Taking in the stubborn set of Ransom's jaw, Victoria realized she wasn't going to get what she wanted, not without an argument. That did not sound fun...or productive, not when they were going to be stuck living together for God knew how long. Victoria narrowed her eyes and contemplated her options. Living on canned soup and sandwiches was one option, one she didn't feel like entertaining. *Unless there was another way to convince Ransom to leave her refuge.*

"Unless you want to take me out for dinner?" she asked the one thing she was sure would encourage Ransom to give in to her demand. She asked it sweetly, abandoning her argumentative tone for something less aggressive and much more evocative. Basically tying up her suggestion in a knot she knew Ransom had no intention of unraveling.

*Thank you, Samuel,* she thought, developing a newfound appreciation for good intelligence. Too bad the only other person that could appreciate that talent was the one she was using it on.

"Fine, we'll go. I suggest you make a list...enough to last a week at least or we will be eating soup and sandwiches," Ransom said, pissed that her guest had outmaneuvered her so easily. She would rather brave the grocery store than put up with the sideways glances and attempts at overly friendly and well-meaning conversation she would have to endure at Two Sisters, the only restaurant the town had.

"I'll go get the Jeep."

*** 

*Where is she? How can I keep screwing with her if she isn't here?*

# Chapter Seven

Ransom met the delivery driver at the front gate.

"This is an awful lot of stuff, Ms. Greathouse," the driver said, handing the stack of boxes off to her. "You having problems with poachers again?"

Ransom made a noncommittal noise in her throat, tucked the boxes onto the back of the ATV and strapped them down, expecting the man to leave. No such luck. He was too curious and being rude wasn't going to keep what she was doing unnoticed. *Dammit*, she thought. Small talk was not on her list of things to do today. She closed her eyes and focused on her breathing, then turned and smiled at the nosy delivery man.

"No. Not yet, at least," Ransom said, patting the overly obvious boxes. "These are for the conservation area. I'm trying to get shots of the herd; get a better idea of how many are up there."

"Oh, okay. Well, be safe. I know some folks weren't too happy when y'all made half the mountain a no-hunting zone."

Ransom nodded and kept strapping down her delivery, hoping he would get the hint and leave. *Doesn't he have other deliveries to get to?*

"I don't care much for poachers," she growled. At that point she didn't care if he thought she was being rude. She didn't give a single damn that some of the locals were pissed, hell, she grew up with most of them...so they should know better. It was high summer. There was no excuse to hunt now, not with all the young fawns on the ground. It was also illegal as hell, and she had no sympathy for greedy folk who thought they were above the law. She climbed onto the ATV and let the engine noise do her work for her. She waved goodbye and headed back up the hill, stopping just past the first curve to check behind her. The box van was gone.

Ransom pursed her lips and concentrated on breathing through her nose. Long, slow inhalations that stretched out her lungs as far as they could go, expanding her chest until she was forced to exhale.

As much as she hated these little interactions, the idea of driving to the nearest city for supplies was worse. The guy wasn't trying to be annoying. They probably knew each other from high school or something like that and he was just trying to be friendly. If she tried hard enough, she was sure she could pinpoint where and when.

*That was in another life. Another time.* Opening one door would open the next, and she didn't want to visit the old ghosts living inside those walls. They belonged in the past, and in the past they would stay, no matter how hard they tried to get her attention...and no matter how hard Samuel tried to convince her she would be better off talking about them.

The ATV flushed a small flock of birds away from a shallow ravine just ahead of her and she pulled over. Crows, about a half-dozen of them, bitched at her with their rough voices...upset that she had disturbed their meal.

"Shoo!" She waved her arms at them, sending a few of them up into the trees. A couple of the bolder ones eyeballed her with those bright obsidian eyes. Heavy and awkward on the ground, they hopped from foot to foot and tipped their heads, watching her with open curiosity.

"Don't worry, I don't want to steal your meal," Ransom said, crouching down to get a better look. Just a rabbit, nothing more. She had been worried it was one of her deer. Ransom stood up and brushed off her jeans. "Have at it, boys. It's all yours."

The biggest crow bobbed its head at her, then called to its brethren. Before she even made it back to the ATV, they were back to doing what they did best. *A murder of crows*, she thought, amused at the reverse anthropomorphism. There was nothing malicious or deadly over what they were doing, unlike their human counterparts, who were often malicious and deadly.

Victoria's stalker came to mind. The natural response to such strange behavior was to assign some mental problem to the person involved. Who else but a crazy person would stalk someone so ravenously? *Who else, indeed*, she thought, making a mental note to talk to Victoria about past lovers.

"Heaven has no rage like love to hatred turned, nor hell a fury like a woman scorned." The poet's quote made her smile, she did love her poetry.

Half way back to the ATV she stopped in her tracks, her mind working furiously. Why would she assume Victoria was involved with a woman? Statistically, it was more likely her stalker was a male. Methodical and cruel, their campaign to terrorize included some dangerously escalating features that went beyond an awkward attempt at romance. The threat behind those photos was very real and revealed a mind overly fascinated with Victoria's life, as if they were trying to imbed themselves inside it.

As much as she hated having her sanctuary invaded, she had to admit that Samuel was right to send Victoria away. The stalker was working their way up to something bold. In fact, she was certain that Victoria might have already met the person...a chance meeting perhaps or a seemingly innocuous interaction she wouldn't even remember.

The minute she hit the top of the hill, her phone started beeping at her. "Shit." She'd missed a call from Samuel. No message, of course so she had to call him back.

"What's up, Sam?" The connection was horrible. Samuel's voice kept breaking up and unless she stayed right next to the ATV she could barely hear him at all. *Damn, that's going to make things more difficult.*

"Hold on, Samuel. I can't hear you." She was starting to get frustrated. When he didn't answer she looked at her phone. The red slash and circle flashed at her. No service. *What the hell was wrong with the phone?* She always got bars here, and now the damn thing was dropping calls.

Holding the phone in one hand and driving slowly with the other, she had to travel several hundred feet before the phone clicked back into service, and that was only by switching to roam. A call blew through the instant it beeped back alive and she answered it only to be barraged by a frantic and overreacting Samuel. "I'm fine, Sam. She's fine. I'm having trouble getting reception this morning."

She tucked her cell phone against her shoulder and started unstrapping one of the boxes. The brightly colored box, replete with glossy camouflage and a raccoon with freaky reflector eyes watching her from behind the packing label. This was the reason the delivery man was so damn noisy. Rather than use the requisite plain brown box, the company she ordered from had to use their original packaging. *Last time you get my money*, she vowed. No one needed to know what she was ordering, from whom, or why for that matter.

"You sound grumpy," Samuel noted, his voice carried a hollow, tinny quality to it that made Ransom's ears want to bleed. She flipped him to speaker phone and spun the box around to face her and whipped out her pocket knife. Her knife blade flashed in the sunlight, appearing in a fraction of a second with the merest flick of her left wrist, a magician's flourish she had perfected over the years. Only the crisp snick of the blade locking into place gave away the trick.

"Mm. You think? Your counselor friend has been trying my patience, but don't worry. I haven't locked her in her room yet," Ransom said, "other than that, I'm just bumping up the security here. Is this just a check in call or do you have something new to report?"

Ransom stopped unpacking and started listening. "Holy shit, Samuel."

"That's what I said. I have a PI willing to stay there, but now I'm not so sure. Maybe I should cancel."

"Female?"

"Yeah."

"Hmm. That's your call, Samuel." Ransom thought for a minute before speaking again. "Look, I know this seems bad, but not necessarily."

"They were in her home, Ransom, how can that not be bad?"

"Because they're getting desperate, that means they're more likely to get sloppy and make a mistake. Sloppy gets you caught. What did the cops say?"

"Nothing. There's no sign of forced entry, so they took a report and left it at that. I'm not sure if they believed me or not."

Ransom squeezed her eyes shut and counted to ten, slowly. *Stupid, stupid woman.* Once she got her shit back together she very quietly and calmly gave Samuel a list of things to do, including looking for a key somewhere in the yard. "Look for a rock that doesn't look like a rock, that's the most likely place. Jeez, I can't believe people still buy those things, like it's not super obvious to everyone in the neighborhood what you're doing."

Who picks up a rock before leaving the house, then picks the same one up when you return? That would have to be one of the strangest rituals in the world. That, and who has a rock garden next to their front porch? Nope, one little plastic rock that looked more like a dried dog turd than stone...not obvious at all.

"Will do, is there anything you need from me?" Samuel asked.

"Nope, I'm on it here. Everything is going through the Sanctuary accounts, so expect to see a few odd purchases." If Victoria's stalker was watching Samuel, they shouldn't be able to trace anything back to him personally. "If you have your lady PI stake out the house, make sure she stays out of camera range. As long as our stalker thinks Victoria is still around, they won't be looking for her anywhere else."

*Which means they won't show up here.*

"That is a good thing. I'll talk to her and see what she thinks." Samuel sounded relieved. "I have a client in a few minutes, I need to get back to work. Unless there's something else?"

"No, I'm good. Wait!" She caught him before he hung up. "I was thinking about it this morning. Is there any chance this stalker is an old flame? Someone Victoria was seeing, and it ended badly?"

Ransom could hear Samuel breathing, but he didn't answer right away.

"Samuel?"

"No, Ransom. Not that I know of." He seemed reluctant to talk to her all of a sudden, and that immediately sent alarm bells off in her head. She stopped what she was doing and focused all of her attention on the phone.

"No one at all? No ex-boyfriends, or?" Ransom's heart sped up with the always unexpected rush of adrenaline that heralded an impending panic attack.

"Or?"

Ransom swore she could hear him laughing at her. She could even imagine him shaking his head and leaning forward, resting his elbows on that ridiculous desk of his and fiddling with his favorite pen. Tap, tap, tap...like a woodpecker working its way around an old stump. She wasn't sure if it was a nervous habit or a way to stall while he ticked off points in his head, but right now it was setting her teeth on edge.

"Look, Ransom. The last person I know for sure Victoria was involved with was a couple of years ago, and as far as I know it was just a weekend fling. If you want to know any more, you're going to have to ask her. Our conversations don't usually involve discussing her sex life." The tapping stopped. "I will say one thing. I don't think this is the right avenue to pursue. I'd bet my money on a prior client. It wouldn't be the first time a client became fixated on their therapist."

"I'll keep that in mind." Ransom ground her teeth together. She needed to get off the phone now. The taste of cold iron and fear made her mouth run dry and her legs start to shake. "I gotta go, Sam," she heard herself say, one part of her brain noting how very normal she sounded before the world tilted around her.

"Dammit," she growled, managing to swipe the end call button before going down on her knees. The breeze kicked up around her, teasing her hair and whispering in her ears. Accusations flew, familiar ones that threaded their way through her brain like a hot wire.

"Not my fault, I'm so sorry," she rasped past the sensation of acrid smoke choking her and burning her nostrils. Foul with the scent of burning flesh and red-hot steel, her stomach rebelled, and she gagged, dry heaving until she lost her breakfast.

She pushed, and they shoved, all those memories she didn't want...all those emotions that tasted like bile and burned like Hell, until she finally won and they were safely back behind their locked door. The emptiness that followed was more than the hollow feeling in the pit of her stomach, it was blessed numbness...the divorce of her emotions from the pain of the past.

Slowly, she became more aware of her surroundings. Her fingers ached and her head was pounding. At some point she had leaned against the ATV, pressing her forehead against the back of her hand to relieve the pressure building there. She looked down at her hand. The Glock, black and hard and unforgiving, was locked in a death grip that turned her knuckles white. She didn't even remember drawing it.

She forced her hand open enough to feel the sting of blood rushing back into her digits, then tucked the weapon back into its holster.

"I hope you're happy, Samuel."

***

*She missed her morning jog, and I didn't see her come home last night. I wonder if she is finally learning what it is like to be afraid.*

70

# Chapter Eight

Victoria was two cups into her liquor and pissed in more ways than one.

*Three days!* Three days of boring nothingness that was starting to make her skin crawl and her brain turn to underutilized ooze.

Ransom had been in absentia most of that time, choosing to be locked in her office or doing only God knew what out and about the Johnson Estate. Victoria couldn't call the place a farm, not after walking inside the house and snooping around a bit. The place was almost, not quite, but almost a mansion. It reminded her of the old governor's mansions the south was so fond of.

"Oh, duh. Why didn't I make that connection before?" Victoria muttered. "What other secrets do you have, Samuel freaking Johnson of Johnsonville? Was daddy the town mayor, or maybe it was granddaddy?" The house was old enough for either, or both for that matter.

She took another sip of the fine whiskey Samuel had so kindly left behind, toasted to his lineage before refilling her glass. She waited for the burn to hit her stomach, welcoming anything that would warm her from the inside. *My babysitter certainly wasn't going to do it*, Victoria thought. Ransom's presence had played havoc on her subconscious, taking advantage of what she could only describe as torn desires every time she tried to sleep.

Hence, the liquor cabinet. A poor excuse for drinking too much, but perhaps she could actually make it through the night without waking up hot and bothered, her sheets soaked in sweat and her pulse racing towards a destination that eluded her.

Ransom was very good at playing the cool, collected protector when she had a mind to. And Samuel? He hadn't contacted her either. Irritation at the man had kept her from calling him on the burner phone for an update, but she wasn't sure how much longer she could hold out. She needed to know what was going on. Victoria pinched the bridge of her nose and tried to let the liquor do its job but Samuel's last words of advice about dealing with Ransom kept returning to haunt her.

*She needs somebody out here with her, someone that won't let her bullshit them. I just need you to be here so she has something to do, something else to occupy her mind other than the past. Don't let her bully you, she's isolated herself for a long time so her social graces are lacking a bit, and she can be quite the pain in the ass.*

Well, so far she'd done a smashing job, if alienating, upsetting and generally just being a total bitch qualified as "don't let her bully you."

"What are you doing, Victoria?" she asked herself. Shopping with Ransom had turned out to be a very trying experience. She had never seen someone fidget so much at being in public, and they were only in the store for an hour. Ransom wouldn't meet anyone's eyes, and she seemed tense the entire time they shopped, her full lips pressed into an uninviting and stern line that was reflected in a cold expression that was right at home in the freezer isle. The only contribution Ransom made was to grab an entire case of Red Bull and a handful of energy bars. Not exactly a grade A diet.

On the way back to the jeep, Victoria discovered an unexpected and delightful vision. This tiny little town had a designer clothing store, right next to a lingerie store. Her hunger forgotten, she insisted on going across the street to shop for some decent clothes. Ransom was not happy, but she finally gave in to her demands.

By the time they made it back to the house, the sun was setting and so was Ransom's willingness to entertain her. The minute she was sure Victoria was safely tucked away, she was out the door, mumbling something about rounds and being behind schedule. The sound of the ATV soon faded away, leaving her alone with a pile of grocery bags.

Dinner was out of the question, and after putting away her purchases, she was too tired to even think about cooking.

***

As she stood there, examining the deep tones of the liquor twirling idly in the bottom of her glass and drunkenly contemplating her life, Ransom entered the room.

Victoria turned and leveled a bleary gaze at her over the edge of the crystal snifter. Ransom, in turn, watched her with the same wary expression on her face she'd

73

expect to see when trying to sidle around an angry bull. Cool-green eyes appraised her with all the warmth that chipped ice could muster, then flashed down to the glass in her hand.

"Enjoying yourself?" Ransom's droll question not only rubbed her the wrong way, it smacked of superiority.

"Really? You are actually going to ask me that?" Victoria slammed down her glass, sloshing liquor all over her hand and the serving cabinet. "Dammit all to hell," she cried out, her anger spilling out of her like hot magma and bringing tears to her eyes.

Ransom grabbed a towel and handed it to Victoria, then inspected the bottle she'd been drinking from. From the amount of liquor missing, she'd been busy for quite a while. "Samuel's not going to be happy. That's his favorite brand."

"Fuck Samuel."

Ransom recoiled at the ferocity behind that curse. Red tinged eyes, whether from crying or too much alcohol, locked on hers with all the malevolent intent of the emotionally wounded. She knew that look, having seen it in the mirror all too many times before she realized she was killing herself slowly. She glanced back at the cabinet again. The various bottles there had been old friends of hers at one point, appreciated for their subtle taste as well as their ability to deaden her senses, but it was all a lie. The pain was still there when you woke up, just like the pain was there...as plain as day...in Victoria's face right now.

"Look, Victoria, I don't know what you expected when you came here, but..."

"No! You don't get to make excuses." Victoria raised her voice, gesturing wildly at her with one accusing finger. "I've put up with this for three days and I am done! I've gone along with everything Samuel has asked, abandoning my practice, my home...hell, my whole life! Just because he thinks this, this admirer I have might be dangerous. MIGHT, Ransom."

"I don't think Samuel was wrong, Victoria." Ransom frowned at the inebriated woman. She wasn't making any sense.

Victoria held up three fingers and swayed, a lopsided smile on her face that was more a sneer. "Three fingers, hah...no, that's not right. Three days, Ransom. I've been here all alone while you gallivant around, doing God knows what." The slur was back. She narrowed her eyes into thin slits before spitting out the rest. "If I was in so much danger, Little Miss War Hero, why haven't you been here with me, protecting me from this stalker, instead of outside playing woman of the woods? Hmmm?"

Victoria ran out of steam, and the ability to stand up at the same time. She wobbled and Ransom barely had enough time to grab her before she fell.

"Sit down," she growled, angry beyond belief. Victoria must have gone into her office today.

"You've been snooping around, haven't you?" Ransom asked. She needed to know what else she'd found.

"I needed the key to the liquor cabinet. I couldn't find it in here so I looked in your desk for it." Victoria hunted around on her person for something, then pulled out an ornate, antique key and held it up like a trophy. She saluted Ransom and giggled. "Mission accomplished."

Ransom snatched the key out of her hand and tucked in her pocket. This was getting out of hand. "That's not funny, Victoria. Do you always drink like this when shit gets too hard to deal with?"

Victoria leaned back on the couch and gazed up at her, one eyebrow raised and just the slightest hint of a smile on her face. "Why, of course I do, Ransom dear. But I thought you already knew that."

Ransom took two steps back, her expression turning cold and hard. The mask that Victoria hated with all her heart and soul slipped into place in an instant and took away everything she remembered about Ransom from that night so long ago. Through the haze of alcohol, she wondered how far that mask dug into the woman's psyche. Something ingrained that deep could damage a person, like tree roots wrapped around and through a foundation. Remove one and the other topples over.

"I'll make you some coffee so you can sober up," Ransom spoke coolly. "Then, I'll show you what I've been up to and why it's so important."

Two hours later a very red-faced and embarrassed woman knocked on the doorframe leading into her office. Ransom looked up from her desk, a troubled expression on her face that made her look much, much older than her twenty-eight years.

*So much history in such a young face, so much conflict,* Victoria thought, mentally wincing at her earlier cruelty. She couldn't even imagine some of the things Ransom had seen, let alone experienced herself.

"Hi," Victoria said, ducking her head sheepishly.

"Are you feeling better now?" Ransom asked.

"Except for my pride," Victoria admitted. "I think it's still cowering in the corner of the bathroom."

"Sit down, please." Ransom was glad for the desk between them. This wasn't going to be comfortable for either of them, but the physical barrier would help.

"I feel like I've been called into the principal's office," Victoria said, as she took a seat.

"Hmmpfh. Not quite. But I do need to ask you not to come in here again. Not without me. I don't care about the rest of the house, but this is my office. I'd prefer not to keep the door locked."

"Got it." Victoria tried to smile, but it took too much effort. She was going to have one hell of a hangover in the morning, but right now she was in that uncomfortable middle ground where she was still drunk but the nausea and body aches were starting to make their presence known.

"Are you sure you're okay? You look a little green." Ransom didn't want to go through the entire spiel just to have to repeat everything all over again tomorrow.

"I will be. I need to know what's going on."

Ransom nodded. She could understand that sentiment. There was nothing worse than going into a situation without as much intelligence as possible. That was a surefire way to walk into a shit storm that might get you killed. She also knew that the best way to go in is hard and fast so she brought out the big gun first. Victoria had to understand exactly what she was dealing with.

Keeping things hidden from her wasn't protecting her, it was leaving her uninformed and vulnerable. That was why she pulled out the rose first, placing it on the desk between them without a single word of explanation.

"What's this?" Victoria eyed the black rose suspiciously, swallowing against a sudden surge of fear so strong it made her stomach flip-flop. The black rose, each thorn tipped with the same shade of red lacquer that graced her fingernails, was limp and half dead...the silken petals flattened and dull from lack of water, yet it carried a malevolent aura that made her shudder.

Ransom leaned forward, resting her elbows on the desk and gazing directly into Victoria's eyes. "This is why you should be concerned, and why I've been gone so much. I have security set up all over the property, but I've been upgrading it and rechecking all the entrances. There's over a hundred acres to patrol, and a dozen entry points that could be used by someone determined to get on here. I can't be everywhere at once, so I need mechanical eyes to help me."

"Oh." Victoria leaned back in her chair, not to distance herself from Ransom, but to put as much distance as possible from her and the black rose.

Ransom shook her head and grinned, it was time to drive her point home so she wouldn't have to deal with this ridiculousness again. "So you see, I need you to take all of this quite seriously, as seriously as I am taking it...and I am taking it very seriously. This rose here? It's not the only one Samuel found. Its twin was found the day after you left. On your bed."

"In my house," Victoria whispered.

"Yes," Ransom answered simply. Victoria's response was to turn several shades of sickly green.

"Um, I think I need to go lie down." Victoria's voice was so faint Ransom had to strain to hear her. Blind fingers sought the edge of the desk, relying on the hard edge to pull herself up from the chair.

"Do you need help getting upstairs?" Ransom stood up immediately.

"No, no. I'll be fine." Victoria waved her away. She had a pretty good idea that the next few minutes were going to involve praying to the porcelain goddess, and she didn't want an audience. Her trip upstairs was a trial that required all of her semi-inebriated concentration, by the time she reached the landing she was exhausted. All she wanted to do was find her room and crawl into bed. Being horizontal was so much easier than standing; although she wished the room would stop spinning wildly around her.

Ransom watched Victoria's pinball alley climb up the stairs, hovering close enough to make sure the fool woman didn't kill herself falling backwards until she cleared the last step.

*Samuel would never let me hear the end of it*, she thought, *and I wouldn't be too thrilled either.*

Tired but too wound up to sleep, Ransom returned to her office and plunked back down in her chair. She rubbed her eyes then ran her palm across her face, plucking at her lower lip thoughtfully before surging forward. A plain flat box sat inside the top left drawer right where she had left it two years ago. She hesitated, then snapped it open, exposing the off white silk lining cradling a medal she didn't want and didn't think she deserved.

Medals never told the whole story. They gave pomp and circumstance to acts that ordinary people call brave when all you were trying to do was stay alive and keep the people you cared about in one piece. They fail to remember the ones that didn't make it. It was all about the numbers of saved souls, while the ones who went home in a flag covered casket were conveniently left out of their carefully worded histories.

"Damn it, Victoria." Ransom snapped the case shut and slammed it back into the drawer, then dug deeper, past the two-inch-thick medical folder that detailed her path back to the land of the living and pulled out a small packet of letters.

There were only a dozen of them. Dirty, the edges creased and folded from being crammed inside a sea bag, but they all had two things in common. They were unopened, and they were all sent to her while she was deployed. The nurse at the hospital had been so thrilled to hand them to her, these letters that had chased her through the snail mail system from place to place and never making it in time. By the time they did reach her, all of them rubber banded into one neat bundle, it was too late. She wasn't the same person she had been; those letters were just a reminder of how much she'd changed.

She tapped the letters on the desk, then flipped through them like shuffling a deck of cards. The same name appeared in the upper left hand corner of every envelope, scribbled in the messy scrawl of someone used to typing more than writing.

Victoria Carrillo.

***

*Come out, come out...wherever you are. I see you, Victoria, your shadow behind the bedroom window. I knew you would come back. You can't stay away from your client's for long. They make you feel too important.*

# Chapter Nine

Ransom struggled to wake herself up. Covered in sweat, her throat wrapped around a silent scream so painfully tight she could barely breathe, she fought and lost the battle inside her head. Every breath pulled acrid smoke into her lungs. They burned in memory of the heat and fire that almost consumed her. She blinked away the hot tears streaming down her face, then scrubbed at her eyes, trying to erase the images of torn flesh and hot metal around her but it was no use. She knew what came next. The smell of burning gas, followed by a blast so loud it turned the world around her silent, then the excruciating agony. A dozen pinpoints of white hot pain exploded through her shoulder, rendering her left arm useless. Then sound returned, whooshing back into the world like a whirlwind and carrying with it the terrible screams of the wounded. Hot sand and burning shrapnel licked at her uniform and sliced through her sleeves, leaving a bloody trail behind her as she crawled away from the burning Humvee. The blaze was a beacon of light that was sure to attract attention and make her vulnerable to detection. Her heart beat painfully inside her chest, trying to keep up with the demands of her body.

"No!" she shouted, sitting straight up in bed. She had relived this moment in her life way too many times and it always ended the same way, no surprises, and no straying from the script. Sometimes she was lucky and could pull herself out before the end, like tonight.

"Jesus," she muttered. She hadn't had "The Nightmare" this bad in over a month. She had started to believe that it was fading away on its own, but that hope was shattered when Victoria showed up. *I never wanted to be responsible for anyone ever again. Yet, here I am.*

Ransom threw off her sweat-soaked sheets and crawled out of bed. She had to do something, anything to get the nightmare out of her head. Slipping into a pair of sweatpants and racer back tank top, she padded down to the basement where she had set up a gym. She cranked up the stereo to an appropriate decibel level to drown out the sounds of gunfire bouncing around in her head, then spent a few minutes wrapping her hands. Her shoulder still ached, whether it was from the old injuries or from the nightmare she didn't know, and she had to roll and stretch out the tight tendons and muscles before she could even begin.

It was all a part of the ritual, and she felt the dream fade with each exercise as she started punching and kicking the specialized training dummy she had bought to stay sharp with her martial arts training. She was really getting into the groove of it, her punches and kicks hitting the lifelike target with a steady rhythm as she changed up the combinations instinctively, her eyes focused on some inner vision as she took her pent-up emotions out on the inanimate body.

She spun around, her hands up in a defensive posture when she heard a soft step behind her followed by absolute silence as her music was turned off—not just down but off.

Victoria stood in the doorway, her finger still on the off button, wearing nothing but a very short, silk like pajama set that would have easily gotten Ransom's attention three years ago.

"What the hell Victoria, you have no right!" Ransom yelled. She wasn't really in a very good place right now, and she definitely wasn't in the mood for Victoria's word games.

"Is it really necessary to play it that loud? And at three in the morning? I could hear it all the way up in my room." A wave of nausea hit her, followed by painful throbbing that somehow managed to make her eyes feel like swollen balloons. It hurt. She closed them against the painfully bright fluorescent lights and rubbed her temples. Bright spots danced behind her eyelids, which felt like two pieces of sandpaper rubbing against her corneas. "Ugh, my head. I swear it feels like someone's taking a jackhammer to my sinuses."

"Whose fault is that?" Ransom snarled. Red faced from exertion and covered in sweat, she glared at Victoria with more fury than being interrupted from an impromptu workout session warranted. "I wasn't the one who told you to go hunting for the liquor cabinet key and get hammered."

"No, you didn't," Victoria admitted. "And you have every right to be angry at me."

"Is that an apology?" Ransom's entire demeanor changed. She crossed her arms and stared at Victoria. She didn't blink, or fidget, she just watched and waited.

Victoria swallowed nervously. Never had she met a person, let alone a woman who could pull off such casual potentiality. She had to cast about for the right word, and that was as close as she could get. The potential for action, even violence, while remaining completely still unsettled Victoria. The longer she stood there, arms crossed, legs shoulder width across, hips loose and ready to move in any direction at a moment's notice...the more nervous she became.

"Yes?" Her answer became a question the moment it left her lips. *How did she do that? Make me question myself and my motives with just a question and a look?* Doubt was not something she was used to, and lately there was a lot of it going around. Too much. She dropped her shoulders in defeat.

"You're right. My behavior was inexcusable. I'm sorry."

"No. Never say you're sorry." Ransom dropped her arms and smiled. "You can be a sorry ass, but sorry isn't an apology."

"I'm sorry, now I'm confused." Victoria shook her head, then winced when her brain didn't like being bounced around inside its box like loose change.

"Sorry implies you hurt my feelings, Victoria. An apology is all about accountability. That's what I was taught in the military. No one says they're sorry. You apologize for failing to meet expectations, face the consequences, and move the hell on. From the look on your face, I have a feeling you're already feeling the consequences. I see one hell of a hangover in your future."

"So, what you're trying to tell me is emotions don't matter? I don't believe that. Look at you. It's three in the morning and you're down here beating the hell out of a mannequin. Can you honestly tell me this has nothing to do with what happened between us earlier?" Victoria spoke softly, partially because loud noises were starting to make her want to throw up, even the sound of her own voice, but mostly because it was what she did...ask questions. Even on the cusp of the worst hangover of her life, she couldn't divorce her inner therapist.

"No, I can't, but not for the reasons you think." Ransom looked away. She wasn't about to tell Victoria a nightmare drove her down here. That was none of her business.

"Since you don't know what I think, why don't you let me in on what you know. I can tell that something is bothering you." Victoria found a bench closer to Ransom and sat down. There was something else going on here, something more than her being upset about Victoria drinking too much and making a fool of herself.

"I don't want to talk about it." Ransom closed her eyes, and the nightmare was right there, just waiting for her to return. The inside of her eyelids were an appropriately hellish blood red backdrop for her own personal movie theatre. *They went after one of the transport vehicles first, tossing a backpack into the back of the vehicle before speeding away. The heavy vehicle jumped into the air as the explosion boomed around them, a fireball lighting the darkened sky as Ransom's world slowed down to a crawl. She watched the burning vehicle descend to the ground, it almost seemed to float on the smoke and flames, then reality sped up to painfully pull her into a world of gunfire and insanity. She held someone she cared for in her one good arm and lied to them shamelessly, ignoring her own wounds and struggling to remain conscious so they wouldn't be alone. She smiled up at Ransom, trusting her judgement and content to lie there until help came, but the only thing that happened was death. Ransom watched the light behind her eyes fade, then blink out, bleeding out into the ground around them. Her uniform was soaked with the same damning blood, mixing with hers and staining her camo's a deep, dark crimson red, the true color of hell on earth.* Ransom forced her eyelids open, only to find Victoria right there, watching her closely.

"It's pretty obvious to me that you need to," Victoria spoke softly. The distant look in Ransom's eyes was disturbing. She appeared so far away, like she was watching something behind Victoria that no one else could see. Victoria felt transparent, a ghost in a room full of ghosts that spoke to Ransom louder than she could ever shout. She reached out and caressed Ransom's cheek, just to make sure they were still together on the same plane of existence. "Ransom?"

Ransom blinked. Victoria watched as pain and loss, then conflict and anger shuttered across her eyes. Another blink and there was nothing. In an incredible display of

87

self-control, Ransom clamped down on her emotions until there was nothing left to prove that the last few minutes even happened. She looked at Victoria calmly before speaking again.

"I can't talk about it, not yet, and certainly not with you. I'm sure Samuel's told you why, and if I know him as well as I think I do...he's even given you a few hints on how to deal with me. Filled you in on all the interesting factoids about Ransom's fucked up life, just in case your stay here gives you the opportunity to get through to me." Ransom was on a roll now, throwing punches left and right without worrying about the damage she was inflicting. "I don't need to stroll down memory lane right now. I won't appreciate it if you try to push me, and all you will do is make this more difficult for the both of us."

"I understand," Victoria said. They had a past together. She was too close to her because of it, not because it happened, but because she hadn't let it go. *I still have feelings for her. I can't be her therapist.* It wouldn't be ethical. She swallowed past the pain that came with that realization. "Is there anything else I can do?"

"Right now? You can turn my music back on and give me some space. It's still early. The sun won't be up for a couple of hours. I'll keep the volume down so you can sleep...there's no reason we should both have to be awake."

"I will. But just one thing before I go. I need to know...am I one of those things from your past you don't want to talk about?" Victoria was rewarded with a subtle tell when Ransom inhaled quickly, surprised at the unexpected question. She shook her blonde mane, the sweat dampened hair moving sluggishly against her sharp movement.

"Memories are tricky things, Victoria. Pluck the wrong one out of the past, no matter how pleasant, and the rest come tumbling down with it. I'm not sure I can survive that avalanche."

"That's a terrible burden to bear, Ransom."

"Perhaps, but it's my choice. I can't be who I need to be if you insist on playing therapist with me. I have to be this in order to keep you safe." Ransom tapped her chest, just above her heart.

"And afterwards, when this is all over?"

"When this is all over, you get to go home." Ransom's face reshaped itself into something else altogether, something far beyond grief or regret.

She turned her back on Victoria and tightened her gloves, focusing on the practice dummy in front of her. The bust was realistic enough, down to the heavily muscled torso and square jawed visage of a real opponent, but the human qualities ended there. No matter how hard she struck out, she couldn't break bones or damage organs. There was nothing there. He was as hollow inside as she felt, lacking emotion or desire. Ransom dropped her hands and her head. "Please, just go back up to your room. I'll be up in time for breakfast."

Victoria left Ransom in peace, the stereo thumping in the background at a more reasonable level that became gratefully muffled as she climbed the stairs back to the main house. Her head still throbbed painfully. She sought out a bottle of water and some aspirin before falling back into bed. She could feel the beat of the music through the mattress, but there was no sound accompanying the mild vibration. As she fell into a blissful sleep where her pounding headache could be ignored, she focused her last coherent thought on what Ransom had said, or rather what she didn't say. Home. After traveling halfway across the world and back again, Ransom still hadn't found her way home.

***

*It's not her. Who is that woman in her house, and where is Victoria?*

# Chapter Ten

When Victoria woke up again it was well past 10 am, and despite Ransom's prediction, the sunshine streaming through her window didn't make her want to cringe and crawl under the bed like a vampire. Other than the old shag carpet coating her tongue, she didn't feel nauseated and surprisingly enough, she even felt hungry.

"Wonderful," Victoria murmured. She was in a surprisingly good mood this morning. The promise of a beautiful day and no lingering hangover was a grand combination she couldn't ignore.

She tilted her head back and soaked in the heat radiating through the paned glass window. In the time-honored tradition of making lemonade when life gave you lemons, Victoria decided to make a conscious effort to approach her situation in a different light. If she was going to be stuck here for a while, she might as well enjoy the little things—like sleeping in late and cooking for herself. She didn't have to be the victim, or the helpless maiden waiting for someone else to rescue her. She had resources. There were things she could do to help. With that decision came a renewed sense of purpose that put a bounce in her step. The first thing she needed to do was sit down and talk to Ransom.

After getting a good look at herself in the mirror, she amended her plans. Her hair looked like a small flock of finches had tried to build a nest, and she was still pale enough to warrant makeup today. There were dark puffy circles under her eyes, and her hands shook just the slightest bit. She wasn't about to give Ransom any ammunition to tease her about her little indiscretion last night. Her stomach growled, choosing that moment to complain about being completely empty.

"Breakfast, but only after I make myself presentable," she promised, patting her middle to calm the rumbling. Food would help, so would a cup of strong coffee.

She was halfway to the bathroom door before she snapped her fingers and did a one eighty, bee lining it back to the bedside table to grab the cheap burner phone Samuel had given her. She frowned at the ugly, boxy thing and hesitated before picking it up and stuffing it in her back pocket. It was an ugly reminder of why she was here. She didn't have to like it, she didn't have to look at it, either. The phone had been holding down a piece of paper, plain lined paper torn from some kind of notebook and folded into a neat rectangle. The script inside was equally neat, crisply following the lines with a precision that made her cringe. Her own handwriting was a messy scrawl worthy of any doctor and just as hard to read.

*Victoria,*

*My cell number is programmed into your phone. If you need me, text or call.*

*I have my phone on me.*

*Stay in the immediate area of the house and barn. You know the rest of the rules.*

*Ransom*

Victoria smirked, then crumpled the note into a tiny little ball and tossed it into the trash can. If Ransom hadn't insisted she keep the phone with her at all times she would have missed her note.

It was nice that Ransom was concerned, but she wasn't a child that needed a reminder to stay close to the house. "I hope Ransom knows I have more sense than that," Victoria groused. *Besides, nobody knows where the hell I am.*

Victoria changed into a pair of jeans and a comfortable looking button-down shirt she found in the bottom of her suitcase. She didn't recognize the shirt when she shook it out, so she checked the tags before slipping it on. It was her size, but she didn't remember buying it. *Hmm, not really my style, but comfortable enough*, she thought, smoothing the brushed cotton fabric down her front before shrugging and heading out the door. Samuel had helped her pack, who knew what dark corner of her closet he found the thing in.

A couple of aspirin and a huge glass of water later and Victoria was ready for the day. Someone had put the bacon in the freezer and it needed to thaw out before she could start cooking, so she went looking for her wandering protector, purposefully tagging each building like a baseball player running the bases after hitting a home run. She knew she was just doing it to be rebellious, but it made her feel better. It didn't take her long to realize Ransom was gone, off zipping around the property on her ATV.

"Well, I'm sure she'll be back soon," Victoria said, resorting to chatting with an insistent orange tabby brushing up against her shins. He looked up at her with saucer eyes and meowed pitifully past the worst purr she'd ever heard. It reminded her of a pickup truck her college roommate owned. It was old as hell and between the misfires and rough idle, it sounded like Chitty-Chitty-Bang-Bangs grumpy older brother. "Where did you come from, huh? Are you hungry? Well, me too so why don't we head back in and find something good to eat?"

Victoria didn't have to ask twice. The tabby zipped up to the house with her and slipped inside the door when she opened it, owning the place as cats were prone to do— immediately and with an air of disdain. It was the first time she had seen the cat, but he seemed quite at home in the kitchen, setting up shop on one of the wooden chairs so he could watch her.

"You are one lucky, pussycat," Victoria continued speaking to the cat so she wouldn't have to talk to herself. A quick search of the kitchen and pantry came up empty. No cat food anywhere.

"Huh. Well pussycat, you're out of luck."

*Uh-oh*, she thought, pursing her lips and raising one eyebrow at the feline. Ransom barely fed herself. Why would she think she'd remember to feed a cat?

"You little stinker. Well, I won't punish you for boldness. You get people food today." Victoria grinned. She didn't think the obviously entrepreneurial feline would mind that at all. "You earned your bacon if for no other reason than you're good company."

94

*Speaking of company...I wonder if Ransom ate this morning.* The woman didn't eat enough or often enough, and when she did eat? Cold sandwiches and protein bars would keep the body moving, but that was it. The prospect of living like that made her shudder. Food was meant to be enjoyed, savored, not just be human fuel you put into your tank to keep you running.

Samuel had asked her to take care of Ransom and that's what she would do. She laughed, loud enough to startle the semi-somnolent cat. Samuel had nothing to do with it, she would make breakfast for the both of them because she wanted to. Last night wasn't actually a success for either of them, but Victoria was willing to call it a minor breakthrough. They had managed to talk, actually talk to each other. She felt like some sort of unspoken truce had been called and that was worth celebrating. Cooking a real meal for the both of them was a great way to start.

Victoria didn't want to keep self-analyzing, but her mind rebelled, forcing her to review the last twenty-four hours critically. She had no logical explanation for her behavior, only that she wasn't handling the stalker problem as well as she had hoped. Of course, discovering that the woman who was supposed to protect her was also the same woman she had to admit she still carried a flame for had thrown her way off her game.

She knew what her inner therapist would say, that tiny little voice inside her head that relied on Freud, Jung, Adler and logic. Inner therapist constantly reminded her it wasn't healthy, holding onto somebody like that for so long, especially considering the circumstances. She fought inner therapist for months after Ransom left, but eventually she won out and Victoria was forced to come to the inevitable conclusion. Her feelings were decidedly one sided. She stopped writing Ransom, convincing herself that it was the right thing to do, the healthy thing to do.

She convinced herself that she didn't care anymore because that was the easiest way to throw a Band-Aid on her feelings and move on. *But, I do.* She shied away from continuing that line of thought, at least for now. Now, it was time to make some breakfast and maybe explore the land around her. At least it was something tangible to focus on, rather than the fact that she was in hiding because of a stalker.

"So, call or text?" Suddenly nervous, she looked to the cat for advice. It just blinked at her and went back to sleep. "You're no help. Text it is."

She pulled up Ransom's contact info and sent a quick text about breakfast then stuffed the phone back in her back pocket and went to work.

Taking over Ransom's kitchen was interesting. Most of the stuff was new, or rarely if ever used. She had free rein and set about her kitchen conquest with vigor.

When the phone buzzed against her left butt cheek, she squeaked and jumped so hard she almost burned herself. Her happy morning fizzled as she read the text, a frown forming at Ransom's negative reply.

*Come in for breakfast.* Her fingers flew across the keyboard. There was no way all her effort was going to go to waste. Just in case she shot off a second text. *Come in for breakfast or I will come find you. That's an order!*

*Fine.* Victoria swore she could hear an exasperated sigh tacked to the end of the message.

Ransom had actually been pretty close to the house when the text came through. She hadn't gone far today, just enough to check the fence lines and make sure no one had tramped onto the property in the night. It was her job to protect Victoria, and that's exactly what she would do.

The phone was supposed to be for important communication, not to tell her to come to breakfast. That Victoria felt she could blackmail her into being sociable did not sit well with her. Ransom was not happy about being ordered around.

"Victoria," Ransom greeted her guest coldly. Lack of sleep chafed at her already short temper. She had never made it back to bed; instead she had stayed up till daybreak and then headed out at soon as it was safe to ride the trails.

"Good morning, Ransom. Did you enjoy your ride?" Victoria plastered a smile on her face. That was not the response she was hoping for.

"Yes, it was a nice morning."

"I take it you got my text?" Victoria tried again. Pleasant conversation required two people.

"Obviously since I replied back." Ransom sat down at the kitchen table. Victoria had place settings set up for two, and there was enough food for at least two people heaped onto her plate. Bacon, eggs, and hash browns was the trifecta of breakfast perfection and it all smelled wonderful.

It reminded her of past visits to the Two Sisters, where she was guaranteed as much bad coffee and artery clogging goodness that the cook could whip up. The coffee sucked, but it was hot and enough sugar and creamer could fix even the bitterest Navy coffee.

Then Victoria returned to the table with a plate full of steaming biscuits and Ransom almost moaned in ecstasy. She reached out to grab one and Victoria swatted at her. She missed, of course. Ransom was too quick for her. Her victory was short lived when Victoria surprised her by swiping her plate away as neatly as any waitress, taking her freshly stolen biscuit with it.

"Please, wash your hands first."

"Why?" Ransom looked at her hands, they weren't that dirty.

"It's hygienic and proper."

"You're at the wrong place if you think I worry about proper." Ransom snorted. "But if you tell me those are homemade biscuits I'll wash up without arguing."

"They are." Victoria smiled at Ransom's enthusiasm. Such an old trick, but it seemed to be working.

"Awesome." Ransom stood up, scraping the chair across the floor and using the distraction to snatch a piece of bacon from Victoria's plate, then promptly took a huge bite out of it. "Mine now."

Victoria shook her head. The woman managed to surprise her again. "If cooking for you makes you smile like that; you might have to run a few extra miles every day to burn off the calories."

Whatever possessed her to say that? Victoria watched Ransom stiffen, then turn around slowly from the sink. She spent a few more seconds drying her hands off than Victoria thought was necessary, then inspected her hands before looking up at her.

"I don't know how to respond to that," Ransom stated flatly.

"You don't have to. It's just nice to see you smile." Victoria made sure she kept her tone light and friendly. "I got the impression you don't cook much, and I learned the hard way yesterday that I can't just sit around and do nothing."

Ransom nodded and returned to the table. She still looked a little skittish, but she wasn't running away. In fact, she looked like she was thinking about what Victoria had said.

Ransom cleared her throat. "You have a point. I hadn't thought about it until now." She could understand where Victoria was coming from since she wasn't one for being idle and doing nothing all day herself.

"What are you going to be doing today?" Victoria asked. "Maybe I can tag along?"

"I'll go out and jog the trails again to make sure there are no unexpected tracks or signs of intruders. A neighbor rents some of the acreage to pasture his cattle and I need to make sure they don't damage any of the fences. We can't have them getting into the refuge lands and ruining the ponds there. I do it every day, either on the ATV or running. Sometimes both." Ransom finished with a shrug. That was more explanation than Victoria had gotten since she arrived.

"Can I come with you on one of your runs? It would be nice to see more of the farm."

"Sure, but if you get tired, let me know. It's about a five-mile loop or so for the shorter run. I'll start you on that one," Ransom warned her, wondering how fit she could be living in the city. Some of the photos showed her jogging, but running a flat trail around your neighborhood was way different than hitting a dirt trail wrapped around and up what was essentially a mountaintop.

"I'm sure I can manage," Victoria drawled, secure in her ability. She jogged every other day at home and had run more 10K's than she could count. She had no doubt she could keep up with Ransom. "When do we start?"

"Tomorrow morning." Ransom had to see a man about a new phone and find out why the signal was so crappy lately. "Oh, and one more thing. Try to remember that the phones are for emergencies. I appreciate the breakfast and all, but I'm going to assume something is wrong if I hear from you."

Ransom stood up and took her plate to the sink, leaving Victoria at a loss for words and stuck staring at the wall in front of her. Her initial response was anger, but then she realized something. Ransom was just being practical. If it felt personal, that was her problem, not Ransom's.

"Okay, I won't do it again." Victoria bit her lip. It was going to be interesting, trying to keep tabs on Ransom without the phone, but she would manage. "But, I think if you want to reserve the phone that way, we should make sure we have sit down time every day to discuss things."

"Like a plan of the day?" Ransom asked.

"Sure. That works," Victoria agreed. She couldn't help but feel a bit disappointed. Somewhere along the way their nice meal together had turned into a business meeting. She half expected Ransom to pull out a notepad and start outlining a plan, but something else entirely different happened.

"Uh, Victoria?" Ransom's voice sounded strange. Victoria twisted around in her chair to find Ransom standing next to the sink, staring down at a very bold ginger cat licking the grease out of the frying pan on the stove. "Where'd the cat come from?"

***

*Come out, come out whoever you are. You don't belong in Victoria's house. I need to know who you are and why you are in there instead of Victoria.*

# Chapter Eleven

*Holy smokes! When Ransom said she went out for a run she meant she went out for a RUN.*

It was early, which she was used to, but the trail was hilly...something she wasn't used to, especially with the ego bruising pace Ransom set for them. Five minutes after they took off, even her thoughts sounded out of breath and Victoria started to question her ability to keep up.

This was no casual jog, this was ground eating reconnaissance with a purpose, and Victoria was the slow kid...the green recruit everyone was watching to see if they would make the grade or fall out on the side of the road to heave their guts out. Sheer stubbornness kept her moving. Despite the sharp stitch stabbing just below her ribs, she had to admit the views were perfect...when she wasn't staring at her feet. Between Ransom, the amazingly beautiful landscape and the difficult trail, it was no wonder she was having a hard time concentrating, let alone keeping up.

The thin dirt path ran alongside a long wooden fence and, in Victoria's less than thrilled opinion, barely qualified as a trail. The only distance markers along the winding path were randomly placed tree roots that popped up at the worst moments and delighted in stubbing toes and ruining her perfect one-two rhythm. There were no flat runs on the trail, it was either up or down, and both required more from her leg muscles than she was used to. And while she was used to avoiding the occasional idiot driver, those reflexes were useless to her when a deer jumped in front of their path, then bounded away into the woods.

She screamed and skidded to a dead stop, almost spraining her ankle in the process. Ransom spun around faster than lightning, then broke out laughing. Embarrassed, Victoria could only hope that her face was already so red from exertion that Ransom wouldn't notice any difference.

"That's not funny!" Perhaps Ransom would have taken the heart stopping encounter more seriously if she could actually yell, instead of sounding like a crotchety old man wheezing at his neighbor's bratty children.

Forewarned now, the second deer only received a surprised squeak and the third one she managed to see first. A wolfish grin followed the deer until it disappeared behind a small copse of trees. Evidently it was only fun to play jump-in-front-of-the-city-slicker until she stopped screaming. After that, they ignored her, and she ignored them.

"Ransom, can we slow down? I'm not used to going this fast." Victoria finally broke down and admitted she was hurting.

"Sure," Ransom said, slowing to a walk before realizing she had lost her completely. Victoria was about twenty feet behind her, bent over, clutching her side, and breathing heavily.

"Damn, Victoria, are you okay?" Ransom rushed back to her running companion.

"I'll live." Victoria waved in Ransom's general direction, her open hand a white flag of surrender. She managed to straighten up, her fingers digging into her side to get rid of the stitch. After a few deep breaths, her heart stopped banging so hard against her chest, demanding more oxygen than her lungs could give her. "Not...used...to...the...hills," she rasped.

Ransom frowned, more upset at herself than anything else. She had been in her zone, legs pumping against the familiar burn. The difficult terrain was a welcome challenge, but she had to watch the trail beneath and in front of her while scanning the landscape for anything out of the ordinary. She had assumed that as long as she could hear Victoria moving behind her that she was okay. That was a mistake.

"You should have said something sooner."

"I'm alright, really. I just need to walk for a little bit," Victoria said, trying like hell to not sound like she was totally winded, but she couldn't quite ignore the sharp stabbing pain of the stitch in her side that flared with every breath she took.

"This is a lot different than home." She wasn't just talking about the jogging difficulty, the land was beautiful, so green and lush under the canopy of trees. It was a far cry from the manicured city trails and constant noise. She usually ran with earbuds in, but here there was too much nature to absorb to need the distraction of music. She noticed that Ransom didn't play music during her runs either.

"I'm sure it is. Let's go ahead and start walking back." Ransom flashed a quick look at Victoria before scanning her surroundings again. So far, she had only seen animal tracks mar the surface of the trail, which was normal for this time of year. She usually only discovered the occasional trespasser in the fall and winter when hunting season was in full swing. The locals knew better, but there was always one or two yahoo's who ignored the no trespassing signs to try and hunt on the property.

The forest suddenly opened up into a large pasture that crowned the hilltop they were walking along. The tree line rose along and below the horizon line, creating a leafy green border that stood dark against the bright sunshine lighting the open fields.

"It's beautiful here."

"Yeah, I've always thought so." Ransom smiled. She looked peaceful and relaxed, the light sheen of perspiration the only evidence that she had just ran the last few miles at what Victoria could only call a punishing pace. She didn't look the least bit winded; in fact, she looked like she could go several more miles before even thinking about being tired.

"Are those horses?" Victoria asked. She had seen some cows earlier, but the silhouettes emerging from the pasture in front of them were definitely not cows. As they advanced down the trail, she was able to discern color. There were two horses, one pale and the other dark. They moved in unison, their heads down as they grazed on the lush grass, giving the illusion that a single horse was grazing with its shadow.

"Yeah. We're right on the edge of Samuel's property. Those two belong to the next farm over. Do you want to meet them?"

"Oh, can we?" Ransom abandoned the trail, wading into the tall grass without a moment's hesitation. Victoria was close on her heels. The only horses she ever saw was the occasional mounted patrol, and they weren't big on letting people pet their horses.

"The blond one is Casper and the other one is Mac. Don't tell Casper, but Mac is actually my favorite," Ransom whispered like it might actually hurt the other horse's feelings.

"Okay, it will be our secret," Victoria whispered back, enjoying the playful nature of their conversation. She was thrilled to see Ransom's lighter side make an appearance.

Ransom stopped at the fence and whistled. Still mirroring each other, they lifted their heads in unison and trotted over.

Victoria hesitated until Ransom waved her closer. The two geldings were hanging their heads over the fence, rolling their eyes at each other in jealousy as they tried to keep Ransom's attention all to themselves. "They're amazing."

"They won't hurt you, just pet them like this," she said, showing Victoria how to keep her hand flat and all her fingers out of the way of hungry lips. All of a sudden she was their new best friend and Ransom was out of favor. Casper, the less dominate gelding actually pushed Mac out of the way to get to Victoria.

"Traitor," she muttered, chuckling at the show.

Mac got tired of sharing scratches with his pasture buddy and returned to Ransom with an apologetic snort. "Yeah, now you want me, huh?"

Mac was a laid back boy, but you wouldn't know that just from looking at him. He was very muscular, with the thick neck and heavy mane of a stallion. Not surprising since his owners had kept him as such until he was older. Combine that with the solid black coat and you had a very impressive looking horse that tended to make people nervous, unless you were familiar with him. All he wanted in life was a good scratch and a friendly voice and he was putty in your hands. Mac was so easy, such a pushover really, and he was her favorite.

She looked over at Victoria and found Casper pretty much in the same pose, his pale-cinnamon eyelashes drooping as Victoria found a particularly itchy spot between his ears. It was funny to see the other woman cooing over him, but was delighted that Victoria didn't exhibit any of the fear she had seen in others. Horses were big animals, and it was easy to be intimidated by their sheer size.

"It looks like you made a friend."

"He's beautiful." Victoria lightly stroked Casper's nose, bringing her open palms down in front of his inquisitive nostrils so he could sniff at her, letting him get her scent. "They both are. Do you know how old they are?"

Ransom had to do some quick math.

"Uh, I'd say they're both around eight. I helped Mr. Petersen get them under saddle right before I left for boot camp."

Ransom's face turned pensive; a look Victoria was learning to recognize. It happened whenever Ransom stopped talking but kept thinking.

What happened to make her retreat from society so thoroughly? Victoria knew the only memories you had that woke you up at three in the morning and required you to work out as violently as Ransom had been, were nightmares you couldn't escape or ignore. Victoria's old job had put her in contact with some of the worst cases of abuse and neglect she never wanted to imagine, so she understood nightmares. It was hard not to be affected by the stories, especially when confronted with hard evidence. The casual cruelty that one human being could mete out to another amazed her as much as it repelled her, and that was just everyday life. War was something else altogether.

"Can I ask you a question?" They had been walking in quiet for a few minutes, just enjoying the walk and at least for Victoria, each other's company.

"Have I been able to stop you yet?" The rhetorical question was laced with sarcasm, but Ransom found she was also curious about what Victoria wanted to know. This was a new thing: she really hadn't been curious about anyone or anything in a very long time. It was easier to simply exist day to day without thinking about anything too much.

Victoria had placed demands on her to engage more with the outside world, partially because she had brought the outside world crashing down into her private little refuge, partially because she brought with her forgotten memories. Memories of a happier time that made the months that followed all the more bitter and painful, she amended. She glanced over at the newly familiar face and felt time fold back on itself like a single sheet of paper, hiding all of the text between point A and point B. *If only life was that easy*, she thought, *just folding over the pages of your life you'd like to skim past.*

"Good point. Okay then—and please don't be upset. If you don't want to answer, just tell me to mind my own business."

"Victoria just spit it out. This foreplay is getting tedious."

"Fine, what had you up so early the other morning?" Stunned by Ransom's unusual choice of words, Victoria's well scripted inquiry completely fell apart. Finding Ransom downstairs working herself to exhaustion in the middle of the night still disturbed her. She had promised not to play therapist, but the need to know was still there. *I'm not breaking my promise. I'm asking as a concerned friend. I can still be that.*

"I couldn't sleep."

"I think I figured that part out, unless you were walking, uh...boxing in your sleep." Victoria's droll reply was met by a stony glare.

"I thought we had covered this already," Ransom said, every word bitten off between clenched teeth. "I don't need a therapist."

"I'm asking as a friend, Ransom." Victoria closed her eyes and prayed she wasn't making a mistake, then cleared her throat before glancing up at Ransom's face. She was as still as a stone and looked just as hard, but Victoria convinced herself that she couldn't keep avoiding the past, their past. "Not only a friend, but as someone who knew you before whatever happened to make you like this. I haven't forgotten you, Ransom...and I know that you remember me, too."

Ransom backed up a step, then turned her back on Victoria. It was her own damn fault. She had given Victoria permission to ask her a question, hell, she had practically demanded she just spit out whatever was gnawing at her, she just hadn't expected her to go there. She'd been avoiding the past long before Victoria arrived on her doorstep, living alone and like a hermit for the last two years because that was what she needed. Victoria had a bad habit of waking *things* up in her, things that clamored for her attention and disrupted any sense of peace she had managed to gain.

"Just memories. Memories best forgotten." Ransom chose to answer the least of her questions.

"What type of memories?"

"Bad ones." Ransom's jaw twitched. *The woman was stubborn as hell.* "Let's just drop it, okay? I need to get you back to the house."

Casting one last longing glance down the thin path, Ransom veered left onto a wider path that turned west and back towards the house. The ATV path was less tasking than the deer trail she had chosen this morning. The return trip would be quick, if not necessarily easy. As it was, she was behind on her rounds and would have to make up the lost miles this afternoon on the ATV.

"Sounds fair," Victoria murmured, feeling nothing of the sort. There was nothing fair about it, but Ransom held all the cards.

***

The walk back turned into a second, slower run. This time it wasn't Ransom setting the pace, it was Victoria trying to move past the awkward situation she had created. She accepted the burning lungs, the cramping leg muscles, as penance for trying to push her own agenda.

"I'm going to take a shower."

Victoria sounded defeated, wobbling her way down the hall to her room and closing the door behind her. Ransom followed her slow procession, then ducked into her own room to do the same. She barely made it to the shower when she heard Victoria screaming.

"Ransom!!!?" Victoria's voice, sharp and edged with panic, sent her rushing into the other woman's room, gun drawn and expecting trouble.

"What? What's wrong?" Ransom asked, skidding to a halt just inside the door while simultaneously scanning the room for any signs of danger. *Odd,* she thought, *there's nothing out of place. So what the hell is Victoria screaming for?*

"I have a tick on me," Victoria squealed, practically dancing around the room in nothing but a matching pair of blue silk and lace panties and bra. Perfectly bronzed skin contrasted sharply with the deep hue of the underwear, and she had brushed her still wet hair back from her face, reminding Ransom of another time and place. Ransom found it hard to concentrate on what she was saying. It wasn't like the spandex shorts and tank top she wore this morning had left much to the imagination, but this was different. *Very different, indeed.*

"Are you serious? I thought something was seriously wrong," Ransom huffed, trying to get her emotions back under control.

"There is something wrong. Get it off me." Evidently the ick factor for ticks was high in Victoria's world. If she hadn't looked so distressed, Ransom would have been tempted to laugh at her.

"Come on." Ransom took Victoria back into the bathroom and dug out a pair of tweezers.

"Where is it?" Ransom asked. Victoria pointed at the offending bloodsucker and Ransom groaned. *Great, just great.*

Like most ticks, this one had found a nice warm place to set up home. Unfortunately for Ransom, that place was a lovely piece of real estate along Victoria's inner thigh.

"Oh, please, please...just get it out," Victoria begged.

"Okay, okay…just stop squirming. I'm going to have to get up close and personal here."

She was forced to get down on one knee to pluck the little bugger from Victoria's inner thigh, but that wasn't the worst of it. Victoria needed to move her leg so she could get to the darn thing, and that meant exposing even more of her inner thigh to her. Victoria gasped when she touched her, then bit her lip and apologized for being such a baby. Ransom could barely hear past the sound of her pulse whooshing past her ears, a tide of hot blood that matched the hammering in her chest. The smooth flesh beneath her fingertips trembled, and Ransom found herself having to practice the same breathing exercises she used to steady her hand before pulling off a shot with her rifle. Inhale, exhale, hold your breath and go for it.

She quickly pulled the tick out, the offending insect hanging on for dear life before releasing its hold on Victoria's flawless skin. She inspected it carefully to make sure the head was intact before tossing it in the toilet, then dabbed the bite with antiseptic.

"Got it!" Ransom crowed, then attempted to get up from the cold floor. She hadn't meant to grab at Victoria's scantily clad hip—really she hadn't, but her left calf cramped up from the lactic acid buildup, and it threw her off balance.

*Holy shit, she feels so good.* Victoria was lightly muscled like she did yoga or Pilates regularly; but not so lean that she wasn't soft in all the right spots. She was nothing like Ransom, who was all hard muscle and definition from years of military training; it would make a good combination in bed. Ransom tried to tamp down that thought immediately, pulling her hand away from the enticing combination of smooth skin and cool silk that nonetheless felt like pure fire beneath her reticent palm.

"There you go, all gone. You should be okay, it wasn't in there long enough to make you sick, but we'll keep an eye on it to make sure it doesn't get inflamed."

"My hero." Victoria could barely breathe. She had seen the heat flaring in Ransom's eyes, the color in her lips darkening with desire. The spot where Ransom's fingers had touched her, where her hand had rested for a moment before she snatched it away—those places tingled like her skin was more awake there.

Victoria leaned in and lightly kissed those lips, startling Ransom as much as herself for her boldness.

"Thank you," she whispered, pulling back from that subtle meeting of lips and walked away. She was sure she could feel those enticing green eyes staring at her ass. A quick glance behind was all it took to confirm her suspicion. Ransom's eyes were definitely glued to her backside, her expression openly hungry enough to make Victoria shiver. For a moment, she thought Ransom would follow her into her room and make the decision for the both of them. Instead, Ransom turned and went out the hallway entrance to the bathroom, leaving her alone and wanting.

Victoria slipped on a thick robe and pulled the collar up close to her neck. The room felt cold and empty and she wasn't willing to give up the heat Ransom's touch had sparked inside her.

"Ransom." Victoria ran her fingertips across her lips and smiled. It was a small victory, but so worth it. Ransom tasted like summer promises no amount of winter storms could erase.

***

*Got you. You will never be in Victoria's house again.*

# Chapter Twelve

"You have got to be kidding." Disgusted with the entire ordeal, Ransom filled her lungs with as much air as they could hold and blew her breath out slowly, ticking off the seconds it took to cool down. There was no getting back the last twenty minutes of her life, and the extreme level of stupid she had just been exposed to made her brain hurt.

"It's settling in," she muttered. What the hell does that even mean? She had asked the smug technician the same question, and he had launched into a circular explanation meant to make her exasperated and hopefully, just give up and end the call. She did, but not until she had let him know exactly what she thought of his excuses. Ransom shook her head again. People settled in, foundations settled, hell, sometimes people settle for less, or settle a farm...but to say an upgrade on a cellphone tower was making her cell service worse instead of better because the upgrade was still "settling in" made no sense. What did the tower need to settle into? Was it still unpacking, did it plan on moving somewhere else?

Stupid answers deserved stupid questions, but they didn't help her temper any.

What she really wanted to know, and what he wouldn't or couldn't tell her, was when her phone would work properly again. That meant she was stuck manually downloading last night's data from each and every one of the new camera's she bought last week, a tedious process that involved positioning the ATV just so and balancing on the seat to reach the hard plastic box containing the latest and greatest in field camera's. If anyone or anything waltzed by since the last time she checked them, she would know immediately...and get a nice little candid shot to identify them with. Every camera had to be checked personally. There was no way to tell if the flashing light meant someone had been trespassing, or if a good size buck had bounced by and got a selfie on the way up to the high meadows.

Her job was to check the memory card and find any non-four-legged critters running around on the farm and convince them that it wasn't a good idea to trespass on conservation land. Now, the cameras were a helpful second, third and tenth pair of eyes she could use as backup. If or when Victoria's stalker found her, she would have evidence. A face was all she needed to find him, and the stalker would find out what it was like to be hunted by someone with a hell of a lot less patience than he'd exhibited.

"Damn, this freaking sucks," Ransom growled. She jumped down from the ATV and rubbed her forearm vigorously to take away the sting, then inspected the damage. Luckily, there was no blood, but the patch of linear scratch marks looked like she'd been attacked by a gang of crazed chipmunks. Rug burn had nothing on bark burn, especially the gnarly old oaks populating the farm and that was the third time she had slipped and scraped the hell out of her arm.

117

A yawn big enough to impress a hibernating bear made her jaw ache and reminded her that she was down more than a few hours of sleep.

"Nightmares, bullshit phone issues, and now this, what more could go wrong?" Ransom uttered the five words every military person knew should never pass their lips, even when everything around them was FUBAR. Her phone buzzed before she could kick her own ass for saying it.

"Dammit." Ransom rubbed at her forehead, trying to smooth out the wrinkles before answering, then gave up. Today was so not going to be a good day, she just knew it, her forehead knew it...so did the pressure building behind her eyes. Pinching her nose and scrunching her eyes closed in preparation, she put the phone to her ear. "Hey, Sam, what's going on?"

Samuel launched into his updates. Ransom sighed and found a fallen log to rest on.

"Shit, Samuel." Ransom rolled her neck to get some of the kinks out. The couch was not as comfortable as she wished it was, and she had a feeling after tonight, it was going to become even more familiar. "Are you sure it was an accident?"

"That's what the traffic cops are saying. A simple hit and run. It was nighttime, and she was wearing dark clothing."

"What the hell was she doing out so late?"

"She must have gone out for some groceries. Maybe she figured it was safer after dark?"

"Or maybe she was following someone?" Ransom found a rough patch of nail and chewed on it. Samuel knew this person. He wouldn't have hired someone stupid enough to step out in front of a car and get themselves thrown thirty feet, and while she'd met some pretty sleazy PI's, they were usually pretty street savvy.

In Ransom's world, there was no such thing as coincidences, and accidents were rarely just that. Too often they were due to lack of planning...or more likely, someone taking advantage of a moment of carelessness.

"I don't know, Ransom. It's troubling, and I'm not thrilled she got hurt." Samuel's voice was barely audible and what she could hear sounded like he was stuffed inside a metal drum.

Ransom growled. *Damn phone.* "Look, Sam...I've got to go. Call me back when she wakes up or you hear anything useful."

*If she wakes up.* Ransom wasn't too sure that was going to happen. Whoever took a run at her made sure it wasn't just a love tap. From what Samuel told her, they had done some real damage. Broken ribs, fractured pelvis, and a collapsed lung weren't something you just snapped back from. If someone hadn't heard tires screeching and come running, the PI wouldn't have made it to the hospital at all.

"Come on, tell me what you're up to." Ransom stared blindly ahead of her, her vision turned inward on itself. Her mind raced along old but familiar pathways, trying to play out the game ahead of the action. It was what she did best. An old friend of hers had tried to put words to the process, telling her that she was prone to thinking around corners and chasing possibilities down dark alleys. At the time she thought it was a great compliment, until the day the world exploded around her, and pain rained down on her in the form of glowing shrapnel and liquid fire. That day reminded her that no matter how good you were, it didn't do a damned bit of good if no one was listening to you. *And people died, remember?* Ransom's heart contracted painfully in her chest. Of course she remembered.

*This time will be different. This time I won't be constrained by rules and regulations,* she vowed, pushing back the paralyzing doubt that threatened to make her a liar. Fingernails digging into her palms, she rode the storm out in silence when all she wanted to do was scream in defiance. She would protect Victoria. Not for Samuel, not because it was her job, but because she wanted this for herself and the possibility of a future she had thought was lost and gone forever.

"I didn't want this, but I can't undo the last week now," Ransom told the trees what she couldn't admit to anybody else.

The stalker had just upped the stakes on what was already a dangerous game. Attacking the PI like that, it didn't make any sense. Or did it? The PI was staying at Victoria's house...living in her home. Somewhere they didn't belong. That they had lashed out that violently showed a disturbing level of possessiveness that went way beyond jealousy.

Ransom jumped up and headed for the ATV. She needed to get back to Victoria. Her days of running around the farm by herself were over. From now on, she needed to keep Victoria close to her. The stalker had just made a huge mistake, losing control like that.

The stalker knew Victoria was gone now, that left only one question of any importance. How long would they wait before they went looking for her?

***

*That felt so good. The sound of her body hitting my car, the way she screamed. I had no idea that would happen. She deserved it. Sleeping in Victoria's bed, acting like she belonged there. She made a huge mistake, following me like that. My only regret was not being able to make her talk. She might have known where Victoria was. I won't make that mistake again.*

# Chapter Thirteen

The familiar tinkle of old brass bells announcing the presence of a customer, along with the scent of ancient wood and dusty shelves always brought a smile to Ransom's face. She loved this place.

"Ransom Greathouse, it's been ages since you've been in. What have you been up to, girl?" The hearty greeting came from somewhere inside the maze of aisles and cubbyholes that made up the old country store.

"Hey, William." The grizzled older man emerged from out of nowhere, close enough to touch Ransom's sleeve. When she didn't jump, the lines around his eyes crinkled in amusement. *Damn, he's still quiet as hell.*

"I've been telling you to call me Buddy for years now, Ransom, when you gonna listen to me?" Buddy held out his hand and she took it. The firm handshake was their idea of a hug, and it held just as much warmth as one, even if it did feel like she was gripping a piece of gnarled oak wrapped in barbwire. Buddy was tough as hell, no matter how gray he was getting or how many wrinkles were carved into his face.

"That's what my dad called you. I'm barely comfortable calling you William. And it hasn't been forever, I was just here a month or so ago," Ransom responded, grinning as they went through the same programmed banter they always did before getting down to business.

"Six weeks, but who's counting?" Buddy grinned back at her. Merry blue eyes that saw and noted everything danced beneath tangled eyebrows that still retained his original hair color. Fuzzy caterpillars in startling black that contrasted with a gravity defying crop of salt and pepper hair that stood at attention across the top. Once a month he went into town for a regulation high and tight, and he would probably do that till the day he died. That was Buddy in a nutshell. Literally, the best friend you could ever ask for and the worst enemy you could ever possibly have. That sort of life balance wasn't something you saw every day. Buddy was unique.

"You are, evidently. Good to see you're keeping a close eye on everything and everyone still."

Buddy didn't deny it, he just shook his head and winked at her. "You got it. What brings you in? I think you've outgrown sneaking off to buy too much candy."

Buddy had owned the country store for as long as she could remember, it was only a couple of miles down the road from where she grew up, which meant it was close enough for her to reach on her bike as soon as she could ride that far. Her parents never caught on, or maybe they just chose to look the other way, so her trips to the country store always felt like a forbidden adventure. The inevitable stomach ache that followed was part sugar overload and part fear factor. She never knew what her parents would do if they caught her and that made it more fun.

It was easier to disappear during summer break, when the sun didn't set until prime time and she was pretty much allowed to roam free as long as it wasn't full dark by the time she wandered back into the house. She would sit at the long bench near the check-out counter and listen to Buddy, he always had the most interesting stories even if some of them were scary.

He had been in the Marine Corps during Vietnam and was one of the few who actually seemed to like being there. There were a lot of rumors about Buddy. Some say he went back after his discharge to become a mercenary, but he never confirmed or denied the allegation. Either way the compact, nondescript man didn't seem like much to look at, but he could be deadly when the situation warranted it, especially when someone he cared for was in trouble. No one ever considered robbing his store, and that was exactly why she was there.

"You're right, although I might be persuaded to take some of that Salt Water Taffy you keep hidden behind the counter before I go. But, really...I have something special in mind that I think you can help me with."

Buddy leaned forward against the counter, cocked his bad leg up on the bottom shelf and waited. He knew exactly what Ransom meant by something special. "Oh, really? What kind of trouble have you gotten yourself into this time?"

The bells rang again, followed by the sound of the door creaking shut. Buddy stood up straight, shedding the mercenary gaze and attitude between one blink and the next. A seasoned actor couldn't have done it any better.

"Afternoon," he called out, busying himself behind the counter. A second woman entered the store, someone he'd never seen before. Out of the corner of his eye, he noticed Ransom stiffen up. From the way the two women's eyes met for a second, their gaze holding more familiarity than a casual acquaintance, he found himself instantly curious.

Ransom had been holed up at the Johnson estate for a couple of years now, to find her in the company of a beautiful woman today was something he would have bet against any day of the week. Flipping his gaze back and forth between the two, he had to admit that they were as different as two people could be. Ransom was fair under her tan, with blonde hair and green eyes gracing a lithe but powerful body. Her companion, on the other hand was petite and dark, her brunette hair almost black in the dim light of the store. Her skin had that translucent feel to it that someone with naturally tan skin held when they spent most of their time indoors. *Light and Dark*, he thought, fascinated with the contrast. They made a most impressive couple.

"Victoria, why don't you just wander around for a bit, I need to talk to William for a sec."

"Of course, Dear."

Ransom paled a little before turning back to Buddy. She really had expected Victoria to make good on her threat to sit and sulk in the Jeep.

"She's a little pissed right now," Ransom explained when she saw Buddy looking at her funny. "Really, just a little misunderstanding, I asked her if she wanted to come with me to do some shopping, and I guess she assumed it meant going into town."

"Uh huh. You said you wanted to talk? Does she have anything to do with our little talk?" Buddy nodded in the other woman's direction.

"Yes, no...not in the way you think." Ransom couldn't seem to make up her mind.

"Right," Buddy drawled. "Are you trying to send the Town Elders into a mass heart attack?"

"Hell, no. No one knows she's here, except for you." Ransom started to make excuses then wondered why she was bothering. "Although you might have something there. Maybe they'd leave me alone if their little pet project was persona non grata, eh?"

"She's cute, I give you that. You always did have good taste."

"She's not my girlfriend, William." Ransom held up her hands when he glared at her. "My bad, Buddy. She's in trouble and I agreed to hide her out here, keep her safe until things blow over."

"And you want me to keep an eye out for anything strange?" Buddy asked.

Ransom sighed in relief. She did the right thing by coming here. "Thanks, Buddy. I can always trust you to know exactly what's needed."

The object of their conversation had disappeared somewhere in the store. Ransom couldn't find her, but she could hear footfalls somewhere in the back.

"She's shopping. I think I'm going to have a good day's sales from what I've heard so far. Let me just lock up and we'll get down to business. While we're doing that, you can tell me all about this mysterious woman and why

126

you've decided to take on a case after all this time. If you want me to keep an eye out for you, I need to know what it is I'm looking for."

Ransom nodded. "I'll pay for everything today, including her purchases."

They headed farther back into the maze to gather up the supplies she needed while she explained why Victoria was staying with her. As she explained, Buddy stood there quietly. He wasn't fazed in the least bit, and he even had a few pointers on how to keep the farm secure while she was there.

When Buddy straight out asked Ransom if she had told Victoria that she was falling for her, Ransom almost choked on her lies. He just smirked at her denials as he handed her the last box of ammunition.

"Ransom, that woman in there really likes you," Buddy said, "and you must think I am an old fool if you think I can't see it. You are just as much into her as she is into you." He let Ransom sputter and carry on for a minute before holding up his hand to silence her.

"Stop trying to bullshit the bull-shitter, Ransom. What I want to know is why the two of you are still batting eyelashes at each other instead of taking advantage of your time together. You obviously want to."

"Yeah, I do. It's just not that simple, Buddy. What happens if I let her back in and something happens to her? I don't think I could handle losing another person."

"You can't live in the past, Ransom. I'm not saying you can't honor the memory of your friends and family, but you can't use the past as an excuse to keep running from your future." Pausing to let that sink in, Buddy's face softened perceptively at the anguish crisscrossing Ransom's face. He didn't want to cause her pain, but he couldn't let her keep wallowing in the past, either. Not if there was someone in her life that could bring her back to her former self.

Buddy spoke softly but urgently. Victoria could only walk around the store for so long; eventually she would find them or get upset at being left alone for so long.

"You can't blame yourself for still being here, Ransom. You didn't do anything wrong, so why do you keep blaming yourself for other people's actions? Dammit, Ransom, you aren't living your life. You're just existing, waiting until the day you die and not even realizing you are acting like you're dead already. You don't offer any honor to those who did die. Do you think they would want you to be this way?"

Buddy felt awful, putting it out there like that.

Ransom's eyes shone with long overdue tears, still unshed, she blinked them away as rapidly as they formed. "No."

"Now like I said, that pretty lady out there seems mighty keen on you and from what I've heard, you seem pretty keen on her, too."

Ransom didn't speak, she just nodded, accepting his appraisal of the situation.

"I may be old, but I'm no prude, and if she makes you happy, well, you need to embrace whatever the future holds between you two."

"And what happens when this is all over and she's ready to go back home? What do I do then?"

"Well, then...at least you will have new memories, good memories to combat the bad. You never know. Just because she may leave, doesn't mean she won't come back. From the way she is looking over at you now, I don't think she could stay away from you for long." Buddy's gaze shifted past her, warning her that Victoria was heading towards them.

She needed to wash her face; it wouldn't do if Victoria found out that she'd been crying. Mumbling something about needing fencing supplies, Ransom escaped before Victoria found her way around to them.

"Hello, Victoria." Buddy took it upon himself to make introductions, grabbing the slightly shocked woman by the hand and leading her farther into his store. "It's so nice to meet you."

By the time Ransom was able to compose herself and pick up the fencing supplies she said she needed, she found Buddy and Victoria hanging out quite comfortably together. Without a single ounce of guilt for commandeering her house guest, he sidled up to the cash register to check her out. They said their goodbyes, and he helped bring out some of the bulkier supplies to the waiting Jeep.

Before Buddy headed back inside, Victoria walked up to the old man and hugged him. His face told Ransom that the unexpected gesture was just as shocking to him as it was to her. They weren't demonstrative people.

"Thank you, Buddy," Victoria murmured, then turned and climbed into the Jeep, apparently ready to go.

Ransom noticed that Victoria was holding a small paper bag on her lap, and while she didn't seem angry at her anymore, she was unusually subdued.

"What's in the bag?" she asked curiously.

"I don't even know. Buddy handed it to me right before we left. He said it was something special for dinner?"

"Huh, I guess we'll find out when we get home." Ransom didn't have a clue, but it wasn't unlike Buddy to do something extravagant when the mood hit him.

***

*I have to think smarter. There has to be a way to turn this to my advantage.*

# Chapter Fourteen

A brief summer storm popped up, soaking both Ransom and Victoria down to the skin and making the drive home much more interesting.

Victoria held up her hands so she could feel the rain beat against her. The rain was warm. Giant, soft blobs of water that made her feel alive...a part of nature.

"What are you doing?" Ransom yelled. The whooshing sound of the rain falling through the trees, added to the road noise of wet tires, made it hard to hear anything else.

"Enjoying this. It's magnificent!" Victoria yelled back, grinning like a fool.

"You're nuts." Ransom shook her head at the foolish woman sitting in her passenger seat, enjoying getting rained on. The open cab of the Jeep hadn't spared either one of them. Her jeans were a sodden mess from the thighs up and her shirt was plastered to her body—just not as nicely as Victoria's was. Ransom swallowed and concentrated on the curves ahead of them before a different set of curves ran them off the road.

She glanced sidelong at Victoria's face once they hit a straight away and had to admit to herself. She looked happy today.

*Damn, and all I have is bad news.*

Ransom bit her lip. They were close to home now, and she was pretty much driving on automatic, shifting without having to think about it. That freed up too much of her brain, which meant it wanted to have another chat about what she was doing and why.

She hadn't told Victoria about the PI yet. Yes, she was still waiting to hear back from Samuel for an update, but that was no excuse. Neither was the fact that she was operating on pure instinct when it came to the nature of the woman's injury. Victoria should know what had happened and be allowed to form her own opinion. Forewarned is forearmed, and Ransom wasn't the type to hold back information from one of her charges.

So why was she waiting now? There had been plenty of time to tell her when she came back from her rounds, then on the drive out to Buddy's. Both missed opportunities.

Laughter broke through her troubling thoughts.

"Look, Ransom. It's so beautiful."

The sun had come out, transforming the world into something fresh and new. Every drop of rain seemed to gather the bright light and reflect it back into a world that actively breathed around them. Small tendrils of steam rose out of the ground and curled around the rocks like fog, adding to the heavy, almost ethereal haze softening the distant landscape.

"It is," Ransom absently agreed, plucking at her wet clothes and trying not to fidget. The sun trying to steam dry your clothes while you were still in them was an unpleasant sensation, it tended to dampen her enthusiasm for enjoying nature's delights.

"Pish. Party pooper," Victoria continued, then twisted in her seat towards Ransom. "I want to have a picnic. It's too gorgeous of an afternoon to crawl back inside that house."

"It's too wet to have a picnic," Ransom replied, drolly reminding Victoria that it just rained.

"Okay, a barbecue then. I know you have a grill. I saw it the other day. And, if it rains again, there's the covered porch."

Victoria's sudden enthusiasm was infectious but Ransom couldn't help but feel the teensiest bit suspicious. *What had she and Buddy been chatting about while I was gone? On the other hand, when am I not always a bit suspicious about everyone's motives? Maybe she just wants to forget about all this stalker crud for an afternoon and enjoy herself.*

"Please, Ransom? I just need a few hours to destress," Victoria practically pleaded. "If you don't think it's safe, I understand, but you've put up all those cameras and no one's heard a peep from the stalker in days."

*That's not true,* Ransom grimaced, keeping that unpleasant knowledge to herself. Victoria did get one thing right. She had this place locked down tight. Unless this stalker was some world class hacker-slash-secret agent type, there was no way they could find this place so soon.

"Yes," Ransom agreed to the barbecue before she could change her mind. *Let her have one evening of fun. Tomorrow. Tomorrow I will tell her about the PI...and a few changes I have in mind. It's time Victoria learns how to defend herself.*

"Yes to which one?" Victoria asked, unsure what question Ransom was answering.

"Yes, we can have a barbecue."

Victoria leaned back in her seat and smiled. The wind had already started to dry her hair, and she just wanted to enjoy the feel of it while she could. "Wonderful. It's been ages since I've done this."

***

Ransom bounced out of the Jeep as soon as they arrived back at the farm, taking charge of the groceries and running them onto the porch before running back out and helping Victoria with the rest of the bags.

"Um, what's this?" Ransom held up a bag of cat food and kitty litter supplies. She had been so busy dealing with Buddy she hadn't really paid much attention to what Victoria had been adding to the pile.

"They're for Whitman," Victoria said, relieving Ransom of the cat food and trying not to smile too smugly.

"Whitman? Since when do we have a Whitman?"

Ransom's confusion was actually kind of cute. She stood there, still holding the kitty litter and refusing to bring it in the house. Never mind the fact that she had said "we", which Victoria noticed immediately. *Try not to make too much of that Freudian slip,* she warned herself, but that didn't mean her heart was paying much attention. It had skipped a beat or two when Ransom said it.

"Whitman is..." Victoria pointed just in time for Ransom to skip aside and miss the orange streak making a beeline for the open door. "Um, right there. He's quite the gentleman and keeps me company when you're not here."

He hadn't shown up at the front door with a name, but when she found Ransom's copy of *Leaves of Grass* sitting on the coffee table, she thought it was the perfect name for the regal looking tabby. *Walt just wasn't going to do it, it sounded too much like someone's mechanic uncle,* she thought, casting a quick apology up to the poet.

"A cat. There's a cat now," Ransom muttered, stomping into the house.

Victoria sniffed and ran her palm over her lips to keep from laughing. She could still hear Ransom stomping about and muttering, but she refused to take the blame for adding a cat to the household. Ransom didn't have a dog, so why not a cat? Every self-respecting lesbian had to be either a dog or a cat person, it was a prerequisite to joining the club...along with the imaginary toaster oven.

Whitman came running up to Victoria the minute she walked into the kitchen, rubbing across her ankles in a figure eight motion that was either meant to say "I love you" or "let me trip you so you can drop whatever food you're carrying."

"You'll get fed, never fear," she said, petting the insistent tabby on the head. She checked to see if Ransom was anywhere nearby. She wasn't, but she lowered her voice anyway. "And if she doesn't want you, you can come home with me."

Victoria froze. Home. The concept was an interesting one. Where was home, exactly? Was it the place you slept every night, the place you hung your clothes? Where you made your meals? Or, was it something entirely different? She knew what she'd tell a client. Home was where you were happy. Home was family and being around people you loved. It wasn't a place so much as a place in your heart. *So where does that leave me?*

"Stupid, stupid woman," Victoria berated herself. She'd been here, what? A week? Strange thoughts to be having for anyone. *Unless you're a creepy stalker with no sense of boundaries,* she thought, snorting at the comparison. *Maybe if I was more like Ransom, I wouldn't have this problem. She's tough and fully capable of taking care of herself. I doubt a stalker would have the balls to mess with her.*

"What was that?" Ransom asked. Victoria practically jumped out of her skin. Whitman hissed and ran for the exit, his claws clattering against the wood floor ineffectively until he got some traction and managed to skid out into the living room.

"Okay, now that was amusing." Ransom chuckled at the cat's antics. This time she managed to stay out of the path of the orange streak and save her shins. She dug through the last bag left on the kitchen table and found the plain white wrapped package Buddy had snuck in at the last minute. She brought it over to the counter and thumped it down. "Did you need something?"

"No. I was just talking to myself." Victoria busied herself at the kitchen counter. "Did you need to go up and change? I'll just get everything started in here and then head up myself. I'm still soaked."

"No, I'm good. The heat from the grill will dry me off. Oh, you might want to put those burgers away. I think Buddy likes you, he gave you a present you might enjoy more," Ransom said, patting the plain white paper packet.

"Really?" Victoria dropped what she was doing to unwrap Buddy's care package. She found two perfectly cut Delmonico steaks within the white butcher paper. "Ooh, these are going to be lovely. That certainly changes my plans. This is less barbecue now and more outdoor chic...I wish we had something more elegant to go with it than soda or juice."

"Mm. I guess. Come with me." Ransom disappeared into the mudroom, literally. As in, Victoria was right behind her and she just disappeared.

"Uh, Ransom?" Victoria called out, checking the back door. It was still locked. "Okay, what's going on?"

"I'm right here."

For the second time in less than a dozen minutes Victoria jumped out of her skin. She whipped around to find Ransom standing right behind her, a cheesy grin plastered across her face. "Dammit, Ransom, you scared the snot out of me."

"Sorry." Ransom's face was anything but contrite. She nodded towards the wall and pulled Victoria closer. "Here, you should know where this is."

She touched a part of the wall and it made a slight snick noise, then swung in to reveal a small stairwell leading into an even smaller basement. A bit of mental geometry told Victoria that this room wasn't a part of the main basement where Ransom kept her workout equipment.

"A hidden room?" Victoria let Ransom lead the way, one wary eye on the stairs and the other one checking the low ceiling for spiders.

"Yeah. Neat, huh?" Ransom flipped on the light to reveal a roomier space than Victoria expected. "This house is old, turn of the century. I'm sure this started off as a root cellar but then prohibition came, and someone in the Johnson family wasn't willing to give up their liquor. I hear there was a lot of moonshine running going on back then, but if you ask Samuel about it, he'll get all testy and huff at you."

"I might just do that sometime," Victoria drawled. *Samuel, you sneaky bastard, you. So much about you I don't know.*

Row after row of dusty shelves attested to Ransom's history, until she noticed a more familiar set of shelves, ones designed to hold wine bottles at the perfect angle for years while ensuring the cork stayed nice and wet. Those were new. She made a bee line for the non-dusty shelf and pulled out the first bottle.

"Nice," Victoria whistled, then carefully put away the bottle. "Are these...?"

"Samuels? Yes. He has quite a collection. The drinkable stuff is over there. As in, stuff he won't mind

138

losing to a guest." Ransom winked. "Why don't you find us a nice bottle of wine; you probably know what goes better with steak than I do?"

Victoria gave Ransom a sharp look.

"You're going to drink?" she asked, then backtracked when she realized how that sounded. "I'm sorry, I didn't mean anything..."

"No, that's quite alright. I don't drink, but that doesn't mean you can't enjoy a glass of wine with dinner." Ransom ran her hand along the smooth oak cabinet. Victoria would laugh at her if she knew what she thought of this place after the first time she saw it. This wasn't just a hidden cellar; it was a perfect safe room, complete with internal bolts and a few extras she had added when she found the place. *And now Victoria knows where it is, too.*

"Listen, I've got to get the coals started if we're going to eat tonight. You take your time and find something you like. I'll let Samuel know so he doesn't freak out when he finds one of the bays empty. Just come up when you're done."

Victoria stood in the middle of the room and turned in a small circle. The place was almost too small, it made her feel claustrophobic, and she had to fight the sensation that the walls were shrinking around her. Worse yet, she couldn't decide if Ransom was being exceptionally nice today or if this trip to the wine cellar was a test of some sorts. Either way, she could still enjoy a nice bottle of wine and prove to Ransom that she could drink responsibly.

Victoria pulled out a cabernet and wiped the label clean. It was going to be a beautiful evening, and the prospect of a good meal with an intelligent and handsome hostess was too perfect to ignore.

Victoria mounted the first stair before turning and clicking the light off. The cellar plunged into darkness, leaving only a distorted rectangle of light from above to guide her way. Hugging the bottle to her side like a football, she took each stair one at a time, carefully avoiding the cobwebs.

Somewhere there was a clock ticking, marking off the time she had left to spend with Ransom. She wasn't going to waste one minute of it.

***

*Today I tried to get Samuel to talk about Victoria, but he was being awful closed mouthed. I will just have to find another way.*

# Chapter Fifteen

As Ransom busied herself with the grill, the unexpected advice from Buddy kept popping up, reminding her that she had the right to live and enjoy her life. While she knew this intellectually, irrational fear kept creeping back in. Like some cobwebbed old boogeyman from her childhood, the cause of those fears refused to leave their cozy home, having taken up refuge in the darkest corners of her mind for so long they practically owned the place.

Yet here she was cooking dinner for her guest, substituting one appetite, one hunger, with another. She doubted that Victoria would appreciate the distinction, but that was all Ransom had to give. Her nightmares were ramping up, occurring almost every night. Even the lumpy couch wasn't able to fend them off, and if she drank any more caffeine to stay awake, Victoria would wake up one morning to find a zombie bouncing around the living room.

Was it guilt that made her promise this one pleasant evening? Victoria needed this, she had made it very clear that everything was starting to get to her, and rather than respond logically Ransom had given in and said yes. That wasn't like her. She was letting her emotions in on the decision-making process, no matter how hard she tried to tell herself that she was just trying to be nice. She didn't do nice. She did efficient.

"Is everything okay?" Victoria showed up at her elbow with a glass in each hand and a pleasant smile for Ransom. "You looked thirsty. I brought you some iced tea."

"Thank you." Ransom forced herself to move. She had been standing in one place for a very long time, and she could feel the strain across her shoulders and back where the shrapnel had torn through the muscles there. No amount of physical therapy ever got rid of that ache, or the stiffness she woke up with every morning and the rain and humidity hadn't helped today.

"Everything's fine. Just thinking about a few things. Boring things that don't matter right this minute." Ransom backtracked quickly before Victoria got it into her mind to start asking questions. She grabbed the long fork and poked at the meat sizzling on the grill. "The steaks are ready if you are."

***

They ended up eating beneath the deep, covered porch. Neither woman seemed interested in retiring indoors, preferring to stay outside and silently enjoying each other's company.

When darkness fell, Victoria was sure that Ransom would suggest going back inside. Instead, she brought out a small radio and moved to the porch swing overlooking the sloping grounds along the side of the house. Victoria poured another glass of wine, then took a chance and poured a second, smaller one before joining Ransom.

"You don't have to take it, I just didn't want to be rude and drink alone."

Perhaps it was the shy way Victoria asked, or maybe it was Buddy's reminder to try and live a little more, but Ransom broke from her longstanding rule and took the glass. *Besides, a single glass of wine with a beautiful woman is a far cry from drinking a bottle of Jack all alone with your pain.*

"Thank you," Ransom said, noting how Victoria let out her breath before sitting down, as if she was relieved nothing else came of her offer.

"This place is amazing. Sitting here like this, I can imagine myself transported back in time. It's so peaceful." The heady scent of something flowery made the air taste sweet and there was constant noise in the background, as if the entire bug world was singing about the earlier rain, joining the music playing on the radio.

"It is." Ransom found herself more content and mellow than she had felt in a long time. She had accepted the glass Victoria offered her, expecting to nurse the dark red liquid throughout the night. That was until she had tasted it. It would be a shame to only offer lip service to such an exquisite vintage. Samuel had expensive tastes in wine and Victoria had a good eye. She wondered how upset he was going to be when he found out that Victoria had plucked one of the choicest jewels out of his wine cellar.

Ransom looked up from her silent contemplation of her wine to catch Victoria openly appraising her.

"Yes?"

"Could I have this dance?" Victoria asked.

"Why?"

"I have the need to dance with an attractive woman." Victoria spoke lightly despite her heart fluttering dangerously fast. Would Ransom take her up on her offer?

Ransom was instantly cautious; still, she couldn't find one good reason to argue against Victoria's request. How far could a single dance on the porch go? It was a beautiful night, and she had a beautiful woman sitting next to her, looking at her expectantly. It would be rude to deny her something as simple as a dance.

Ransom stood and held out her hand, which Victoria accepted gracefully.

A slow song was playing on the radio and somewhere between her finding the courage to ask for a dance and Ransom agreeing, the moonless night had come alive with stars. The Milky Way was visible as a band of light traveling across the heavens in a display of celestial wonder she had never seen before.

It was a rare night in the city where you could see more than a smattering of stars, and Victoria had lived in cities most of her life. The covered porch had become a small oasis of soft light floating on a river of darkness. The illusion that they were alone in the cosmos made it seem like anything was possible. From here, Victoria felt like she could create her own universe, if only Ransom would join her and show her the way. That feeling was so overwhelming, so overpowering, that she began to tremble against the unseen force lashing out at her psyche.

"You're cold, we should go inside," Ransom suggested, feeling Victoria shiver in her embrace.

"I don't want to," Victoria admitted, she was far from cold but she couldn't let Ransom know that. The night had been too perfect, more than she could have asked for and definitely more than she had expected.

"But you're shaking."

"I'll be alright for a little while longer." Victoria stilled in Ransom's arms. "Before we go back inside, can I ask for one more thing?"

"What?"

"A kiss. Just one single kiss to complete this perfect night?"

Ransom searched Victoria's face for any sign of artifice and found none. She honestly believed what she said. Ransom didn't know what to say, she was afraid of what would happen if their lips touched. "I don't think that's a good idea."

"If you kiss me, I promise you, I won't ask for anything more tonight." Victoria was not one to beg, ever...but the overwhelming need to connect with Ransom tonight had a tight hold on her.

"Just a kiss and nothing more?" Ransom's head was spinning, far more than she could blame on a few sips of wine, and certainly not when she was being offered something much more intoxicating. Somehow, she knew that this wouldn't be just any kiss, that if she chose to close that short distance between them something would irreversibly change in her life. That short distance represented so much more than Victoria could possibly realize. That kiss sealed a breach between one moment in time and another, but what about all those moments in between, would they come flooding through as well?

"Just a kiss," Victoria breathed as she tilted her face up towards Ransom, full pink lips already parted and waiting.

"You don't know what you're asking me to do." Ransom felt warm hands slide eagerly through her hair to press firmly against the base of her skull, drawing her down to meet eager lips.

"Then tell me."

"I don't think I can," Ransom protested, twisting away from Victoria and moving as far away as the deck rail would allow. She couldn't explain how she was feeling, she barely understood it herself.

"Don't shut me out, Ransom." Victoria didn't feel cold anymore, her blood ran hot with emotion.

"Victoria, please...you don't want this, you don't want me, not the way I am now," Ransom pleaded with Victoria to stop whatever this was that was happening between them.

"Don't." Victoria stopped Ransom with one word. "I said, don't...don't speak, don't make apologies, and certainly don't assume anything about me that I don't tell you myself."

Ransom didn't stop. "You don't understand. I can't bring back the past, no matter how much you want me to. I know you think there's still something between us, but..."

She knew they were bald lies, but they couldn't stop her from remembering, from feeling the memories she spent so much time trying to forget. Her heart thudded painfully in her chest, the blood rushing through her temples a steady drum beat in her head. It was primal, primitive in its rhythm and it made her painfully aware of how close Victoria was standing to her. She closed her eyes and swayed a bit at the intoxicating sensation, all she had to do was bend her head down the least little bit and their lips would meet.

Opening her eyes, she found herself staring into deep-brown eyes that held her, captivated her and demanded more from her. She had been standing like stone before Victoria, but that look, that look challenged her to take action. A low moan reverberated in her chest, becoming almost a growl as Victoria looked up at her and smiled. It was a knowing smile that Ransom recognized as one of victory.

"Why are you smiling like that?" she demanded.

"Oh, Ransom." Victoria reached up and caressed Ransom's cheek. She flinched, but didn't move away. She was like a wild animal, barely used to a human's touch, uncertain whether to run or bite. "I'm smiling because you've finally given me the only thing I've wanted since I arrived here. You do remember me."

"Of course I remember you," Ransom choked out. If Victoria had crowed over her victory, had made her mistake a matter of conquest or ego, Ransom would have walked away without another word. "You were the last good thing that happened to me."

"Then why go through all of this, pretending not to know me?"

"That's not a fair question." Ransom closed her eyes. "I never pretended a thing. When I saw you on the road with Samuel, it brought everything back...but I couldn't let myself remember. I didn't want to remember."

Ransom had trouble thinking past the thunder roaring in her head, deafening her to everything but the sound of Victoria breathing, she wanted to hear that sound quicken and go ragged, to gasp and growl and howl against her like a summer storm.

She moved quickly, quick enough for Victoria to gasp in surprise before demanding lips found hers, a quick tongue pressing along her teeth until she opened her mouth to the invading muscle. Their tongues fought and slid against each other, each seeking dominance over the other. It was no gentle kiss, this bruising clash of lips on lips, feeding off all the pent-up emotions from the last week.

"Christ, Victoria. What you do to me." Hating herself for doing it but having no other choice, Ransom pushed away, awkwardly untangling herself from Victoria's embrace.

"What?" Victoria asked, breathless and confused by Ransom's sudden withdrawal. "What do I do?"

The two women stared at each other in the dark. Ransom's face was a mysterious shadow. Victoria couldn't read a thing in her expression other than the pain in her voice.

"You make me feel too much," Ransom murmured. Then she was gone, the enigmatic statement cutting through the blood red haze of arousal as effectively as a hard frost.

Victoria sat down, blindly finding the swing they had abandoned not so long ago and wrapped her arms around herself. Ransom was right about one thing; it was getting cold outside. She would have to go inside soon or risk getting chilled. She stood up and leaned against the railing. The stars winked at her, oblivious to the human drama playing out beneath their watch. Victoria cast her gaze across the heavens then back towards the house, finding her resolve somewhere in between the two. She took a couple of deep, cleansing breaths and headed for the front door.

"You might be right about a lot of things, but you're wrong about me," Victoria said. Regardless of Ransom's denial she did want her, and she wanted her just the way she was.

\*\*\*

*Fuck, fuck, fuck. That old coot put that woman in Victoria's house.*

# Chapter Sixteen

Victoria jumped out of her skin at the loud roar reverberating through the house. *What the hell?* She looked at her watch and realized that over two hours had passed since she'd gone upstairs. A second bellow loud enough to shake the rafters followed the first, sending her heart pounding up into her throat.

That was Ransom.

Without a second thought for her own safety, Victoria jumped out of bed and ran down the hall and towards the other bedroom. Ransom was there, her hair and body soaked in sweat as she thrashed violently against the covers tangled around her legs.

"Noooo," Ransom cried out in a ragged and broken voice that made Victoria's soul ache. It sounded like she'd been screaming for a long time.

\*\*\*

Ransom was caught in a nightmare world of fire and smoke, where the night screamed in agony and what didn't move in slow motion was happening way too fast.

Images of the past flipped through her troubled mind. Like a tumbler running through the numbers, they settled on a day and time and clicked into place, opening the door to a world where pain ruled and hell stood aside and watched in awe.

150

Then that world exploded.

Ransom groaned. She was lying face down on dirt that tasted lifeless and dry. The faint aftertaste of diesel fuel and old oil was more pleasant, but only because it reminded her of her old Chevy back home. She blinked, trying to work the grit out of her eyes but she couldn't find enough moisture to clear her vision.

For a moment, Ransom was alone in a completely silent world, then sound came crashing back around her. Gunfire mixed with the screams of both metal and flesh and the rough bellow of orders all sounded like they were happening inside her head, but she considered the pain in her ears a blessing. The blast could have deafened her permanently. Lost in the dust and smoke, she tried to make sense of the confusion around her before attempting to move.

Hot fire lanced through her left shoulder when she tried to pull herself up. Spots danced in front of her eyes. Tinged with a sickly black, the pain threatened to make her pass out. She dropped back to the ground and panted for a few moments, trying to keep the darkness at bay. She couldn't afford to lose consciousness, not now.

"Fuck," Ransom rasped, barely recognizing her own voice. She couldn't remember why she was lying on the ground, or why her arm wasn't working, but she knew she had to move. The impetus to get out of the open was part training and pure instinct and couldn't be denied. The vehicle behind her was on fire, it cast too much light and made her far too visible. She rolled over and managed to get her feet under her. Turning in a wobbling circle, she realized the burning vehicle was the one she had been riding in, now minus a few chunks and the rest of its passengers. Staggering away, she scanned the area for the other occupants.

Where was everyone? She could hear voices, harsh, guttural. Not her people. She tried to swallow, but it felt like razor blades working against her throat.

She spotted a soft form a few feet ahead of her, soft only in that it was obviously flesh and blood and not torn and twisted metal. She bent down to check for injuries and woke up a small fury.

"Easy, Sailor," Ransom said, keeping her eyes up, scanning the area around them for danger. "Are you in one piece? Can you move?"

"Yes, I think so." she spoke in a voice as raspy and strained as hers. "Sorry about that just now."

"Don't worry about it."

They grinned at each other. Despite the shitty situation, they were still alive.

"It's good to see you, Jones, and in relatively one piece."

"You too, Greathouse." Jones pulled herself up with a little help from Ransom's good arm. "Let's get the hell out of here. We need to find the rest of our unit."

The scene reset, twisting upon itself and rewriting Ransom's carefully scripted edits.

Ransom stumbled through the smoke and flames, her shoulder burning cold and hot at the same time. Her flak jacket was a joke. She could smell her own flesh, burnt and broken, the hot trickle running down her back told her that she was bleeding somewhere.

She had managed to get up yet again, her arm dangling uselessly at her side. The wiry MP at her side lurched with every step and sent sharp pains through her back. Petty Officer Jones was new to the unit, but was someone she knew from her first tour of duty. Ransom promised herself that she would look after her old friend. A stupid thing to do, considering where they were headed, but they had been close at one point and she felt she owed it to her, especially since she was so close to retiring.

"I lost my weapon," Jones apologized. Hell, from looking at her, she barely had half of her body armor. Ransom was sure she didn't look much better. "Do you have ammo left in your Nine?"

"What?" She looked down the length of her arm and found her sidearm still grasped in her hand. She didn't remember pulling it. Her entire arm was numb from the shoulder down. She also couldn't feel the cold steel, nor her fingers. She tried to move her hand, to wiggle a finger, but she couldn't even get a twitch.

"I can't..." Ransom never finished her sentence. A dark figure swirled out of the smoke, the AK-47 in desert hardened hands coming up to bear on them. Ransom lurched, trying to move away from his line of sight. She cursed her nerveless fingers as the end of a barrel swung up and pointed at them. Her vision narrowed until all she could see was that small black circle. She knew that black nothingness would soon flash the brightest of whites.

They fell, toppled over each other really. It was an inglorious way to go, and Ransom couldn't stand the thought of it. She willed her arm to raise, her teeth grinding together at the sharp pain running along her side and across her shoulders. She managed to raise her weapon, but couldn't pull the trigger.

"Goddammit!" she screamed her frustration. She wasn't sure what happened next. The man paused at the sound of her voice, just for a second, just long enough for another hand to grasp the top of hers. Her nine millimeter fired, then clattered to the ground, the recoil releasing her hand from its death grip even as it offered death to the enemy. Petty Officer Jones grunted, then collapsed next to her. It was only then she noticed the hot trickle of blood staining her BDU's. She was bleeding from somewhere.

"Fuck!" This wasn't happening. She was trapped. Jones weighed less than she did so she was at least able to pull her around into her arms. She ran her fingers all along the blood dampened uniform but couldn't find the wound. She couldn't move her and she was slowly bleeding out.

"No, Goddammit, I'm responsible for you!" Ransom screamed

"Corpsman...I need a Corpsman here!" she bellowed, even though she knew it was too late.

A weak voice struggled to be heard over her bellowing. "Lieutenant, stop yelling." Petty Officer Jones fumbled against Ransom's uniform, grabbing at her collar.

Ransom glared at her. Anger was her only friend now. "Don't call me that. You know I haven't said yes yet."

"You will. It's in your nature." Jones coughed, wetly, and something dark and thick appeared at the corner of her mouth. Her hand managed to snake inside Ransom's uniform, just above her heart.

"What?" Ransom asked, her heart pounding. She felt dizzy, probably from the smoke. She needed fresh air.

"This isn't all my blood, Ransom."

"You'll be okay, you're okay. Someone's coming. Just hold on, okay?"

"Corpsman! Where the fuck are you?" she bellowed one more, then broke out into a racking cough that left her breathless. A slight hand reached up and stroked her face.

"Stop."

Ransom looked down at the woman in her arms.

Dark, almost black eyes that reflected the blazing sky gazed up at her peacefully, the way a person does when they know death is approaching. Her helmet slipped off, revealing familiar chocolate-brown hair.

"Victoria?"

"Victoria, NO!"

\*\*\*

Ransom sat bolt upright in bed, drenched and chilled to the bone. Her lungs burned, and despite the great drafts of air she sucked in, all she could smell and taste was fire and blood and loss and agony.

"Ransom? Are you okay?"

Ransom jumped. The tentative voice, following so closely behind the one in her nightmare, startled her. *So real.* The woman who had been dying in her arms now stood in her doorway, alive and well and afraid to approach her. The dream had changed and had brought with it a new set of fears.

"I'm responsible for you," Ransom whispered.

Her entire body vibrated with the memories of her nightmare. She tried squeezing her eyes shut against the stubborn images, but that only brought them into clearer focus. Victoria had died in her arms while Ransom had been forced to watch, unable to save her. It was odd, how you could tell when someone was not there anymore. Every emotion, whether it was love, fear or pain, flared wildly in those last few seconds before the soul fled, leaving a dull vessel behind whose sole purpose was to remind you of what was lost.

"Ransom it's okay...it was just a nightmare," Victoria murmured. *Another nightmare, the same nightmare that came to Ransom night after night despite her attempts to hide it.*

"You don't understand; it won't let me go. Jones was shot and I couldn't save her, and then she became you. You were shot and dying, and there was nothing I could do." She could still taste the metallic tang of fear and blood. The bitter smell of smoke and ash stung her nostrils, the faint cries of distant wounded as her nightmare followed her into the waking world. This was what she was used to. This was why she stayed alone and uninvolved in the rest of the world.

"I'm fine. I'm right here. You've kept me safe, just like you promised." All Victoria could do was hold her tight and reassure her. She took Ransom into her arms and kissed her. Tearing Ransom away from her nightmare meant she had to bring her back from her visions of death and loss. She brought Ransom's hand up to her chest, letting her feel the strong muscle that beat beneath her breastbone. "See? I'm fine."

A deep shudder ran through Ransom's body. Her tear-stained eyes found Victoria's, but there was something about the way she stared at her, or rather, through her that terrified Victoria. Ransom wasn't quite all there with her and she needed to come back. She guided Ransoms hand to her breast, then leaned in close until their foreheads touched. "Please, Ransom. I am here, now. In this place with you, and I want you to feel me."

Ransom made a sound then, a desperate and needful sound that was so heart-wrenching Victoria almost changed her mind. Despite her physical toughness, Ransom's soul had taken one hell of a beating, one that many survivors never recovered from. She deserved time to heal and someone who could help her do that. *I'm not her therapist. I want to be something so much more than that for her. There are other paths to healing. I can still help her.*

The tension between them was a silent whirlwind that built upon itself until it was almost unbearable, then the pressure shifted with an inaudible crack.

Without warning, Ransom's lips were on hers and she was falling back onto the bed. Victoria moaned, her body arching into the desperate caresses, the feel of a hot mouth on her breast. Her silk pajama's melted away from her body like they never existed, until only Ransom's body covered her. When Ransom's searching fingers found her already wet and ready for her, Victoria shifted to give her more access. Ransom settled between her hips, trapping her hand between them and slipping inside her. Victoria cried out and grasped at Ransom's back, urging her on. This was no gentle lovemaking; this was sexual catharsis.

Ransom pushed into her only to withdraw a second later, starting a rhythm that was fast and hard and left them both gasping for air. Victoria managed to get her hands under Ransom's tank top, running her fingers along the tense back muscles as she rocked against her, pulling her closer until she could grind her hips against every thrust. She could feel her orgasm building, her body tensing in anticipation of the delicious tumble into blinding oblivion. Victoria's hands stumbled across a puckered rough patch of skin along Ransom's shoulder where hot shrapnel had found a home in her body. Sobbing, she tucked her head into Ransom's neck, letting hot tears fall as she tumbled into bittersweet ecstasy.

\*\*\*

*The man sitting in front of me added a dozen packets of sugar to the crappiest coffee I've ever tasted and sipped it, smacking his lips like it was the finest champagne before holding his cup out to the waitress for a top off. She smiled at him and he beamed at her like she was the freaking*

*Queen of Sheba. Being institutionalized would do that to your taste, for both the coffee and women.*

*I thought I had planned everything so perfectly, then Samuel ruined it by taking her beyond my reach. Victoria won't come back until she thinks it's over.*

*I need to make her think that danger is gone. Then we can continue where we left off. He's perfect for what I need.*

*"Are you sure?" he asked, leaning towards me, eager for some sort of confirmation.*

*"Oh, yes," I said. I was very sure he was the perfect man for the job.*

*"I just want to apologize to her, to let her know how terribly sorry I am."*

*His lip trembled. I thought he was going to cry. Weak. Pitiful. My lip curled, but I forced it to keep moving until it looked like a smile. That made him look like he was going to cry even more. Jesus. What a sad sack. It took every ounce of willpower to touch him, but I did, patting his arm like a child.*

*"You'll get your chance, I promise. I'll talk to her, get her to see how different you are. She doesn't have to be afraid of you anymore. You're a changed man, now."*

*His eyes lit up. "I am, oh, I am. Thank you, oh, thank you for helping me. God has blessed me, bringing you into my life."*

# Chapter Seventeen

Victoria woke up the next morning alone in Ransom's bed. She sat up and looked around. Ransom wasn't just missing from the bed, but the entire room. The bathroom door was open and she could tell she wasn't in there, either.

Victoria drew her knees up to her chest and stared at the empty space next to her.

*Poor Ransom.*

No, the woman was too strong to pity. She didn't think she could carry around that much pain and suffering inside her and still function, and the fact that Ransom had managed to make it this far alone was a testament to her inner strength.

Then there was her own sense of guilt. Samuel hadn't said anything about Ransom suffering from such violent nightmares. More than likely that meant she had simply hidden them from him and, Victoria suspected, her therapists at the VA. She wanted to believe that, but after what she witnessed last night she could only come to one conclusion. Her presence here had only made Ransom's symptoms worse.

"Christ, I wish I could talk to Samuel," Victoria muttered, knowing that would never happen. She could never, ever, tell him about last night. The way Ransom looked at her, the wildness in her eyes, the desperate need...and then. *Oh, God, and then.* Victoria shivered. She had offered herself to Ransom, and Ransom had taken her, taken what she needed from her without apology. Afterwards she had curled up around Victoria, sweat dampened hair clinging to her brow and her breath coming in great, ragged draughts that eventually evened out when she fell into a fitful sleep.

Victoria wasn't far behind her, despite trying to stay awake for as long as possible. Without wanting to wake Ransom, she tried to project calm, carefully brushing the hair away from her face so she could watch for any signs of another nightmare.

She had no idea how long Ransom had stayed with her. Had she left the bed as soon as she had fallen asleep? She would feel awful if Ransom had retreated to the couch because of her.

Victoria climbed out of bed and found her robe. It was time to find out. She couldn't just stay in bed all day and hide. She had to find out how Ransom was doing after last night.

Surprisingly, Victoria located Ransom in the kitchen—not a place she would normally expect to find her.

Victoria noticed three things immediately. One. A laptop was open and running at the end of the table. Two. Whitman, that traitorous orange fur-ball, was sitting on the kitchen table. And, three?

Ransom was sitting cross legged at the kitchen table, but that wasn't what made her stop in her tracks and scratch her head. Nope. It was what she was wearing. Bright yellow Joe Boxer smiley face boxer shorts and a black form fitting tank top that accentuated just how easily she managed to pull off the Yoga like posture.

Victoria wasn't sure she could pull off that position so casually and balance on a chair at the same time. What really made her eyes want to pop out of her head was what Ransom was doing at the kitchen table, because it wasn't the standard fare you'd expect. The table was strewn with a medley of metal bits and pieces. They looked vaguely familiar but didn't register completely until Ransom brought two of the larger parts together, then manipulated something under her thumb that joined them into a recognizable form.

Ransom was sitting at the table assembling a decidedly wicked looking rifle. With her blonde hair, skimpy outfit and the dull gray/black rifle resting in her hands, she looked like a center fold expose on hot women with guns for Soldier of Fortune magazine.

"Um?" Victoria managed to stutter a one syllable sentence. Sadly, that was all her brain could come up with at the moment. Her tongue felt stuck to the roof of her mouth as she tried to get words out that weren't even coherent inside of her head.

"Morning," Ransom said, not bothering to look up from what she was doing. There were a lot of little pins and springs involved in putting a gun together.

"Um..." Victoria tried again, but got just about as far as her first try. She licked her lips before trying to speak again, but that worked about as well as washing up with a piece of sandpaper. Her mouth was even dryer than her lips. Apparently eloquence wasn't going to happen right now.

"Don't worry, I put a towel down."

"Huh?" Victoria managed to switch words. *Jesus, get it together.* It wasn't like she'd never seen the woman before. *True, but not sitting in a kitchen cleaning and assembling guns in her boxer shorts.*

Ransom finally twisted around to look back at Victoria. She took in the open mouth and shocked expression on her face.

"A towel, you know...to keep the table from getting gun oil on it," Ransom spoke levelly, as if it made perfect sense to sit at her kitchen table and clean her weapons. She wasn't even sure why she had to explain. It was her table and her kitchen, well, technically it was Samuel's...but that didn't mean she had to answer to Victoria.

"Okay." Ransom seemed blissfully unaware of the effect she was having on her, and for a moment Victoria felt lost. What was going on? She was pretty sure she hadn't imagined last night, her body surely hadn't. She was still sensitive where Ransom had touched her, the nerves subtly charged with residual energy that hummed whenever her thoughts landed back on last night.

"Do you always clean your guns in boxer shorts?" Victoria mentally clapped herself on the back. *Yay!!* She had formed a complete sentence this time.

"Only when it's raining outside," Ransom quipped. She kept her eyes on the small towel in front of her while she assembled the AR's bolt. Whitman kept trying to help,

163

and she didn't want to go hunting for a spring somewhere on the floor.

"So, this is a thing with you? It rains and you strip to your underwear and clean guns?" Victoria tried so very hard to sound casual as she asked the question. She finally made it to the safety of the kitchen counter and found a clean coffee cup for herself.

"Yep." Ransom managed to keep a straight face as she slid the bolt home before snapping the rifle back together.

"Are you serious?" Victoria turned around and leaned against the counter.

"Maybe." This time, Ransom looked up when she spoke, her smile widening into an amused grin.

"Would you like breakfast?" Victoria decided to change the subject. She knew she was being teased now.

"Sure, just give me a minute to finish up." Ransom packed her supplies together quickly, her military training showing in the quick, efficient movements. The rifle went into a hallway closet, taking the acrid smell of metal and gun oil with it. The more familiar pistol stayed on the kitchen table. She didn't have anywhere to tuck it.

"Um, Ransom?" Victoria couldn't help herself, she had to ask.

"Yes?"

"What do you do when it snows?" Victoria took a sip of her coffee, then choked and spluttered on the hot liquid when Ransom answered her.

"I sharpen my knives." Ransom looked up at Victoria, her face carefully blank.

"Are you serious?"

"Absolutely." Ransom held Victoria's incredulous scowl for so long that Victoria started to believe her. Then Ransom raised one pale eyebrow, her lips twitching just the slightest bit. Just that and nothing more, but it was enough to ruin the game.

Victoria burst into laughter. "You have one hell of a poker face, Ransom."

"I'll take that as a compliment. Here, you're wearing some of your coffee," Ransom said, tossing Victoria a dish towel before wandering into the laundry room.

"Speaking of what we're wearing, what happened to your clothes?"

"I got soaked riding the trails this morning." Ransom's disembodied voice carried through the open door.

"Why didn't you just find something else to wear?" Victoria asked, thinking that was a very reasonable question. Certainly more so than cleaning guns in your underwear.

"It was easier to throw everything in the dryer down here," Ransom said, reappearing at her shoulder without a sound. She had pulled on a pair of jeans and was absently buttoning them up.

"Don't do that!" Victoria scolded. "Are you trying to give me a heart attack?"

"Nope." Ransom refilled her mug and returned to the kitchen table, her bare feet moving as silently as a ghost across the wood floor.

Victoria shook her head, sure that Ransom made a point of moving as quietly as possible after her comment. It wasn't right, being able to do that so easily, not when she was prone to falling over her own big toe. It might have been her imagination, but even the cat seemed a little jealous right then.

"So, you weren't avoiding me this morning?"

"No, why would I? It was raining, and you were sound asleep. There wasn't any reason to wake you." Ransom didn't mention the rest of it, nor did she explain why she went out into a deluge without any raingear. "You'll have to wait another day for our run, though. It's pretty much a crapfest out there right now. I had to take the ATV this morning and from the look of it, this isn't going to let up anytime soon."

"No, that's quite all right." Victoria sighed. She didn't have to look outside to know Ransom was right. The sound of the rain beating against the house came in waves, and somewhere in the back of the house a tree branch had started slapping out a secret message against the siding. The rain was turning into a full-blown storm and there was just her and Ransom and last night sharing the house together. *How perfect is that?* Victoria asked herself, not sure if she was being sarcastic or not. "I'm surprised you went out in all that, even with the ATV."

"Still have to check the cameras," Ransom said, rolling her shoulders to work a few kinks out. This morning's recon was a bit more exciting than she expected. Slick mud and wet roots made for a slippery ride that required all her skill, and most of her muscles, just to keep from skidding off the side of the mountain.

"Well, considering what it sounds like out there now, I guess I should thank you for letting me sleep in. I was pretty wiped out after last night." Victoria slid a sideways glance at Ransom. What was up with her this morning? It wasn't that she didn't appreciate seeing a more playful side of the woman, but after last night, it was just weird. *Avoidance technique?* Victoria worried her lower lip. *This was going to get awkward.*

"Yeah, I noticed. Did you know that you drool?" Ransom avoided the obvious gambit with another joke.

"I do not," Victoria said, instantly indignant.

"Sure you do. You left a giant puddle of drool on my chest."

"You're teasing me again, right?" Victoria scrutinized Ransom's face for the slightest tell.

"Yeah, I am." Ransom let her smile touch her eyes this time. She might have been teasing the woman to misdirect her, but that didn't mean it wasn't fun to do.

"That's just mean."

"Sorry." Ransom grinned. "I was just having fun."

"I know. Me too," Victoria admitted, dropping her gaze. Pretending to watch her coffee cool might hide what she was really thinking, but it did nothing to stop her growing frustration. *I'm not fooled by this little comedy show, Ransom Greathouse.*

"Ah, listen. There's something I wanted to talk to you about." Ransom pulled a small plastic box closer to her and unlatched it, then turned the box around.

Victoria peeked inside, then sank down into the seat closest to Ransom, her hands clasped together between her knees. She stared at the gun with the strangest expression on her face, then looked up at Ransom. "What is this?"

"It's a .380 semiautomatic. Compact, easy to use and a good concealable weapon for a woman." Ransom pulled out the gun and launched into a quick demonstration. After a few minutes she realized Victoria wasn't really listening to her. "I thought it would be a good idea if I started training you to protect yourself."

When Victoria still didn't answer, Ransom leaned forward. "Is there a problem? I mean, I understand if you don't like guns. A lot of people don't. We can start on something else first."

Victoria, calm, cool and oh, so therapeutic Victoria exploded. "A problem? Yes, there's a problem. First, we spend all afternoon together for what felt very much like a date. That falls apart. Then I wake up to you screaming, caught up in some night terror that did almost give me a heart attack." Victoria took Ransom's hands and gazed directly into her eyes. Her pulse quickened. Part of her wanted to run away from this conversation, but the part that wanted to fight was stronger. She forced herself to smile past the jumbled mess of emotions making her want to cry. "I can't even tell you what's going on inside my head about last night. I'm not talking about us sleeping together, or me drooling on your chest. I'm talking about what happened before that. What happened between us. Don't you think we should talk about that?"

168

Ransom winced and pulled away. "We don't need to talk about everything, Victoria. I know that's the way you roll, but I don't. Can't you just let things be?"

"No, I can't." Victoria took a deep breath and exhaled. Yelling wouldn't solve anything between them. Neither would be pushing Ransom to the point of shutting down. "Okay, let's table that for now."

The relief flashing across Ransom's face was short-lived.

"There is something going on. I know it. Your nightmares are getting worse. You're obviously afraid of something. Now you want me to start carrying a gun? A gun, Ransom? What aren't you telling me?"

Ransom stood up, very slowly. Victoria took a step back without meaning to. Ransom looked very dangerous in that moment. "I won't lie. There's a very good reason why I want you to know how to defend yourself."

Victoria gasped, her thoughts going immediately to the only other person in her life that mattered. "Is Samuel?"

"He's fine." Ransom made a chopping motion with her hand. "It's the PI he hired. She was involved in a hit and run the day before yesterday."

Victoria felt the floor drop out beneath her. She licked her lips and had to try twice before she could get her voice to work. "Was it...was it the stalker?"

"We don't know. Whoever it was covered their tracks too well. As far as the police are concerned it's just a coincidence. It was late at night. She was wearing dark clothing, and the visibility was poor. Their chalking it up to a drunk driver."

"Do you believe that?"

"No. But then, I'm paranoid as hell, or so some say." A toothy grin as sharp and deadly as a sharks accompanied that statement, at total odds with the casual shrug that followed. "We'll know more when, if she wakes up. Right now she's in the ICU. Until then, I'm going to assume the stalker knows you aren't going to be home anytime soon, and that means he might start widening his net. I want you to stay close to me as much as possible, but just in case we're separated, I want to know you can protect yourself."

"Oh." Victoria's mind spun with the news. Someone had been hurt. Someone had been hurt protecting her. She needed to do more than sit here and wait. Victoria frowned, narrowing her eyes as one idea after another came to her and was discarded. *I'm wasting my talent, sitting here being the victim when I could be using my time trying to figure out why this person is doing this.*

"Oh?" Ransom interrupted her thoughts. "Just oh?"

"No, not just oh." Victoria was about to ask for the computer when another thought hit her. She grabbed Ransom's sleeve. Her words tumbled over each other almost manically "Wait. You said the day before yesterday?"

"What?"

"You said Samuel told you about the PI yesterday. If you knew then why did you wait until today to tell me?"

Brilliant green eyes held Victoria's gaze steadily before looking away again. "You seemed so stressed out. All you wanted was a few hours, one nice day, where you could forget about the stalker. I thought I could give that to you."

"That was very sweet."

"That was a mistake. My job is to keep you safe. I let my emotions get the better of me. It won't happen again." Ransom picked up her pistol and tucked it in her jeans. "I need to make a phone call. When you're ready, we'll start training."

***

*The problem with sending a hound out on a field hunt is making sure they remember there's a leash waiting for them at home.*

*It's a good thing they don't know I'm counting on them being a bad dog.*

# Chapter Eighteen

Ransom spun around to face the window and tried not to let her frustration get the best of her. So far, Samuel hadn't been able to tell her anything useful.

"That's too bad, Samuel, any timeline on when they expect her to wake up?"

Ransom was back in her study, slouching in the heavy leather chair she was sure was a leftover from Samuel's first office, as was the oversized desk that now served as a catch all for her personal papers.

"Not right now. She came through surgery just fine, so that's good."

"So, what we have right now is crap. The stalker has basically dropped off the face of the earth. The only person that might be able to identify him is attached to a machine in a hospital, and we still don't have a clue who the hell this person is," Ransom muttered. "That doesn't bode well for a resolution any time soon."

"Well, when you put it like that," Samuel coughed into the phone. "No, it doesn't."

"Do you think..."

"Hold on."

Ransom spun back to face the desk and started rummaging for a pad of paper. She could hear him speaking to someone in the background, their voices muffled and distant, but the other was clearly female.

"I'm back," he said, just as her fingers found the small packet of letters that had followed her to the Navy Hospital. She had saved them all this time, still unopened, all from Victoria.

"Who was that?" she asked, tapping the packet on the desk. Their contents distracted her. What would she find inside if she dared open them?

"Just Bridget, the receptionist. She had a question about a client."

"Bridget? Do I know her?"

"No. She came on board right after you left."

"Does she know about the stalker?" she asked sharply. It didn't take much for paranoid Ransom to surface.

Samuel chuckled, dismissing her concern instantly. "I don't think so. I certainly haven't said a thing. As far as the office knows, Victoria is away on a family emergency."

"Don't laugh, Samuel. You know how I am."

"I know, Ransom, I know. I'm sorry. But look, Bridget's a good kid, sensitive, smart as a whip and good with the clients. She's going to school at night to get her degree in psychology. I don't think she would say anything even if she did know."

"If you say so, Samuel," Ransom said, rubbing her eyes to clear them. She was tired, more tired than she was willing to admit after last night. "I'm sorry, what?" She had missed Samuel's next question.

"How did Victoria take the news?"

Ransom rewound the conversation and found the missed question.

"About the PI? I just told her."

"Wait? Just now? As in this morning?" Ransom could practically visualize Samuel leaning forward, punching his finger against the desk with each question. He was that agitated.

"Yeah, what's the big deal?" she asked, schooling her voice carefully. Samuel was too good at reading her.

"That's not like you. You're too big on transparency to keep something like that hidden from a client. What gives?"

And just like that, their conversation was ruined. *First Victoria, now Samuel, the only problem is that he's absolutely correct. I've never withheld information before, not to save a client's feelings.* Ransom groaned. "You know what, Samuel? You headshrinker types really get on my nerves."

"That's not the first time I've heard that."

She was sure Samuel had a hell of a lot more to say but a rapping at the door gave her a quick way out. She looked up to find Victoria standing there. "I gotta go, Sam. Just keep me updated on any changes." *And stay the hell out of my head, I'm doing just fine on my own.*

"I thought I closed that door."

"Not all the way." Victoria smiled politely and let herself in. "This feels weird, I'm usually on the other side of a desk like that. Actually, I gave up using a desk a long time ago. It's easier to talk when there's nothing between us."

"Nothing between us or in between us?" Ransom shot back, sliding her note pad and the letter packet back into their drawer while Victoria was busy trying to get under her skin.

"Now that is a very good question." Victoria sat down across from her, crossed her legs very primly, and studied her. With her elbow resting on the chair arm and her jaw propped up on her palm, she looked like a woman very much in charge of her life.

"Are you enjoying the view?" Ransom asked sarcastically.

"Very much, actually, but that's not why I'm here."

Those dark eyes caught hers, and perhaps it was a trick of the light in the room, but Ransom felt like Victoria was staring right inside her...peeking at all those shadowy corners she kept hidden from the light. Only years of training kept her from squirming in her seat. She hadn't felt this uncomfortable since she'd been in boot camp, surrounded by five DI's intent on breaking her down. Making eye contact with any one of them meant a quick dressing down. Unfortunately, with five of them surrounding you there was no way to avoid the inevitable. Kind of like now.

"I told you before I wasn't much for verbal foreplay Victoria, just spit it out."

"I need you to tell me why you keep fighting this." Victoria gestured between them. "What's happening between the two of us."

"I just think it's a bad idea."

"You can't make that decision for me, Ransom. You don't have that right. Not without a damn good explanation," Victoria argued. She needed to hear

Ransom's reasons. Those reasons were the walls that had been built between them, each excuse a single block that needed to be torn down until only honest emotion was left.

"It's not a good idea because you are dangerous to me." Ransom shifted her focus, staring at a point somewhere just past Victoria and off to the left. She couldn't look at her; it was too hard.

"How?" Victoria asked; this wasn't what she had expected Ransom to say.

"Dangerous, because you make me draw a fine line between desire and duty."

"Okay, I respect that, but I have to confess I don't understand." Victoria struggled to understand where Ransom was coming from. "One can't co-exist with the other?"

Ransom stood up, violently enough to send the chair spinning away from the desk. Her eyes flashed, like lightning dancing across Caribbean waters, both beautiful and deadly.

"I can't afford to find out. This stalker of yours, he's a dangerous man and I have no doubt he would harm you if he gets a chance." Ransom's emotions were all over the place, her anger at Victoria waxing and waning as she tried to put a voice to the whirlwind of emotions flying around inside her. She wanted Victoria, more than she wanted to admit, the desire so palpable she could feel it as a low thrumming sensation vibrating through her body. She paced because she had to, the need to move a poor substitution for the need to move against HER, to move in HER.

"So what you're telling me is that I distract you too much?" Victoria asked.

"Distract? Oh, yes, you've done a good job of doing that." Ransom smiled past the bitter taste in her throat. "I would be thrilled if that was all it was, but it isn't. Samuel tasked me with protecting you, with no regard for protecting me from replaying my greatest fear and greatest failure. He knows me too well. He knew that if you came here for protection that I would do it. But he didn't give a rat's crap what it might do to me."

Ransom covered her face, scrubbing at her cheeks and pressing her fingers against the eyelids. The afterimages of a hundred nightmares had left their mark there, etched in the veined patterns of her inner vision. Victoria's presence had brought back the past with a vengeance, her nightmares returning the first night Victoria had arrived.

"That is the danger, Victoria...I know in my heart that I will protect you from this person who you fear so much. If I have to kill him, I will be justified because he is a bad person who was planning to do bad things." Ransom stopped, drawing in another ragged breath that burned like fire in her throat. "But, if I fail, if he is better than me, I risk losing you and I risk losing everything I have. I...I can't lose another person I care for. If this person gets to you, I don't think I could come back from that, not again."

Anger that had burned red hot blew out just as quickly, leaving her suddenly empty and cold, like the dying embers of a forest fire after a heavy rain. She shivered against the sudden shift inside her, hoping that Victoria would understand even as she mourned what could have been.

"No, Ransom, NO!" Victoria's voice was strident, insistent and carried the fire that had animated Ransom such a short moment before. The haunted look on Ransom's face was the same one Victoria had seen on so many survivors of violence. It was the look of a person who had reached their limit of pain yet knew they would have to endure more if they let themselves feel anything again. "You're stronger than that."

"Look, Victoria. I'm tired. It's a rainy day. Can't we just let this rest for a little while and try to enjoy a day off?" Ransom flopped back into the chair. This whole thing was exhausting. She was scared to death and there was nothing she could do about it. It wasn't the nightmares; she had dealt with them for years. They were nothing, something to endure, ghosts from the pasts that refused to rest in their graves. This stalker? She would draw on him in a heartbeat, take him out if necessary.

What really frightened her was the depth of her need for this woman. The other night, the way Victoria looked at her, what she said...it opened a floodgate inside her she had thought was permanently closed. Passion had poured from that floodgate and she had let it sweep her up in its wild current. Endorphin laced excitement that sent her pulse soaring without a single tinge of fear or hate attached to it...that is what Victoria brought to the table. After their fierce and unexpected coupling she had fallen asleep, for the first time in so many years to the sound of another woman's heartbeat ticking off the time between them.

"Okay, we'll stop now, but I'm going to leave you with one last thing before I go," Victoria said, pulling herself up from the chair. Ransom looked up, expecting to see her heading for the door. She didn't expect to see her right in front of her, stiff-arming the desk, an inscrutable expression on her face. She tossed her head to the left, in the direction of the drawer holding those damnable letters.

"Yes, I know about the letters. Despite you trying to be slick and trying to hide them from me just now. I noticed you didn't open them." Victoria turned away then, and didn't stop until she hit the doorway. When she turned back, Ransom hadn't moved a muscle. "I'm not going to ask why you never read them, but I'm glad you saved them. That means a lot to me. Seeing them did remind me of something important. Emotions can run strong for a very long time, even in someone's absence. It's time for me to change my focus. Maybe the stalker is my past coming back to haunt me."

She nodded towards the desk. "Read the letters. You might be surprised what you find in there."

"Now, you want me to read them now?"

"No. Whenever you are ready," Victoria conceded. From the look on Ransom's face it was all she could do. Right now she needed to get into that computer and start playing junior sleuth. As long as this stalker stood between them, it was going to be damn difficult to move forward.

\*\*\*

*It's not fair. Victoria shouldn't be allowed to feel safe from me for this long. She needs to feel how I felt, like she felt when she found my presents. The roses were the perfect gift. Black for death, red for blood. Did she tremble when she held them in her hand?*

# Chapter Nineteen

Ransom didn't read the letters. She stared at them for a little while, thumbing through the yellowed envelopes that had been and still were arranged by date and clicked off where her location had been in her head. Each time she moved, the letter made it right behind her.

Snail mail was useless when you were in a unit that moved fast and often. She brought the sheaf of envelopes up to her nose and swore she could still catch the faintest taint of motor oil, antiseptic and the rubbery odor everything that ever saw the inside of a sea bag took on. It was the same smell that assaulted your senses when you walked into every Army/Navy Surplus store that ever existed. The back room in Buddy's store smelled the same way, plus brass, leather and Old Spice.

"Another time," she muttered, stuffing the envelopes back into their drawer. She stood up and stretched, running her fingers across her scalp vigorously before heading for the door. It was time to find out what the heck Victoria was talking about.

An orange flash appeared out of nowhere like a mobile yellow brick road and led the way, guiding her towards Victoria's location.

The kitchen was no Emerald City, but Victoria was managing to channel the vaudevillian energy of the good wizard. Whatever she was reading must have been enthralling because she didn't even notice Ransom entering the room until she popped the top on a cold Pepsi. Then she jumped in her seat, and despite the baleful look she shot her, launched into an excited diatribe about who she thought the stalker might be. When Ransom went to join her at the table, she moved her coffee cup further away from the computer, effectively keeping the evil contents of Ransom's soda can from coming anywhere near the computer or her notepad.

Ransom snickered. If anyone was going to spill anything today, it was the excited woman talking as much with her hands as her lips bouncing up and down in her chair. *Sit or stand already*, she thought. The woman looked like a jack-in-the-box suffering from stage fright.

"So, what you're saying is you think it's not any of these clients. You think the stalker might be someone from before you came to work for Samuel?" Once Victoria started talking about her idea, she hadn't stopped, but from what she had gathered that was pretty much the essence of it.

"Yes. Not necessarily the people I took care of, they were the victims. But there was always someone else involved, a boyfriend, an ex-husband, hell, sometimes there were pimps and drug dealers. A lot of these people were violent, and they didn't like us getting involved in their business."

"The type to hold a grudge." Ransom scratched her nose. She wasn't too familiar with DSS, only that Victoria had worked with families in trouble, usually after something happened or someone called in a report.

"Yes, especially if they ended up in prison."

"So, assuming you're right, how hard would it be to narrow it down to a possible suspect?" Ransom leaned over the table to get a closer look at the computer screen, but before she could see anything, Victoria closed the lid on her.

"I can't let you see any of my notes, Ransom. They're confidential."

Ransom lowered her head and raised an eyebrow at Victoria's sudden bulldoggish behavior. She'd almost got a finger caught in there. "Okay?"

"Look, if I could I would. Don't you think I'd just call Samuel and have him let the cops have at it?" Victoria asked, actually getting up this time. From the way she paced, one elbow propped on the other, her hand raised ineffectually in the air, Ransom got the impression Victoria used to smoke.

"Jonesing for a cigarette?"

"What?" Victoria asked. "What gave you that idea?"

"Just an observation," Ransom murmured, trying not to smile too hard when Victoria's hand casually sagged down to her side.

With nothing else to do with her hands, Victoria grabbed the back of her chair and frowned at the computer. "All this could be a waste of time. Maybe I just need something to do while everybody else tries to find this guy."

"So, basically you're telling me you're searching for the proverbial needle in a haystack, and you aren't even sure if the needle is in the stack you're tearing down."

"Pretty much. I'm just digging around, seeing if anything jogs my memory. You never know, I might stumble on something."

"You're right. You never know," Ransom agreed. It actually wasn't that bad of a plan, and if it kept her busy for a few hours every day that was good, too. "Okay, I understand I can't peek at this stuff. But I do think you should let Samuel know where you're headed with this. He's the one up there trying to keep a fire lit under the PD's ass."

That so was a job she did not want. Ransom was perfectly happy staying right where she was, even if Victoria was a major pain in her ass most of the time.

"I'm already on that. A lot of my old notes are on flash drives at the office. I'll need Samuel to send them to me." Victoria stopped, then looked over at Ransom as if she just thought of something. "What about you? If I'm busy with this?"

"First of all, this doesn't mean you get out of our runs or a little training...as for me? I can find something to do with my time, you don't need to worry about that." Ransom grinned. "Besides, if I can't see what you're looking at, I'm pretty much useless. You're basically sending me to the kiddy table while the grown up's play for a while."

"Ransom!" Victoria exclaimed.

"What? It's all good." Ransom smirked. Victoria was downright cute when she blushed, even cuter when rendered almost speechless. She would have to remember that. "I'll just take my drink here, find something bad for me to eat and watch some TV. When and if you find anything you can share, just let me know."

Ransom was determined to enjoy her rainy day. Like most vets, she had come to appreciate unexpected downtimes and learned to take advantage of them when they popped up. So far, Victoria had managed to keep herself busy, but Ransom had a feeling the enforced inactivity was going to start wearing on her so this new project couldn't have come up at a better time.

Ransom flipped through every channel on the television and found absolutely nothing interesting to watch. She left it on something boring for background noise and contemplated her options.

An old tattered copy of *Leaves of Grass* was sitting on the coffee table. She leaned over and picked it up, running her fingers over the creases and worn edges. This was one of her mother's old books. Too sentimental to leave behind, she had brought it and several other classics when she moved here. They had gone up on a shelf to be forgotten. *Until now. Victoria must have found it and left it here.*

"Good enough." Book in hand, Ransom curled up on the couch and started to read. It was heavy stuff, the poem speaking to Ransom in a way it never had as a stubborn and indifferent teenager. She half contemplated putting the book down and finding something else to read, something a little less intense, but she couldn't do it.

***

After several boring hours of pouring through what records she could find online and skimming through her emails for any clues about the stalker, Victoria found her mental state becoming more agitated the farther back in time she went. It was just so frustrating to sit and wait while other people acted on her behalf. A quick message to Samuel was another dead end. Oh, he returned her email promptly, but the cryptic and unsatisfactory message he sent back revealed nothing new other than promising to look for her flash drive.

It was as if the stalker had just disappeared from the surface of the planet after chasing her away from her home, her job...her whole boring life. There was no purpose in his actions, and it drove her crazy not knowing what had happened.

At least Bridget missed her. Several e-mails asking how she was doing sat in front of her right now, each one more concerned than the last. She hesitated, then clicked on the last message. The younger woman was beside herself with worry, and no wonder, they told each other everything and she'd been incognito now for what? Over a week and a half? Victoria bit her lip, feeling guilty as hell about doing that to her. She had been helping her with her studies, acting as an unofficial advisor since last year, and she had bailed on her completely.

*Sorry, Bridget,*

*You'll have to work on that final paper on your own this time. Hopefully my family emergency will be resolved soon and I'll be back at work. Miss you and*

*our lunch dates...especially my favorite Hoagie. We'll*
*go shopping when I get back,*

*Victoria*

Victoria leaned back and reread her message then smiled in satisfaction. No mention of where she was or what she was doing. Not even Ransom should be able to find fault with it. She hit send and closed out her programs, then shut down the computer.

Victoria finally left her self-imposed exile after her eyes started to cross and she couldn't remember what she had just read anymore. She plopped herself down heavily into the small space left at the end of the couch. Ransom pulled her long legs up under her, giving Victoria at least one cushion of her own to sit on.

"I'm BORED!" Victoria exclaimed.

"Ohhh...kay," Ransom drawled, wondering what the hell Victoria expected her to do about it.

"I can't just sit here and do nothing." Victoria practically threw herself into the padded corner of the couch. She was pouting, and she knew it, a grown woman practically throwing a tantrum at being stuck inside with nothing to do.

Ransom sighed; her quiet time was evidently over.

"You could always read a book," Ransom suggested.

"Well, what are you reading?" Victoria pounced, eager for any sort of interaction with another human after being stuck on the computer for so many hours.

"Whitman," Ransom answered, then looked down at the orange ball of fur taking over half of her lap. "Duh, Whitman...of course."

It was Victoria's turn to grin at her. "You got me. I love Whitman. The poet...and the cat."

Whitman heard his name and started purring. Ransom grunted, then spent a few seconds digging happy claws out of her jean clad thigh.

"Read something to me?" Victoria asked, catching Ransom off guard.

"From this?" Ransom's cheeks burned. The last few pages she had read were from Whitman's *Sing the Body Electric.*

*This is the female form;*
*A divine nimbus exhales from it from head to foot;*
*It attracts with fierce undeniable attraction!*
*I am drawn by its breath as if I were no more than a helpless vapor—all falls aside but myself and it.*

It didn't help that it was Victoria's face and form that flashed through her mind's eye while she read. That it was the memory of how she smelled as she lay in her arms last night that drew her breath in and made her helpless. She sure as hell was not going to read those lines to the dark-eyed woman staring at her like a hawk sighting a field mouse in an open meadow.

"No."

"Well, then you need to find something to entertain me." She had meant it as a joke, but Ransom's terse response had thrown her.

"Do I look like the court jester, Your Majesty?" Ransom scowled, tossing the book down as she stood up from the couch, her long legs unfolding from under her gracefully before stalking away.

Victoria winced; she had probably deserved the sarcasm. Still, she had just asked Ransom to read a poem, not talk dirty to her. There was a difference.

"Well, there has to be something we can do." Victoria followed Ransom into the kitchen. Ransom stood at the sink, washing out a coffee cup. She seemed tense, and as the words faded into the air between them, the cup slipped from Ransom's soapy hands. The sound of porcelain shattering was followed by a creative string of curse words, half of which Victoria was sure she'd never heard before, let alone in those combinations.

Ransom gripped the edge of the sink and tried to get her shit together. Her favorite mug lay in shards at the bottom of the steel sink. She could feel Victoria's presence behind her, could count to the exact number how many steps it would take to travel from where she stood frozen and where Victoria waited for her.

*Have you ever loved the body of a woman? ...there has to be something we can do...*

The damn poem was stuck in her head; the question that had been left unanswered posing itself to her, Victoria's voice echoing closely behind.

"How about we go grab something for dinner? The rain's let up enough to get out of here and I think we could both use some fresh air," Ransom blurted out the first thing that came to mind, making a big production of cleaning up the mess in the sink to avoid making eye contact with Victoria.

"That's sounds wonderful. Just let me go change."

Ransom sighed in relief as Victoria practically bounded up the stairs to get ready to leave. She sagged against the kitchen counter and wiped her hands with a dish towel.

"Oh, boy. This is going to be fun."

***

*I made Victoria run. I need to remember that. She's not on vacation somewhere, enjoying a Mai-Tai. That's got to hurt, being away from everybody she knows, everything she loves. I did that. I made her hurt.*

*Now I need to push, to keep her moving, to make sure she feels unsafe no matter where she is or what she is doing. Maybe then she'll get the tiniest idea how it felt to be me.*

# Chapter Twenty

Like a lot of Ransom's suggestions, they never panned out the way they originally sounded.

In other words, Victoria was way overdressed for the hole-in-the-wall Pizza Parlor Ransom drove them to.

"I thought Samuel said there was only one real restaurant in town?"

"The Two Sisters? Yeah. It's the only sit down restaurant worth going to, but I thought you might enjoy something a little different. I wouldn't quite call Giovanni's a real restaurant but they make the best pizza in three counties."

"Pizza?"

"Sure!" Ransom grinned enthusiastically. "Just mind where you sit and expect the tables to be a little sticky."

Victoria looked down at her silk blouse, then over at Ransom's flannel shirt. "Okay, give."

"You want my shirt?"

"If you want me to go in there? Yes." Victoria smiled sweetly. "Silk beats flannel any day, and I'm not ruining this one. You really don't expect me to spend the entire night remembering to keep my elbows off the table do you?"

"Fine." Ransom climbed out of the plain white utility truck she used for maintenance and yanked off her flannel. It was still raining off and on and the Jeep was topless. Victoria slipped the worn fabric on over her shirt and buttoned it all the way up.

"Uh, no. Not the top button."

"Why not?"

"Just trust me on this." Ransom reached over and neatly slipped the top button loose, then readjusted her collar. "Well, I have to say you certainly look interesting. You ready?"

"Ready as I'll ever be." Victoria took a deep breath and started their zigzag trek towards the front door. The blacktop shone wetly, reflecting every streetlight and sign in slashes of neon color. She still managed to avoid most of the larger puddles, although Ransom's penchant for just blowing through them made it difficult.

Ransom held the door open for her, then politely waited for her to enter first. Victoria balked, craning her head to try and see as much as possible of the interior without actually committing to stepping inside.

Ransom choked back her laughter. It was starting to pour again, and Victoria was acting like she was sending her into a biker bar. "Why don't I go first?"

"Thank you." Victoria's relief turned to embarrassment in three strides.

She was expecting something a little rougher around the edges than the open brick walls and bohemian style atmosphere that greeted her. A few other patrons sat at small, round tables in what she had to admit was a dimly lit, yet cozy setup. They were all young, perhaps college age, but not the disaffected types that sometimes hung out at local joints. If they didn't seem interested in the newcomers, it was because they were busy chatting amongst themselves or furiously scribbling notes.

There were a few laptops up and running as well, but no giggling girls snapping selfies or half-drunk frat boys practicing bull calls after slamming shots. It reminded Victoria of a hip coffee bar, reimagined for late night insomniacs with a craving for carbs and good conversation. It was perfect.

Ransom found them a table in a quiet corner, where she could people watch without being obvious. She didn't know a single person in there, and that was exactly the way she liked it. That was one of the hallmarks of youth, that anyone a few years older than them simply did not seem to exist...which also meant they didn't care to know who she was either.

***

"So, just out of curiosity. In your strange little version of rock, paper, scissors...what beats silk?"

Ransom's question came out of the blue. With the impeccable timing of any good waitress, she had waited until Victoria was taking a sip of her beer. Her throat closed, convulsing around the cold drink and creating enough back pressure to send beer spraying back up through the bottleneck. She slammed her foaming beer down and snatched up a pile of napkins, the last thing she needed was to smell like a brewery. *And things had been going so well,* she sighed.

"Dammit, Ransom, that wasn't funny." Victoria applied the damp towels to the table, wiping up the spill there.

Ransom shrugged, then stole a pepperoni from what was left of their pizza and popped it in her mouth. "Depends on what side of the table you're sitting on. It would have been worth it to see you shoot beer out your nose. That would have shown real talent."

Victoria silently fumed while Ransom scanned the room around her. Both of them had stopped eating a while ago. What was left of the pizza carcass looked like a culinary crime scene, a rough landscape of pock-marked cheese, cherry-picked toppings and pizza sauce. An hour ago, the pie had looked a hell of a lot more appealing and, true to Ransom's promise, was one of the better pizzas Victoria had tasted.

"You know; I was thinking about what you asked. I think bare skin. Yes, bare skin definitely beats out silk. What do you think?" Victoria asked with an air of innocence.

Ransom choked on her iced tea and almost fell off her chair. Since she had donated her flannel to Victoria, the ice cold liquid spilled down the front of her tank top instead.

"Christ, that's cold." Ransom tried to fish an ice cube out of her bra, then gave up when she realized Victoria was just sitting back and enjoying the show. Ignoring the freezing sensation between her breasts, she tapped her forehead with a couple of fingers in a half-assed salute. "Touché, Victoria, touché."

The two women stared at each other, then Victoria bit her lip and Ransom tried to keep a straight face but couldn't. Before they knew it, they were both giggling in that infectious, can't stop until your stomach starts to hurt way. A few irritated glances their way let them know they were being too loud. That just made Ransom laugh even harder. What did they know? Part of her envied their carefree lives, but they had no idea how glorious it felt to be alive when you should be dead.

"What now?" Victoria managed to catch her breath enough to squeak out. It had been a while since she had laughed like that. It felt good.

Ransom fished out a couple of twenties and slapped them down on the table. "I think we should head back now."

***

"Huh." Ransom pulled the truck to a full stop and stared at the house.

"What's wrong?" Victoria asked.

Ransom pointed along the arc of the headlamps. The hazy light danced like smoke in front of the house, everything else was pitch black. "I have security lights right there and there. They should have gone off when we passed that last tree. They didn't."

"Do you think?" Victoria swallowed. She didn't even want to entertain the rest of the question.

"I'm not going to assume anything." Ransom leaned over and popped the glove compartment open, pulling out the familiar 9mm and checking the magazine.

"I thought you were always armed?" Victoria blurted, surprised to see the weapon tucked somewhere other than on Ransom's person.

"I am."

"I so do not want to know where you're hiding a gun," Victoria chattered, letting her nervousness get the better of her.

"Party pooper," Ransom said, flashing a quick smile in her direction. Despite her humor, Victoria shivered at the wolfish grin. That was no cold smile cast in her direction, that was pure heat, one that eagerly welcomed the chase. Yet another mask Ransom hadn't shown her, and one she would not want to face over the barrel of a gun.

"Stay here. Lock the doors behind me and keep your eyes moving. I'm going to check the house. If you hear gunshots, you put this thing in drive and head straight back to town and the sheriff's station, if it's safe call 911. If you see or hear anything out here, anything at all...hit the horn, got it? But do not get out of the truck till I tell you to."

Not trusting her voice, Victoria nodded, sure she looked like a wide eyed extra in a horror movie. As soon as Ransom slipped away, she slid into the driver seat, taking refuge in the residual warmth she left behind. Ransom had disappeared. For some reason, she thought the woman would follow the headlight beams, then realized how foolish that would be. Eyes straining, she had to resist the urge to roll down the window so she could hear better. As it was, she was locked inside a vehicle with nothing but the sound of her heart tapping away like a hammer inside her chest and her breath steaming up the windshield, a rabbit caught in its den while the wolves roamed about outside.

Angry tears formed at the corner of her eyes. No matter how hard she tried, reality had a bad habit of butting in and ruining a perfectly good evening. She had almost managed to forget about the damned stalker, if only for a few hours. *Was that too much to ask?*

Blinding light answered her. Shielding her eyes against the bright glare, she didn't hear or see Ransom until she knocked on the window. She jumped half out of her seat, hitting her elbow on the steering wheel. The horn blared, her heart jumped out of her chest, and she swore she almost died right then and there from fright.

"Jesus, Ransom, you scared the crap out of me." Victoria tumbled out of the truck, her legs not quite working right for some reason, and stumbled into Ransom's arms. "Did you find anything? Is everything okay?"

Ransom gazed down at Victoria with a bemused expression. "Yes. The storm took out the power at the house. For some reason, the battery backups in the security lights didn't kick in. The house is clear."

Relief that nothing was truly amiss opened up a floodgate of emotions. Fear of course, followed by anger, both at herself and the situation, then more fear...terror really. The what if's started rolling in. What if this had been the real thing? What if Ransom had been walking into a trap?

She clung tighter to Ransom, hating her weakness even as much as she sought out the other woman's strength.

"Wait a minute. What's going on?" Ransom pulled back, searching Victoria's face and noting the tears staining her cheeks.

"Nothing. I'm being stupid." Victoria wiped her face. "I'm acting like some freaking weak kneed damsel in distress..."

"But I'm no hero, Victoria," Ransom interrupted her, "and this sure isn't some crappy pulp novel you buy on a whim at the check-out counter. Although at least I don't have to shave my chest to look good."

Victoria slapped her hand over her mouth, but not before something that sounded like a cross between a snicker and a snort escaped. "Oh, oh, one of those underdressed, hunky types that whisk's the desperate woman away to his castle and saves the day."

"Exactly," Ransom drawled. Victoria's emotions were all over the place. She'd seen it before with newbie's when the realization first hit them that the bullets they were using were real, but more importantly, so were the enemies.

"It would be downright scandalous," Victoria whispered, imagining the two of them like this, embracing boldly...perhaps even kissing.

Imagination brought their lips together and reality followed. It didn't take much to draw Ransom to her, a simple nudge...a push in the right direction. She was already that close to her. In the drizzling rain, cold, wet and shivering, it was the most imperfect setting for a perfect kiss, but she didn't care.

They moved together, finding their own refuge from the pouring rain with each other. Ransom's kiss tasted like sunlight and honey, and she felt intoxicated just from inhaling her warm breath. Time stopped for her as she reveled in the feel of Ransom's lips on hers, the universe shrinking until there was just the two of them. It was tempting to remain in that small world, one she wouldn't have to share with anyone else, but the kiss had to end. Reality could be suspended for a time, but not forever, that was the way it was.

"Ah, yes," Victoria stuttered, resting her hand on Ransom's chest. She backed way, not from her feelings, but from the reasons behind the kiss. "I, um, I don't know where that came from."

Being with Ransom felt so right, but this? Tonight would be for the wrong reasons.

"Why don't you go in? I'll follow in a while. I have to replace those batteries just in case the power goes out again."

"Thank you." Victoria made her way to the house alone. She looked back to find Ransom standing where she had left her, the shadows hiding her face from view as she peered out into the darkness and the night sky. Sighing, Victoria walked slowly through the quiet house, picking up the discarded book of poetry before heading upstairs. Her body sang with the need to feel Ransom's arms around her again. It wasn't even a sexual feeling, just an odd sensation that made her feel like she was leaving a part of herself outside with Ransom. She dressed for bed, hoping to find some warmth beneath the heavy coverlets, but she knew she wouldn't sleep...not until she heard the front door squeak open again. Once Ransom was safely back inside the house she would rest, but not until then. Victoria pushed her pillows up against the headboards and opened up her book.

"Until then, Whitman, it's just me and you." The orange tabby stopped chasing a dust bunny in the corner and meowed at her, then sauntered over and jumped onto the bed. Full of self-importance and demanding attention, she gave in and scratched his head. She hadn't meant that Whitman, but she wouldn't tell him that.

\*\*\*

*Someone really ought to update their firewall. As close as I'm getting to her, she's getting to me...if she can figure it out in time. The game is getting more interesting by the minute.*

# Chapter Twenty-One

About two miles into their morning run, Ransom signaled for Victoria to stop.

"What's going on?" Victoria asked.

"Shh. Quiet." Ransom scanned along the trail, doing a complete 360-degree spin before returning her attention to the ground in front of her.

Ransom appeared loose limbed, almost relaxed, but vibrated with a subtle tension. A small, compact dull black pistol appeared out of nowhere to rest in her left hand. Victoria hadn't seen her draw it, but its presence was more effective at keeping her tongue firmly planted against the roof of her mouth than any verbal warning.

Ransom stooped and ran her fingers around a single boot print in the muddy running track, then backtracked a bit until she found another. She closed her eyes for a second and pulled up a mental map of the property. They were close to the edge of the property. The country road that ran along the fence line was one of the old access points from back when it was a working farm. It was gated, but gates could be worked around, especially if someone was willing to hike it in.

Ransom clenched her fists. This area of the property was heavily wooded. She had it posted against hunting and trespassing, but here was clear evidence that someone was doing both. The U shaped imprint of a butt stock was pretty clear farther up. Someone had been lazy or stupid, using their rifle to help them balance to get past a rough patch.

Ransom ran through her options while continuing to scan the area. Normally she would just go after the trespassers, but she had Victoria with her.

A hundred feet down the trail, she found a second set of tracks and a discarded Copenhagen container. She decided against stalker and settled on hunters. The tracks were headed straight for Old Pond. Smack dab in the middle of one of the larger clearings on the property, it was a favorite place for the deer to stop and drink. Every hunter in the area knew that. Ransom grimaced. They also knew better than to come onto the property uninvited. Even so, this was different. It was high summer, and it was illegal to hunt out of season, not to mention downright unethical.

"Poachers," she snarled. Ransom straightened up and tucked the small Smith & Wesson sub-compact pistol she took on her runs back into its discreet concealed carry holster.

"Are you sure?"

"That it's not your stalker? Pretty sure."

"What are you going to do?" Victoria was still worried, but the minute Ransom put away her gun...she relaxed a bit. If she didn't think she needed it that was a good thing.

"Not sure. Usually, I'd follow the tracks...make sure they've left the property."

"Okay." Victoria could tell that Ransom was torn between two duties. "Well, we're already out here. Why don't you just do what you would normally do? You keep telling me I'm safer with you than anywhere else."

"This could take some physical effort, depending on how far they have trespassed onto the property," Ransom warned her.

"I'll do my best to keep up." Victoria smirked. She wanted to brag that she'd been doing just fine all morning, but she held her tongue. With a chase afoot, Ransom was all firecracker and ball lightning. She practically crackled with excitement and it was affecting Victoria. She felt charged, more focused than she had in a long time, and ready to go. The adrenaline rush was intense, invigorating in a sharp-edged way that a sedate park run could never satisfy.

A loud shot rang out soon after Ransom found the tracks. The sharp crack-pop sound echoed hollowly around them. The heavy forest distorted the sound, but Ransom could tell that they weren't firing in their direction. The second and third shots that followed close behind the first told her two things. They were up by the pond and they were really shitty shots. *I hope for their sake they are as bad a shot as that sounds.*

"Assholes. They're still here! Did they really think they'd get away with shooting on the property and no one would notice that?" Ransom looked back at Victoria. The bastards were only about a half mile away, and she needed to get there now if she was going to catch them, which meant she had to haul ass. Hauling ass meant leaving Victoria behind. Her facial expression must have given her thoughts away because Victoria simply waved at her.

"Go, go get them. I'll catch up with you."

"I can't. Tracking behind trespassers and checking to see if they poached anything is one thing, but now we know they're still here and they have weapons." Ransom sucked in her cheeks and growled. This wasn't going to work. More than likely she was dealing with a couple of locals that didn't think the rules applied to them, but poachers could get nasty. If Victoria showed up at the wrong time things could get complicated. She needed a new plan. Leaving them up here shooting at everything that moved wasn't an option either. She'd seen an unscrupulous hunter decimate an entire flock of geese in less than ten minutes, throw them in the back of his truck and haul ass away from the scene before anyone even thought about calling the wildlife officer to report him. She couldn't let something like that happen here.

Ransom pulled out her cell phone. She didn't want to bother Roy, but with Victoria here she needed some backup. "Dammit! I've got nothing."

Not only did she have zero bars, she had no signal at all. Another shot rang out. Victoria jumped, Ransom didn't. She was listening for the echo.

"Okay, change in plans. The Old Pond is about a half mile that way." Ransom pointed to her right. "If you take this trail, it will take you to the ridgetop above the meadow. You should be able to get a good signal from there.

"When you get to the ridgetop, stop and call Roy. He's the Sheriff. Tell him I have poachers at the Old Pond and that I am going to deal with them." Ransom knew when Roy heard that he would come running. *And it will keep her busy and out of my way. She'll be safe up there.*

"But, what if..?" Victoria started to ask.

Ransom held up her hand. "Don't worry about me. Just get to the ridgetop, make the call, then wait for me to come get you."

"I don't know the number," Victoria protested. She didn't like this plan one bit.

"I programmed the phone already. It's #3."

"Three, got it." Before Victoria could say anything else, Ransom took off at an impressive sprint. *Damn, she's fast...and quiet.* The woman loped through the woods with the same silence and grace as a wolf out for the hunt.

Crestfallen, Victoria realized that Ransom had been holding back, slowing down so she could keep up. She was also almost out of sight.

"Be safe," Victoria murmured, raising her hand in a belated wave. *What am I doing?*

Victoria shook herself and got moving. She had to get over this rabbit response whenever Ransom was around. The woman seemed to be able to hypnotize her with a glance.

By the time Victoria reached the ridge top, Ransom was nowhere to be seen. Far below, the sharp glint of sunlight reflecting on water caught her eye. That must be the pond Ransom was talking about.

Victoria shielded the phone screen with her hand and turned in a tight circle until she saw the bars go up.

*Bingo! Got it!* She thought, freezing in place and hitting #3. After a very long pause she finally heard the phone click and then start to ring. Ransom was not kidding when she said the phone service was horrible out here.

A male voice answered and she exhaled in relief. For a second there, she thought the connection wouldn't go through.

"Sheriff's office."

"Um, I'm a friend of Ransom Greathouse and we are out by the pond and there are poachers on the property."

Victoria was winded after her run up the hill. She knew she sounded frantic and out of breath but she couldn't help it.

"Hold on, Ma'am." She could hear a muffled call to find Roy, and then some other rustling noises before a second, older male voice came on the line.

"Victoria? This is Victoria Carrillo, correct?" The professional concern in his voice relieved her instantly; she was worried she was going to have to argue for someone to come out.

"Yes, I'm a friend of Ransom's..." Victoria launched into her spiel again.

"Yes, I know who you are. What's wrong?"

"There's poachers on the property. Ransom went after them. She told me to tell you they are up by the pond." Victoria was so desperate to get her message relayed and get back to Ransom that her words tumbled over each other.

"Poachers, huh? Where are you?"

"Um, I'm not sure. We took the ATV this morning out to the back meadow." Victoria rubbed her forehead. She was trying to remember everything Ransom had told her. Before today, they had only jogged close to the house, but after all the rain, Ransom needed to check the field cameras. "I think, yes, she said to tell you that they were camped out by the old pond."

"The Old Pond? I know exactly where you are. Stay put. I'm on my way." The Sheriff sighed heavily before hanging up. From the sound of it, he had gotten calls like this from Ransom before.

Victoria had nothing to do now but wait. She found that despite the burning pain in her legs and lungs she couldn't stop pacing.

Not knowing what was happening made everything worse. Victoria narrowed her eyes towards the distant pond, trying to figure out a logical excuse to weasel out of her promise. She didn't have to go charging in like the cavalry. It would be enough to make sure she was close enough in case Ransom got in trouble and needed her.

"Ha! Yeah, right. That's a good one." Victoria rolled her eyes at the thin as tissue paper excuse. She started pacing again. It didn't get her anywhere, but at least it kept her muscles from cramping up.

*How long will it take for the sheriff to get here?*

\*\*\*

*Oh Victoria, you will pay for making me work so hard to find you.*

# Chapter Twenty-Two

Ransom found the hunters passing a metal flask between them while they chatted along the edge of the cattail lined pond. From what she could tell, only one of them was armed. The shorter of the two, he held his rifle loosely in the crook of his arm, more concerned with the flask than the rifle.

Both men wore camouflage from head to toe, a good sign they knew they were somewhere they weren't supposed to be, doing something they shouldn't be doing. An honest hunter with tags wore a little orange to keep from getting accidentally shot.

Ransom resisted the urge to just charge in. She bided her time, noting the staggering gait of the first man, the exaggerated gestures. He stumbled about more than shifted position, and from the sound of it, he thought an awful lot of himself.

Ransom shook her head and sighed in disgust. She'd only seen one guy on active duty with a pot belly that impressive, and that was an old as dirt Senior Chief who was short enough to his retirement date he had learned how to smile again. Unlike this wannabe, that old chief had earned his end of career urban spread. After years in the service and inhaling more tear gas and crap than most, his vocal cords had shriveled up into pieces of beef jerky that made everything he said sound like it came through a meat grinder. This man's voice promised to annoy her, whiney with a twist of arrogance.

The second man was skinnier and seemed to defer to the first. Probably an employee or friend cajoled into coming out to try the new hunting rifle. Maybe a climber hoping to earn some points with the boss. Both were in their early 40's, and had the greasy, heavy-jowled features she associated with easy living and no exercise.

She instantly disliked them both.

That dislike turned to something decidedly darker the closer she came to them. The normally pristine spring fed pond was disturbed by a dark shadow laying close to the water's edge. Bright red blood ran freely into water that should only hold the reflection of green grass and blue sky. Holding in the coiled violence tightening around her heart, Ransom schooled her expression into something decidedly more pleasant than what was running through her head. She willed herself, chameleon like, into presenting as a lone woman hiking on a country trail, harmless and nonthreatening.

True camouflage was so much more than an outfit...it was an attitude, the way you walked, talked and held yourself. A woman can learn to bare her teeth beneath a smile and no one would ever be the wiser.

Those men could wear the uniform every day of the week, and any real soldier would peg them as fakes. Ransom prided herself in being who she needed to be to get the job done. Right now, she wanted to see what these two would do, and she wanted them to think they had the upper hand.

What she wanted to do wouldn't work if she approached the two men directly so she continued along the trail, pretending not to notice them. A sidelong glance caught a clearer picture of their kill as she got closer. Now she knew why they felt so proud. Her heart constricted in pain as she saw the distinctive coat and proud antlers of the herd sire. This place was supposed to be their sanctuary, the acreage on this side of the farm protected from hunting for decades.

Having these troglodytes arrested wasn't enough; they had just killed the rarest of creatures. She wasn't against hunting for food, but hunting just for the thrill of it so you could put a trophy on your wall? That was a terrible waste.

Ransom narrowed her eyes, getting a better look at their faces. They weren't local boys. Furious now, she put a mental note in the back of her head to find out how they had found out about this place. Someone had to have led them here.

Ransom felt her nails digging into her palms. The desire to tear through them and demand an answer was almost overwhelming. *Come on, already,* she urged them on, eager to get this over with.

A drunken voice called out, the shorter of the two had noticed her and was waving at her to join them. She smiled, and felt frost at the edge of her lips. *Big hunter, so proud of his kill and ready to present his prowess to the helpless female.*

She stopped and turned, affecting surprise and more than a little trepidation at finding herself alone with two men in the woods. She hesitated, acting as if she would continue on rather than risk the encounter until they called out again, ensuring her that they weren't dangerous.

*That's sweet, boys. Too bad I can't give that same assurance.*

The minute she walked into their impromptu camp, she wanted to throw up. Their sweat oozed with the smell of old beer and too much cologne, so much so she was surprised they managed to get close enough to anything to shoot it.

The farm's protected status had been the buck's downfall. The herd knew they were safe on this property and had lost some of their fear of humans. The Old Pond was their place of sanctuary, until these assholes invaded it.

Ransom put up with their puffery and swelled heads for about two minutes.

"Would you like something to drink?" Asshole #2 asked, holding out the flask and managing not to leer too badly.

"No, thank you," Ransom answered politely, noting the ugly frown Asshole #1 quickly wiped off his face. He obviously wasn't one that liked being said no to.

"Oh." Asshole #1 looked disappointed but he tried again. "We have beer, too."

*Were they really trying to flirt with her?* It was time to set things straight.

"You know what, boys? This property here is owned by a local who really doesn't like people hunting on their

212

land." Ransom kept her voice light in order to keep their guard down.

More blustering verbal accolades as to their physical attributes and ability to fight whatever man might keep them from hunting wherever they please occurred. Ransom didn't even register what they were saying. Their words descended into gibberish until they were nothing more than an annoying humming in her ears.

*Pigs don't get to talk in a human voice.* Stepping closer, she entered the personal space of Asshole #1, the one with the rifle. His smile widened into a victorious leer, no doubt he thought he had won her over. Reaching her hand out to stroke the cold steel of the rifle barrel, she looked directly into the man's bloodshot eyes.

"You know what I like best about a man's rifle?" she asked sweetly, waiting for the light to turn on in his dim eyes before acting. She moved quicker than his liquor addled mind could comprehend, her free hand coming up under the wooden butt stock as she slammed her palm down on the barrel. That sweet smile turned into a wicked grin as she neatly disarmed the man. The rifle spun rapidly, turning against her wrist neatly until it rested in her hands at a perfect diagonal angle across her body.

Pausing dramatically as the man looked down at his empty hands and then up at her, a confused and shocked expression on his face, she answered her own question.

"Hard butts." She reared back and slammed the rifle stock with enough force to drop him like a hot rock.

Ransom chuckled. If he didn't get her joke now, he would later when he woke up with a killer headache and the impression of a butt stock on his forehead.

"Hey, what the hell!" Asshole #2 watched his companion crumple to the ground like a sack of grain, then started yelling. That was just fine with Ransom. Then he made the irrevocable mistake of grabbing her by the shoulder and trying to spin her around to get to the rifle. She did nothing he expected. She dropped the rifle, grabbed the offending hand and twisted, her body movement carrying the man with her as she tucked her body under his arm and held on as she moved behind him. The man found himself on his back, staring up at Ransom and wheezing like crazy. "Having a little trouble there taking a deep breath, hmm?" Ransom asked, stepping away and retrieving the rifle.

"You bitch! You can't get away with this," Asshole # 2 snarled at Ransom before suddenly lunging for her. Something hard whizzed by his head, then connected with a loud thump. Before pain met darkness, he heard the woman's voice above him, the dry tone mocking his assumption.

"Apparently I can, because I just did."

Ransom looked down at her work and felt nothing. She couldn't until they were gone and she could take care of the mess they had left behind.

"Not done with you yet, boys," Ransom muttered, forcing herself to move again. If Victoria had done her job, the Sheriff would be here soon and relieve her of these pitiful excuses for human beings.

***

Victoria spun around. Someone had called out; she hadn't imagined it.

"Ransom?" she called out tentatively. There was no answer. "What the hell is going on down there?"

Not knowing was killing her. Victoria crossed her arms and huffed. *Put in the corner like a child while the grownups played cops and robbers.*

Victoria started pacing again, only this time she conveniently forgot to turn around after a few steps. Meandering slowly down the hillside wasn't technically following Ransom, not if it wasn't intentional.

Then she heard someone make a horrible noise that just suddenly cut off, and she was off and running without regards for her own safety. Just before she rounded the bend that would take her directly to the pond she slipped on the muddy trail, sliding face first before coming to a rest in a clump of grass. "Ugh." Victoria tried to get up, then froze and ducked back down into the grass when she saw Ransom. "Oh, no. What did you do?"

Ransom was standing at the edge of the meadow, near the water. Two very still bodies were laid out on the ground next to her, while a third lay some distance away. Ransom bent down, pulled a large hunting knife from one of the prostrate bodies and tested its edge against her thumb before leaning down again. Victoria gasped as the knife flashed, once then twice as Ransom jerked the blade up in a violent motion. She did the same with the second man then slammed the blade into a nearby log. The loud thunk as the blade sunk into the wood was one of the few things she could hear over her hammering heart. Relief washed over her when one of the men moaned and shifted, raising one hand up to his forehead and trying to sit up. He got Ransom's attention first.

*What is she doing?* Victoria's stomach and arms were covered in mud from her impromptu slide into home base. She was wet, cold and starting to shiver but she was afraid to move, unsure how Ransom would react to her spying.

Ransom grabbed the man's hand and flopped him over onto his stomach while simultaneously pulling his belt free from his camouflage pants. He started mewling like a baby, but didn't seem to have much fight in him. With neat, crisp motions, she tied the belt around his wrists, then leaned over and whispered something in his ear that quieted him down immediately. Then she did the same to the second man, leaving them on their stomachs with their arms tied behind their backs. Victoria shuddered. It looked like a decidedly uncomfortable position...effective, but uncomfortable. Even on the ground and from her hiding place, Victoria could tell that each man outweighed Ransom by at least 80 pounds apiece.

"If you're done with your mud bath, Victoria, you can come on down. I won't bite." Ransom's voice traveled up to her hiding place, the dry humor unmistakable even across the distance between them.

*How the hell did she do that? She hasn't even looked up and she knew I was here.*

Victoria stood up, trying to wipe the sticky mess from her arms and stomach as she walked towards Ransom. It was difficult for her, trying to maintain some semblance of dignity while Ransom stared at her, running her gaze up and down her mud covered body with the strangest expression on her face.

"It's not funny!"

"Yes, it is. You really should see it from my point of view. If you give me my phone back, I could even take a picture," Ransom offered. She even managed to do it with a straight face.

"Don't you dare!" Victoria exclaimed, refusing to admit that it was even the least bit funny. She hugged herself against another, more violent shiver. Ransom's expression sobered immediately.

"You're cold." Ransom dug around the campsite and pulled out a travel blanket. Before handing it over to Victoria she sniffed it, her lip curling ever so slightly before nodding.

"It's wool. Nice quality, too. They never used it so I think it's safe." Ransom surprised her by throwing the blanket over her shoulders and holding the two ends together just below her chin. She felt Ransom's hand tighten around the blanket in front of her, pulling her in closer.

"Didn't I tell you to stay put and call for the Sheriff?"

"I..." Victoria swallowed. She was saved from making up an excuse by the sound of another male voice.

217

A uniformed man popped out of the woods on the other side of the pond and waved at them.

Ransom spun around, leaving Victoria free to tuck the blanket around her and walk away. Ransom was pissed. She had been doing a good job of hiding it, but she was not happy.

"Hello Roy, I have some troublemakers for you," Ransom called out to the approaching Sheriff then turned back to Victoria. "We'll talk about this later."

"Hello again, Ransom. Nice to meet you finally, Victoria." Roy smiled at Victoria and touched the brim of his cap before turning to Ransom and the men groaning on the ground below him. "Jesus Christ, Ransom. What the hell did you do to them?"

He might have sounded gruff but Victoria could see the respect in his eyes as he took in the whole scene. A slight tightening around his mouth appeared when he caught sight of the dark carcass near the pond.

"Oh shit, Ransom...is that?" He didn't finish, and she just nodded and turned away.

Roy squatted next to the two men Ransom had taken down for poaching. They were just starting to get their wits about them, which meant they were already cussing up a storm, their voices thick and ugly and promising all sorts of fun stuff they probably shouldn't be promising in front of the County Sheriff. The louder of the two had a huge goose egg across his right temple, the other one had a bloody nose and kept sniffing like a child with a cold. He sighed; they would have to go to the hospital and get checked out before he could take them to jail.

"Hey, guys." Roy snapped his fingers in front of the two men. They twitched and pulled back from the sharp noise. "Got your attention now?"

They both nodded.

"Good, good." Roy pulled his badge off his belt and held it out in front of them. "See this? I'm Sheriff Jameson. I'm going to suggest y'all might want to reconsider issuing all those threats to Ms. Greathouse here.

"Dammit, Sheriff. I want you to arrest that woman for attacking us." The first one started in on him the minute he was back on his feet.

"Oh, really?" Roy drawled, "So, you want me to arrest the caretaker of this property who, let me see...is a woman. You want me to file an official report that Ms. Greathouse here beat up two strapping men like yourselves, all by her lonesome?"

Embarrassing them was just for fun, but now it was time to get down to business. Roy was done playing with them. He moved in closer to the two men and lowered his voice. There wasn't going to be any doubt as to what he meant by the time he was done with them.

"Do you have any idea how much trouble you are in?" He started listing the charges, ticking each one off with first one hand then the other. The men quieted down right away. Their faces paled in increments, then blanched sheet white when he added poaching and hunting inside a wildlife sanctuary.

"Are you good now, Roy? I've got to get my guest back to the house." Ransom purposefully avoided using Victoria's name now that the poachers were back in the land of the living.

Roy nodded. "Yeah, it'll be a bit of a hike back to the SUV, but I don't think they'll give me any trouble."

The two men lurched and staggered across the rough ground. He had put handcuffs on them, but Ransom's knot work had proved too difficult to negotiate so he had to cut off the impromptu restraints. Both men had to walk funny just to keep their pants from falling off their hips.

"Seriously Ransom? Did you really have to do this?"

"No, I didn't have to, but I wanted to."

"I guess I can zip-strip their pants when I get to the SUV, but did you have to cut their bootlaces, too?"

"Well, it's like you said, Sheriff. It was just little ole me and two strapping men. I had to make sure they couldn't overpower me." Ransom smirked at the Sheriff before turning and walking away. Victoria's gaze remained glued on the two men for a moment longer before she turned and followed her.

"Just make sure you come in and give your statement," Roy called out after them.

"Sure thing, Roy." Ransom was doing her best to put as much distance between her and the scene behind them.

"Oh, and Ransom? The Deputy position is still open if you ever change your mind."

Ransom stiffened but kept moving. She was not going to let him goad her today. She had too many other things to deal with.

"Not going to change my mind, Roy. Stop asking."

***

*Now I know how good her security is.*

# Chapter Twenty-Three

Ransom grabbed her keys the minute they got back.

"This time, do what I say," Ransom said, sliding the barn door shut behind her. "Stay in the house until I get back."

"Where are you going?" Victoria asked, shifting uncomfortably beneath the wool blanket. The drying mud was itchy and stiff; she had hoped to hop in the shower right away.

"I abhor waste; I am going back up to dress out the deer. He shouldn't just lie there and rot."

Ransom's answer left Victoria with a vaguely unsettled feeling in her stomach. She could not in a million years see herself doing what Ransom was getting ready to do. Just knowing that the meat came from such a regal animal would keep her from eating it.

"Oh. I don't know how you can do that." Victoria grimaced at the thought.

Ransom crossed her arms and gazed down at her. "Not for me, Victoria. I know someone that could use the meat, any food actually."

"Oh, I didn't realize."

"Did you really think it was enough just to deny those assholes' their trophy? Those men were arrogant, entitled little bastards who thought they were above the law. That's why I went after them. If we hadn't found them, they would have had their little celebration, taken their trophy and left the carcass behind."

Ransom was getting worked up again. She closed her eyes and took a couple of deep breaths before she felt composed enough to speak again. "Please, Victoria. Just get inside, lock the door and wait for me to come back."

After Ransom left, Victoria walked into the house and did as Ransom requested. She had a lot to think about. The woman really was a mystery. So passionate about her causes yet practical enough not to let those emotions get in the way. She hadn't batted an eye at taking out those two men—but what they did to that animal? That seemed to tear her up more than anything else.

Sooner than Victoria expected, Ransom returned from the pond with a large cooler tucked in the back of the jeep and no desire to engage in small talk.

"You cleaned up and changed." Ransom took one look at her and announced. She looked exhausted, standing in the kitchen trying to guzzle down the last of the orange juice. For some reason, Victoria expected her to be filthier, covered in as much dirt and grime as she had been after her slip and slide adventure down the mountain, but somehow Ransom had managed to escape the worst the mud had to offer.

"You seem surprised," Victoria said, managing to hide her disappointment. Ransom was back to short, terse sentences.

"Not surprised, just making an observation." Ransom tossed the empty carton into the trashcan. She needed to get rid of the stench of old blood and mud clinging to her clothes and coating her skin before it invaded every pore. "I'm going to grab a quick shower and change. Be ready to go in ten."

Ransom vaulted up the stairs without waiting for an answer.

Victoria sagged against the counter. Now that hurricane Ransom was upstairs, she could breathe again.

"Wow." That's all she could say. The woman was somehow managing to run hot and cold at the same time, balancing two storm front's that were bound to collide at any time. When they did, it was going to be ugly.

Ransom blew back down the stairs about five minutes later, fully dressed and ready to roll.

"Ready to go?" Ransom asked, not slowing down on her way out the door. Victoria had to pick up her pace to catch up or risk being left behind.

The Jeep was a sight to see. After all the rain, the trails had been difficult enough to navigate on the ATV, they must have been hell for the Jeep. Every square inch from the fenders down was covered in blackish mud that, surprisingly enough, had missed the passenger seat, although she did have to toe a huge chunk of mud off the floor just to get in.

Instead of turning towards town, Ransom turned the Jeep in the other direction, heading deeper into the countryside. She kept her eyes straight ahead, shifting efficiently if not a little aggressively through the corners, basically ensuring that conversation between the two of them was kept to a minimum.

When the thin county road gave way to unmarked, kidney punching gravel, Victoria started to wonder if Ransom had chosen their route just to torture her. Then they pulled up to a small cabin hidden deep in the woods. The ramshackle building, tacked together with tarpaper and mismatched scraps of old wood looked like it was ready to fall over at any moment.

"Oh, my God." Victoria felt her heart break just looking at the place. This was poverty at a level she had rarely seen, and she felt horrible for doubting Ransom. "Who lives here?"

"Mrs. Johannsen," Ransom answered, looking at the place with a troubled expression on her face. "The place is falling apart but she won't leave it. Every time I come up here, I worry she won't pop out of that door."

"Why? Doesn't she have any family to take care of her?" Victoria had to ask. She desperately wanted to know why one elderly woman would choose to live here, all alone and so far away from the rest of the world.

"Oh, she has family, alright." Ransom narrowed her eyes, furious that her last "pep talk" with Mrs. Johannsen's family had failed to produce any results. She was going to have to talk to Buddy, maybe he could knock some sense into her family. Left on her own, the old house was not going to survive another winter, and neither would Mrs. Johannsen.

"That doesn't sound good at all," Victoria said. "Are they not good people? I mean, who would leave a family member like this?"

"No, they aren't." Ransom shook her head, then blew out her breath. "Mrs. Johannsen, she's a sweet lady. She doesn't deserve this. The problem is, her asshole relatives don't see her as a relative...she was their aunt's 'live-in companion' and the minute the poor woman died, they took control of her house and sold it for a huge profit. Like a lot of women her age, she had married young, was widowed and carried on with her life. This house was the only place she had left to go when they kicked her out of her real home.

"It was a piece of crap when she moved in, and it's gone downhill from there. Me and Buddy, we remind the Smithfield's once in a while that they owe their dearly departed aunt something for taking that house from her partner despite her wishes. That house was worth a lot of money. They can afford to spend a little of it on someone else. From the looks of it, we need to pay them another visit." Ransom paused for a moment and started tapping out an angry beat on her steering wheel. "It's all bullshit. Those women were together for over thirty years."

Victoria watched her suck her cheeks in. She licked her lips, then bit one of them...obviously holding back something else she wanted to say.

"I'm sorry, Ransom," Victoria said. People were so cruel, and for the stupidest reasons.

Ransom jumped out of the Jeep and hauled out the cooler. "This won't take long."

The little old lady who came out to meet them was so wrinkled and shrunken it was impossible to tell her age, only that she was very, very old. Despite her years she walked with a straight back and an air of self-sufficiency that belied her real need. Now Victoria was angry for her, too. The woman had to be at least ninety years old. It was absolutely criminal, what her so called relatives did to her.

Ransom was different with Mrs. Johannsen. Polite and articulate, she was the embodiment of the concerned neighbor. Victoria hovered near the Jeep, uncertain as to what her job there was and too fascinated with watching the two of them to bother inserting herself into the conversation. She realized something by doing that. Separated by many years, they were still two sides of one coin.

Even from a distance, Victoria recognized a similar spirit residing inside both of them.

Strong, resilient...shaped by their experiences, but refusing to let those experiences break them completely. Mrs. Johannsen was their past, with all the knowledge and heartbreak that their history embodied...and Ransom? Her story was vastly different, but she was still willing to take up other people's fights for them. Victoria wouldn't call her an idealist, not by any measure, but she was still a fighter...a warrior down to her core. *No matter how much it made her bleed inside.*

Ransom was wonderfully gentle with the old woman, making sure to respect her dignity while still managing to do all of the work. This was yet another side of Ransom she hadn't seen before, her concern for one old woman purer in heart than most of the charity work she had seen in the past.

Unfortunately for Victoria, that responsiveness was fleeting. By the time they climbed back into the Jeep, Ransom was back to brooding over whatever else was bothering her.

The ride back to the house was much the same as the ride in, silent except for the wind blowing past her ears. When they got home, Ransom went through her security routine, then went straight up to her room and shut the door with barely more than a mumbled apology. The message was clear. Ransom didn't want to talk.

Victoria walked up the stairs with the straight back and determined demeanor she usually held in reserve for a particularly difficult interview. Ransom was going to talk to her, holding everything in like this wasn't healthy. Like it or not, they were stuck together in this house, and that meant they had to communicate. She tapped on Ransom's bedroom door, then opened it without bothering to register what she had said.

"We need to talk."

"Not right now, Victoria." Ransom met her in the middle of the room. Arms crossed and not in a great mood, she waited to see what Victoria had to say.

"Yes, now." Victoria strode into Ransom's room. "Look, I know you are mad at me..."

"Damn right," Ransom's growl, interrupted her abruptly.

"I know I should have followed your instructions..." Victoria tried again. She should have known better.

"Yes and do you know why? Those rules were put in place for your own safety. What you did was beyond reckless." Ransom's jaw clenched, the muscles working as furiously as her temper.

"That's it, exactly." Victoria stabbed her finger towards Ransom's chest. "That's what's screwing us up right now and I don't even think you see it."

Ransom's voice turned cold. "I told you before. You don't get to analyze me."

"Is that what you think I'm doing?" The haughty tone of Ransom's response put Victoria's back up in an instant. If she had been a cat, she would have hissed at the woman. As it was, she could barely contain her own fury at being dismissed so arbitrarily. Ransom was so caught up in her own concerns she was blind to the fact that someone else might actually worry about her. "You really don't get it, do you? You are so angry at me right now for doing something that you wouldn't think twice about doing yourself. Why?"

"Because you could have gotten hurt," Ransom answered.

"And how do you think I would have felt if something had happened to you?" Victoria asked very softly.

Ransom stared straight ahead of her, her expression shedding all emotion until only a stiff mask remained. "It doesn't matter. Your safety is more important."

"That's not true," Victoria shouted. "It would have mattered to me. Do you even realize what it would have done to me if something happened to you today?"

"But you couldn't help and you put yourself in danger by not listening to me. I accept the risk to myself but not to you." Ransom's response left no doubt that she had accepted her role as Victoria's savior, with all the arrogance and self-sacrificing attitude it entailed, and that infuriated her to no end. This conversation was rapidly descending into an arguing match, with most of the yelling coming from Victoria's corner. She needed to shock Ransom out of this ridiculous delusion that her life didn't mean anything.

"Well, too bad, because I am not going to let you put yourself in danger while I just stand by and twiddle my thumbs. Especially not after the other night."

"It's what I do, Victoria. It's why you're here," Ransom answered tiredly.

"I'm not sure I completely believe that anymore," Victoria admitted. "Believe me, I am the last person you'd find spouting metaphysical nonsense about soulmates and destiny, but dammit, Ransom. The odds of us finding each other again? You know as well as I do that this should have never happened."

Victoria very gently pressed her palm along Ransom's cheek. "I know you're hurting. Today was not as easy for you as you'd like me to believe, and you're still very angry."

Ransom made a soft sound in her throat, the first sign that Victoria was getting through to her since she started.

Victoria swallowed past the hard lump of fear threatening to stop her from saying what she needed to say. "I don't know what else I can say, Ransom. I'm waiting for you to tell me I'm either crazy or a damn fool."

"You're not crazy." Ransom thought about those idiot men who had come onto the property just to kill something rare and precious. They did it because they wanted to, not because they had to. They did it for the thrill and the sense of dominion over another being. Men killed other men for the same reason, even if they couched it in nicer terms. People died every day because someone wanted something you had, or simply because they had to have something to hate or demonize and you were the most convenient target. Deep down inside, all of those excuses were just that...excuses. They did it because they wanted to, because there was a thrill in it that got them off one way or another. This stalker was a good example of the worst type of human. He was enjoying toying with Victoria, and every time she thought about him a cold black anger rose up in Ransom's heart...a very personal, icy anger that had nothing to do with her job.

A wry smile that barely touched her lips ghosted across her face. "It's too late to go back, isn't it? That's what you're telling me. For all my trying, I can't keep running away from this."

"No, I don't think so."

"I wasn't lying, Victoria. If something happened to you, I'm not sure I could come back from that," Ransom admitted, then growled at the ceiling. She pressed her palms against her temples and tried calm herself down. She wasn't being fair to Victoria. "Look, about today...I'm not mad at you, okay?"

Red-faced, fingers digging into her scalp almost violently, Ransom was all over the place. The sudden emotional shift was so unexpected; Victoria almost took a physical step backward. "What?"

"I'm not mad at you, I'm pissed at myself." Ransom tossed her head, she couldn't bear Victoria touching her right now.

"Ransom, you're scaring me now." Victoria didn't back down, but she also didn't make the mistake of telling her to calm down, either. "I don't understand. Why are you pissed at yourself?"

"There were so many things that could have gone wrong up there, and there's no one to blame but myself for them. You're not a professional, Victoria. I gave you directions and just expected you to follow them, knowing that you would follow your heart first. I, on the other hand, let myself get so riled up about poachers that I was willing to run off and leave you behind. That was more than stupid. It was irresponsible."

"Not irresponsible, Ransom. Human. Passionate, loving, caring...and yes, a little bit scary at times, actually, a whole lot scary at times." Victoria ignored her pounding heart and slid her arms around Ransom's neck, threading her fingers through the silky tresses to find the soft skin beneath. She needed to be bold now. Slow and careful would get her nowhere.

Ransom was wound as tight as a wire cord. Circling the hard muscles along her spine with her fingertips, she willed her to relax into her touch. "You have got to be the most complex, irritating, fascinating, and exciting woman I have ever met, and you should never apologize for being who you are. But, and I will only say this one time. I am

232

not your damsel in distress, and you are not going to play the self-effacing hero. Your life is worth just as much as anyone else's, including mine, and don't you forget it."

Head reeling, Ransom tried to find some excuse, some reason to stop what was happening. She couldn't find anything other than a thin voice that warned her that this would end in pain and loneliness. She almost laughed at that. She was already in pain and suffering from loneliness. Buddy had scolded her that she wasn't living, just existing, and he was right.

"Still, we need to set some ground rules," Ransom said, stubborn to the end.

"I agree. If this is going to work, we need to make sure we work as a team. A team, Ransom. As in together."

Ransom searched Victoria's face, seeking something there, something that was important to her. "You'll train with me then, including firearms training? No excuses?"

"Yes," Victoria conceded. "Even though I have to admit that part of it frightens me a little bit."

"Then we're even," Ransom whispered. Victoria scared the crap out of her because she reminded her how it felt to be alive, in all its terrifying, soul risking glory. *I wonder if she realizes how much scarier that is than anything else I do?*

"What?" Victoria's question was lost, left incomplete and unanswered when Ransom followed up that enigmatic comment with a kiss. When those lips met hers, she could taste every held back fear, every unfed passion that Ransom had kept locked up tight inside her for far too long. She hungrily devoured those emotions with her own lips, taking what Ransom needed to lose, and sharing with her what she had been missing. She opened her mouth, deepening the kiss until she felt nothing but passion, desire and need flowing between them.

*** 

*It's funny, you know. I thought we had something at some point. The first time I saw Victoria, I was in awe of her. She was so pretty, and she smelled good, too. She always had a smile for me. She made me believe she cared about me.*

*That was a lie. It was all a lie. She didn't care. It was all an act, and very soon, I'll get my chance to prove it.*

# Chapter Twenty-Four

A cell phone was ringing somewhere. Its muted tone infiltrated Ransom's dreams, a semi-somnolent reveille call echoing inside her skull and sending her into full alert mode. Her internal alarm clock had failed her. It was late, at least 7am, and she was still in bed. The bedsheets moved next to her, then moaned. *And not alone.*

"Phone, where's the phone?" Ransom rolled out of bed, landing neatly on her feet and grabbed the first article of clothing she could find.

"I don't hear it," Victoria protested, crawling out of the covers a lot slower than Ransom had. She toed a pair of jeans from where she sat at the edge of the bed.

"I do, just start looking." Kidnapped and gagged by denim or cotton, the damn thing had to be somewhere in the discarded pile of clothing strewn about the room.

"Got it!" Victoria crowed, holding the phone up in her hand like a trophy. Somehow it had gotten kicked under the bed.

"Toss it here." Ransom held up her hand, neatly plucking the phone out of the air with a quick twist of her wrist that made Victoria feel like Quasimodo in comparison.

"I wish I could wake up like that," Victoria said, overtly admiring Ransom's ability to function.

"No, you don't," Ransom stated flatly. She had earned that "skill" out of necessity. Hypervigilance, they called it. Waking up at the slightest sound could be the difference between surviving the night or ending up in a black bag with nothing but your dog tags left to identify you—if you're in a war-zone. Do that when you get back home and all you do is stay up all night, trying to burn off the adrenaline rush. Every sound crashes through your skull at a billion decibels because you're straining to listen for anything that doesn't belong.

"Dammit. I missed the call." The phone flashed a second later. "You've got to be kidding."

The Sheriff was calling back. Ransom muttered something unpleasant under her breath. It was just like him to do that, rather than leave a message. She had the option of ignoring a message, but she couldn't risk ignoring a phone call.

Unfortunately for him, his phone call had nothing to do with Victoria's case and everything to do with the two men sitting in a jail cell. She was only half listening to him because Victoria was doing her best to distract her. She could think of a dozen things she would rather be doing today than going into town, half of which wouldn't even require leaving the house...or getting dressed. Her mind firmly in the gutter, Ransom snapped at Roy when he pressed her for an ETA. "Jesus, Roy. You have the worst fucking timing in the world, you know that?"

"You have something more important going on I don't know about?" Roy asked.

"No, not really." Ransom backtracked before he got curious and started asking questions. Roy didn't need to know why she was being so testy. He just needed a good excuse for why she sounded so damn out of breath. "Just working on some broken fences I've been meaning to mend."

"Uh, huh," Roy drawled.

"Come on, Roy, just say your peace so I can finish what I was doing."

Victoria had been gathering up the rest of their clothes when Ransom said that. She broke into a coughing fit. She couldn't help herself. It was either that or start giggling like an idiot. Ransom frowned at her, drawing her eyebrows down in a stern expression meant to warn her, but all that did was make her laugh even more. Victoria tipped her head towards the bed, taking in the tangled sheets, the small pile of clothing she had just picked up from the floor. Their clothes. From last night.

Comprehension dawned in Ransom's eyes, followed by a bright red glow that crept up Ransom's neck and across her cheeks. Victoria grinned. That had been one hell of a Freudian slip. How could she resist?

"Are you blushing?" Victoria whispered. She didn't think she'd ever seen the woman blush "You are blushing!" In her glee, she forgot that she was naked and far too close to the other woman to get away with teasing her. There were consequences.

Ransom pounced without warning, pulling her close and managing to hold on to her with just one arm. Errant fingertips slipped along the same path as that shiver, up and down...finding the base of her skull and tickling the sensitive skin just behind her ears.

"Tease." The accusation floated out on the slightest exhalation, a ghost of a word uttered so quietly Victoria wasn't even sure she had heard her right.

A mischievous glint sparked across Ransom's eyes, eliminating any doubts she may have harbored. Her lips twitched, reforming into a devilish smirk that meant she was up to no good and was going to enjoy doing it. Victoria gasped. Ransom was going to kiss her...while she was still on the phone.

*Would she risk that?* Roy was a cop. Yeah, he was the Sheriff of a podunk little town in the middle of nowhere, but he wasn't deaf or dumb.

It was Victoria's turn to blush, but the flames licking across her cheeks had nothing to do with embarrassment. She wanted Ransom to kiss her. Her pulse raced, responding to the thrill of having an unsuspecting audience. Her lips parted, anticipating what Ransom's heated gaze promised, only to be thwarted a moment later when Ransom cursed and spun away.

"Dammit, Roy, I shouldn't have to move on their schedule. This is bullshit." Ransom rolled her neck and stared at the ceiling. Roy was not giving up. "Fine. We'll be there."

"What's going on? Did they find the stalker?"

"No, I'm afraid not. We need to go in and give our statements this morning. Roy insists it has to be done now, before the jackasses' lawyers show up."

"And you're upset, why?"

"Because I don't want to go." Ransom rubbed her eyes. It was too early in the morning to feel this tired.

"Fuck. Sorry, Victoria. I know that sounded childish. It's just...well, this is a small town. I know you don't think much of it, and it seems like a nice, simple place to live compared to the city, but the politics here can be hell."

Victoria sat down at the edge of the bed and nodded. "I think this is where I usually ask if you want to talk about it."

Ransom snorted, then pulled Victoria back up into her arms and kissed her soundly. "You, my dear, are becoming very good at saying just the right thing. Not too bad for someone trained to listen to other people pour their hearts out."

"Is that a compliment?" Victoria asked, breathless after Ransom's impromptu kiss.

"Yes." Ransom winked at her, then grabbed her jeans and headed for the bathroom. She walked backwards the last few steps, just so she could toss out one last parting shot. "Just don't mistake the compliment for an open invitation. No one crawls inside my head, not even you."

***

Ransom pulled up to the Sheriff's station and parked next to the Sheriff's SUV. Her movements precise and efficient, she jumped out and ran around to the passenger side and helped Victoria climb out.

"Don't worry. This won't take long. We'll get this done and get you back up to the house."

"You're in an awful hurry. Are you trying to get rid of me already?" Victoria teased. She had noticed a sudden drop in temperature accompanying Ransom's comment and she wanted to bring that lazy, sexy smile back to her face.

Ransom looked at her funny. *What kind of question was that?* "No, not at all. I just thought you'd want to get back to going through your files."

Those files were the only good lead they had, a possible link between Victoria and her stalker she couldn't ignore. She couldn't help Victoria with her research because of confidentiality rules, and it chafed her ass that her hands were essentially tied while everyone else ran around looking for this creep. Ransom felt like a glorified bodyguard with no idea of who the bad guy was or what he looked like. Everyone, and she did mean everyone, they passed by or drove past could be the stalker. She wouldn't know unless he acted or said something to give himself away.

That meant maintaining a constant state of readiness that wore on her, mentally and physically. The only place she trusted was the farm. The house and the land around it was more than just a refuge, it was a buffer from the outside world.

"The files, yes. Of course," Victoria stuttered over her answer. Ransom seemed so keen on helping her find this creep. *That's her job, remember? I can't fault her for doing it,* Victoria thought.

"Come on," Ransom held out her hand. Victoria was acting very strange, but she wasn't about to ask her why right now. Right now they needed to get this situation with the two poachers done and over with. Ransom frowned. Yet another unpleasantness to leave in the past. "Roy's waiting for us inside."

Victoria stared at Ransom's hand, open and waiting for her to take it. A powerful surge of possessiveness welled up inside her, hot and hungry, surprising Victoria with its voracious need to let other people know they were together. Not just other people, she amended, townspeople who knew and had grown up with Ransom.

Ransom strode into the squat building and headed straight for Roy's office, blowing past the stunned secretary who just sat there, mouth gaping open like a bloated fish. Victoria felt sorry for the woman. When Ransom wanted to, she could be quite impressive, carrying an air of unstoppable force that discouraged other people from stepping foolishly in front of her chosen path.

"Where is the paperwork I need to sign?" Ransom asked, unceremoniously bypassing any social graces in her irritation at having to be there in the first place. She had been avoiding the tedious task, hoping that he would eventually get the hint and just drive up to the farm. She wasn't opposed to a quick visit by Roy, not if it would have saved her from a trip into town.

"Good to see you again too, Ransom. Ms. Carrillo." Roy stood up and adjusted his tie, then waved at a youngish uniformed woman to join them. "Actually, I need a statement from both of you. Ms. Carrillo, if you'd just follow Deputy Jones here, she'll take your statement. Ransom, you're with me."

"No," Ransom said, flatly refusing Roy's request.

"No?" Roy raised an eyebrow at her.

"I don't want Ms. Carrillo's name on any official paperwork. She had nothing to do with what happened yesterday. In fact, she had strict orders to stay away from the area and didn't see a thing." Ransom turned, gazing levelly at her companion. "Other than calling you, she had nothing to do with the entire episode. Isn't that right, Victoria?"

"Yes, that's right," Victoria said, taking her lead from Ransom.

"Ransom..." The warning tone in the sheriff's voice was unmistakable.

The air in the small office had been stale before, now it felt absolutely frozen. Victoria's jaw dropped. Between the two of them, she wasn't sure which one of the two was more stubborn...but she knew which one she considered more dangerous. Roy would be disappointed to find out it wasn't him, despite the big ass Colt strapped to his waist.

"Sooo...I think I'll just find a cup of coffee while you two hash this out." Victoria headed for the door, managing to grab the deputy before she escaped.

"Lead me to coffee," she whispered, her expression screaming "help me".

The deputy shot a guarded look back at her boss, then flashed a quick smile at her before leaning closer.

"Sure thing. I don't blame you. Those two are like oil and water, I wouldn't want to be in there either when they go at it."

"Really? Do tell." Victoria grinned. Ransom had taught her the importance of proper reconnaissance...and here was a lady who looked like a talker.

***

"There." Ransom signed the paper work and turned around to leave. She was hoping to collect Victoria and make a quick escape before Roy gave her his usual spiel. She made it as far as the door.

"Ransom, one more thing before you go," he rushed on before she could object or leave, both of which were an equal possibility. "I really wish you would reconsider my offer and become a Deputy. You're wasting your skills sitting up there on that farm all by yourself."

"I'm not by myself, Roy, I have Victoria with me."

Ransom sounded perfectly reasonable, and quite happy to have a new excuse for not accepting his perpetual job offer, and that was the problem. Victoria wasn't from Johnsonville. She had a job, friends, an entire life she had been torn away from. When Ransom found her stalker, and he had no doubt she would, Victoria would run home and leave her behind. She didn't deserve that, and it would only make her dig her heels in even deeper. He would never convince her to leave the safety of her refuge.

"Yes, for now. But she will be leaving eventually," he persisted, somehow maintaining a passive attitude in the face of the deadly glare Ransom threw his way.

"You don't know that."

"Look Ransom. I understand. It's pretty obvious that something's going on between you two. This isn't just about the "job" anymore, it's personal." Roy shook his head at her. "I just don't want to see you getting hurt over something like this."

"Roy, listen to me. I know you mean the best for me, and I know you're only doing what my Dad asked you to do. I appreciate that. But honestly? This is none of your business." Ransom was getting pissed now. "And as for the job? Why would I want to take you up on your offer? The people here, they don't even know what to do with me, let alone how to treat me. Which Ransom Greathouse would you be hiring? In their eyes, who would they see?"

"Now, Ransom. You're being too harsh on the townspeople." Roy stood up, finally losing his amiable country sheriff routine.

"Am I?" Ransom spat. "If I wasn't everyone's favorite war hero we wouldn't even be having this conversation. You know as well as I do that hiring me would be political suicide for you."

She turned her face away and closed her eyes. *No. I will not do this again.* Ransom rapped his desk with her knuckles. "You know what. I'm done here. You have my statement. If anything else comes up, please let me know, otherwise I'm going back up to the farm."

She found Victoria in the breakroom. "Are you ready to go?"

"Yes."

Each lost in their own thoughts, the two women scrambled back into the Jeep and headed for home.

Ransom spent the ride silently fuming at Roy. It was cruel of him to remind her of her shortcomings like that. She barely tolerated short trips into town, a place she grew up, around people she knew all her life...but he didn't know that, did he?

*Dammit, Roy. I didn't need a dose of reality this early in the morning.*

***

*I see you but you don't see me.*

# Chapter Twenty-Five

"Again."

Victoria cursed and slapped the padded mat beneath her. It had been two long weeks of training with Ransom, two weeks of drill sergeant worthy barking and martial arts training that she thought Victoria would find handy "just in case". Two weeks of bruises, cursing, sweating and frustration while they sparred in Ransom's basement for hours on end.

It was also two weeks from the day that Sheriff Jameson had called them in to take their statements over the poacher incident. Ransom had left that interview in a foul, broody and contemplative mood. Once they got back to the farm, she had returned to several of her old habits. She was completely professional, friendly enough in a casual sort of way...but whatever strides they had made as a couple...and yes, Victoria had started to think of them as a couple, just vanished.

The closest she was getting to any physical contact with Ransom now was their workouts and that was not how Victoria wanted to spend their time together. Hours of sweating, grunting and grappling with a woman who made her skin tingle every time they touched. Each time Ransom grabbed her, she was supposed to move in and go limp, but it was damn hard to concentrate when all she wanted to do was throw her down on the mat and have a real workout. Except that Ransom was stronger, faster and better than she was.

"This sucks," Victoria muttered.

"Maybe, but it might save your life someday." Ransom ignored the baleful look Victoria gave her, she'd seen it before and was immune to the expression. She knew she was driving Victoria hard, but she had good reason for it. It wasn't enough for her to know how to perform the moves, she had to be able to do it from muscle memory, instantly, without thinking about it.

"In a dangerous situation, when the adrenaline is pumping through your veins and fear paralyzes any attempt at coherent thought, that is when training like this will make the difference. Boring, repetitive training that performs regardless of your emotion, that reacts only to the situation."

She held out her hand and hauled Victoria back up to her feet.

"Again," Ransom repeated the command for what seemed like the thirtieth time that afternoon.

*Boring, repetitive, emotionless.* Ransom's little lecture was full of unintentional barbs that kept picking at her emotions. Victoria was over it, done. She was pissed and turned on, and so damn frustrated over the entire situation that she wasn't paying attention when the object of both her fantasies and her irritation grabbed her again. She reacted instinctively, driven to strike out at the woman who denied her for so long, yet kept tempting her with her presence. She let Ransom pull her in before turning boneless, falling back just as she put effort into her motion, pulling the blonde down and over her as she purposefully fell to the mat. Her momentum carried her, and she suddenly found herself straddling Ransom, who lay prostrate beneath her thighs on the mat. Wide-eyed, her arms held out to her sides in surrender, Ransom seemed just as surprised that Victoria managed to flip her as she was. Beneath that, a sharp glint of something else flashed across her eyes. Respect?

*Got you!* Victoria smirked, just before her brain ground to a halt and shifted gears, her body reacting to the intimate position almost instantly.

The ragged sound of their breathing was the only noise in the quiet expanse of the large basement. It sounded overly loud in Victoria's ears, competing with the sound of blood rushing like a crimson torrent at her temples in time with her pounding heart. The two women stared at each other for what seemed like eternity, neither sure what to do next. It was Victoria who moved first, her head dipping lower as if unable to fight the magnetic pull Ransom's lips seemed to hold on her.

She half expected Ransom to protest. Instead, Ransom just watched her with a mildly bemused expression on her face. There was no modest lowering of eyelids, no flutter of lashes or looking away in order to break the moment, not a single clue for Victoria to follow.

*Be bold. What's the worst that could happen?* Victoria asked herself, wetting her upper lip with her tongue and tasting salt. Ransom's gaze slipped down, following that simple action with her own. Her lips parted just the slightest, and she inhaled deeply enough to shift Victoria's weight back.

Victoria brushed her lips very softly against hesitant lips, inhaling the spicy scent of the other woman's skin. Caught up in the memory of another night, she moaned and tried to deepen the feather-light kiss.

Suddenly, Victoria was straddling something a hell of a lot less complacent as Ransom's body tensed and bucked violently beneath her, rolling her so quickly her head spun and she found herself back on the mat again, bright green eyes watching her closely, much like a cat did when it was toying with a mouse. Like that mouse, she was tightly pinned, unable to move beneath a very warm and solid body that might as well have been a brick house. She struggled for a moment, then gave up.

Victoria gasped when Ransom lowered her head until they were practically nose to nose. She was so close; Victoria could count the gold flecks hidden within the emerald green depths. Those flecks began to disappear, sinking into a sea of black as Ransom's pupils dilated, until only a corona of pale green held those inky black pools at bay. The kiss that followed was unexpected, quick, powerful, and left her completely breathless as Ransom's full lips pressed against hers. A demanding tongue pushed aside any resistance on her part, then withdrew before Victoria could fight back, leaving only a taste and a promise that made Victoria beat her fist against the hard foam mat in frustration.

"You aren't focused," Ransom accused the woman trapped beneath her.

"Me? Need I remind you that you just kissed me?" Victoria asked in disbelief. She made it sound like it was her fault Ransom was able to overpower her so easily.

"Only to prove how easily distracted you get." Ransom climbed off of Victoria.

"I flipped you, didn't I?" Victoria was moving past frustrated, especially since she was suddenly talking to Ransom's retreating back.

"You know what...I'm done." Victoria rolled away from the training mat and headed for the stairs. *Done with the day, done with Ransom and seriously done with being teased and then left gasping for air like I'm the prize in some fucked up catch and release contest.*

As Victoria attempted to storm past the source of all her anger and frustration, Ransom spun around and grabbed her arm.

"Done with what?" Ransom demanded, then snatched her hand away from Victoria's arm when she realized what she was doing.

Her face paled, and she examined her hand for a moment, staring at it as if she didn't know who it belonged to, then scrubbed her palm across her thigh as if she could erase the physical memory.

"You. Me. Us. You take your pick, Ransom. You keep pushing me away when I know you want me as much as I want you. Well, I can't do it anymore. Nothing has happened in over two weeks. My practice, what's left of it, is in shambles. I'm going back home."

"It's not safe to go back yet," Ransom argued.

"I'll take my chances. Look at you; you are so stressed out trying to keep me safe from some unknown entity that you aren't taking care of yourself." Taking a deep breath to bolster herself, Victoria swallowed hard before continuing. "I care too much about you to watch you destroy yourself for me, so I'm done."

She was surprised at how hard that was to say. As sharp as a razor, the words stuck in her throat and raked across her vocal cords. There were too many painful truths held in that one sentence.

Ransom tried to speak, but she was held off by an upraised hand demanding her silence.

"Look, I'm not an idiot, nor am I deaf or blind. I told you, just because you've taken to sleeping on the couch doesn't mean I can't hear you stay up most of the night, that I don't hear your nightmares. You do know you talk in your sleep, right?" Victoria demanded, letting herself feel all the rage and frustration she'd been holding inside.

"No, I didn't." Ransom's subdued response sounded mechanical, emotionless.

"How are you supposed to protect me, when you spend half your time avoiding me, and the other half running away from your past? Do you know how hard it's been for me to watch you not eat, not sleep, always vigilant to the point of making yourself sick, and for what? So you can protect me when or if this stalker ever shows up? At the rate you're going, you are going to be useless to me and to yourself! I would rather leave now than watch this slow spiral you've fallen into. It hurts too much to watch you do this to yourself because I know you are doing it for me." Victoria gestured, taking in the haunted expression, the dark circles under Ransom's eyes. She couldn't continue staying at the farm with the way things were. Ensuring her safety was one thing, but destroying Ransom in the process was another.

"It's still safer here. No matter what, you know I can protect you," Ransom insisted, not realizing that she would have sounded more convincing if she hadn't retreated from Victoria in the first place.

"Is that the only argument you have left? Because honestly, that's not enough right now. No one's heard a damn thing from the stalker since the attack on the PI. Maybe he's lost interest and moved on." Victoria waited for Ransom to say something, anything to convince her to stay.

She didn't. Victoria knew what she wanted to hear, but she wasn't sure if Ransom did.

"I need some fresh air." Victoria's shoulders sagged in disappointment. She bolted past Ransom and out of the house, managing to make it to the porch before breaking down. She clung to the wooden rail as tightly as a sailor would cling to the deck of storm-tossed ship, and the world around her felt just as unsteady.

Whitman appeared out of nowhere, jumping onto the railing next to her and meowing for attention. She sniffled, then chuckled wryly. Of course. Leave it to a cat to put things in perspective. Your world feels like it's twisted and turned on its head? Wait for a cat to stroll by, balanced on the thinnest beam like it's nothing at all. You're an emotional train wreck? Doesn't matter. It's all about the pets. Behind the ears, if you please. In return, you'll get a purr.

"Well, Whitman. Any sage words of advice for me today, hm?"

All she needed to hear from Ransom was that she wanted her here, not to keep her safe, or because it was her job...but because SHE wanted her here. How hard was that?

*Evidently, pretty hard,* Victoria berated herself, *because you can't even bring yourself to ask her.*

The screen door slammed behind her. She couldn't hear Ransom moving behind her, but she could feel her presence. Starting as a tingling sensation along her spine, it curled around the base of her skull and made the small hairs at her neck stand up on end. She didn't want to turn around. It was too easy to fall into those soulful green eyes, a sensation much more pleasant than drowning, but still capable of stealing her breath away.

"Victoria, I'm not sure what you want from me."

*Just tell me you want me to stay with you,* Victoria thought, squeezing her eyes shut against the deep ache that desire engendered. There were other words, but those would do for now.

"This has nothing to do with anything I want from you. If anything, it's quite the opposite."

Whitman was getting the benefit of her inner turmoil, purring like crazy while she ran her hand across the silky fur, and head-butting her whenever she forgot to keep her fingers moving. The tabby cat was a tiny little orange ball of tranquility in a sea of confusion right now, and she needed that anchor.

"I don't want you to go, Victoria, really I don't." Arms wrapped around her middle as if to ward off some invisible blow, Ransom looked wounded, both physically and mentally.

The protective posture wasn't lost on Victoria, if anything it reinforced what she already knew. Ransom was hurting. It was a deep hurt that had nothing to do with any physical injury and it was tearing her up inside. The military might have patched Ransom up before letting her go, but they sure as hell did a shitty job dealing with the psychological shrapnel left behind.

"I don't want to go either, but unless something changes, I can't stay. We had a bargain, Ransom. You promised me we'd be a team, and you reneged on that deal. I thought you understood what I was offering you, but it looks like I was mistaken." She reached up to capture Ransom's face between her hands. "Look at me. Don't turn away from me. I am offering you this day and whatever days we have together and it is enough. All you have to do is choose!"

"Whatever days we have together," Ransom muttered. "How many is that? Another week? Two? You already threatened to leave even though the stalker is still out there. There's nothing holding you here once this situation is resolved."

Victoria took a step back. "Wait. Stop right there. All of this...sleeping on the couch, pulling away from me, it's because you think I'm going to leave when this is all over?"

"Yes, Roy said..."

"Roy?" Victoria exclaimed, finally making the connection. Now things were starting to make perfect sense. "He told you this, didn't he, that day he called and asked for your statement?"

"Yes."

"Well, with all due respect for his position, Roy is an asshole." Victoria took a deep breath and exhaled. "And I'm not far behind."

"What do you mean?"

"I've been sitting here all this time, expecting something from you that you couldn't give me, all because someone convinced you that I was going to leave as soon as I got the chance." Victoria bit her lip before she said something she couldn't take back. *Damn, and I fell right into that trap by threatening to leave today.* But Roy? Roy had seriously thrown a monkey wrench in their relationship by butting in like that, and she really wanted to know why. Poor Ransom had been put into an untenable position where she was bound to lose either way, no wonder she suffered so badly these last two weeks. "I can't excuse myself for my part in this, but I need you to know...I would never have let things get this far if I had known about this."

Victoria kissed her, just a quick brush of lips along her cheek, then smiled, almost sadly. "We are a pair, you and I. I'm supposed to be so good at talking to people, yet I keep tripping things up with you left and right. The only right thing I've said today is that I'm done. I am done, Ransom. I'm done with fighting. I'm done with us screwing up because we're not communicating. I'm done with trying to be the careful one. I'm going to be you for a second. Blunt, direct and straight forward. It's juvenile, and doesn't even begin to define how I feel about you, but I want you to be my girlfriend. I want us to be together, not because I have a stalker, or just until my stalker is caught, and not when or if you ever deal with your past and all the nightmares that come along with it. I want us to explore what we have now, until there's nothing else left to explore, then I want us to sit back and grow old together so we can enjoy what we discovered. Is that clear enough for you?"

Ransom's body tingled with unseen potential, the raised skin sort of feeling you get when you stand outside in a storm and lightning flashes so close to you that static electricity caresses every nerve ending in your body. The sensation curled in on itself, coiling low in her belly and sending tendrils of liquid fire snaking through her to embrace her heart, melting the fear away. Energy surged through her, the potential demanding action and she vibrated with the need to taste life on the lips of the woman watching her so closely.

"You are a very persuasive woman, counselor," Ransom murmured, kissing her soundly before abandoning the sweet taste of her lips for the tender flesh at her neck.

"It is what I do best," Victoria managed to gasp.

"Is it?" Ransom asked, reclaiming the fiery mouth with her lips and tongue.

\*\*\*

*He might think it was his idea to go off on his own but it wasn't. I'm the one in charge of this game not him.*

# Chapter Twenty-Six

Ransom plunked a clunky looking plastic box down on the kitchen table and cleared her throat.

"What is that?" Victoria asked, barely tearing her gaze away from the laptop to spare the box more than a glance. After staring at the screen for so long her eyes protested the lateral movement. She groaned and pinched the bridge of her nose to relieve the pressure, then blinked rapidly to clear her vision. "Argh, I need to find something soon, this is driving me crazy."

The likelihood of her finding anything in her files seemed to move farther and farther away with each passing day. There were just too many possibilities.

"Nothing in your older files either? The one's from before you started your private practice?" Ransom asked, pushing aside the box for the moment. If Victoria was willing to talk about her cases now, the box could wait.

"No, nothing." Victoria shifted uncomfortably in her seat. "I'll be honest with you. I don't like going through those files."

"Why?" Ransom asked, perking up considerably. *Now this was interesting.*

Victoria closed the laptop and ran her hand over the smooth surface before leaning back in her chair. "I guess it's my turn to talk about the past, eh? It's okay. I don't mind, not really, because you already know a part of it...you are a part of it. That night we met in the bar, do you remember how screwed up I was? That was the night I made the decision to leave DSS and go to work with Samuel. That was the night I left what little bit of idealism I had behind me, along with my resignation letter."

"What happened?"

"What didn't happen?" Victoria asked, then shrugged. She had opened up this can of worms, she might as well lay her own cards out on the table. It was only fair, considering how far she'd pushed Ransom.

"I was tired, Ransom. Tired and sick and wore out from dealing with the bureaucracy and politics. It was all a money game. Cut as much funding as possible, focus on the cases that got air-time that might make us look bad if they weren't handled right, while families who really needed help were left behind, forgotten or put on hold for so long they might as well have been." Victoria ran her hand across the laptop again. So many lives inside there, so many lives ruined that could have been saved with the right help. "These cases. It's painful to revisit them. Joan S. She's one I remember well. Three trips to the Emergency Room, begged for help to get away from her abusive husband. We tried to get her into a shelter. The last time they called me into the Emergency Room, it wasn't for her, it was to take her 2-year-old baby girl to a temporary foster home because she didn't survive the last beating. He was arrested, finally, but it was too late for her."

Victoria was on a roll now. "Erica B? She was only 13 when complaints of abuse were somehow ignored or lost. She was subsequently adopted by her mother's new husband. It was only after he was arrested, again, for drug charges and sexual assault, that DSS discovered he was a known sex offender with prior arrests and convictions in another state. That should have never happened."

Victoria blinked away the tears that still tried to fall when she thought of all the pain and suffering she had witnessed over the years. "The list goes on and on."

"But that's not your fault," Ransom said, she understood politics and bureaucracy. It was a horrible joke in the military that you had to remember that all your equipment, including your weapons, were manufactured by the lowest bidder. That made everything a potential clusterfuck.

"No, but it still feels like it," Victoria muttered.

"I get that."

Ransom's dry, mocking tone got Victoria's attention. Her head shot up, eyes wide and with such a mortified expression on her face Ransom almost chuckled at her overreaction. "Geez, Ransom, I'm so sorry."

"Nothing to be sorry about. We all have our demons to deal with. I'm actually sort of glad you have a few of your own." Ransom shook her head. "Believe me, I'm the last one to make any judgement calls. I used to be just as idealistic...young and stupid and willing to believe I could make a difference. It didn't take me long to figure out that life was way dirtier and not quite as clear cut as I had believed."

People killing people, that's what it came down to in the end. In war, that was something humans managed to do pretty efficiently on an insane scale...but it needed individuals willing to play the game to make it work. Ransom had met some downright terrifying people, ones who could kill without remorse or contemplation. The sad thing was, they weren't even the worst of the bunch. There were truly sadistic bastards out there who weren't interested in killing their victims...they wanted them to suffer. She had seen those victims first hand, mostly woman and children. A slow shudder rolled across Ransom's spine and neck, like someone had just walked across her grave.

*It was always the woman and children that suffered the most in any war, as if whatever made men go insane and start killing each other also made them destroy the most innocent among them. That's what Victoria is talking about, innocent lives damaged and betrayed by those who were supposed to protect them.*

"You've gone quiet," Victoria observed, stroking Ransom's arm to bring her back from wherever she had gone off to. "Can you tell me what you're thinking?"

"I just realized that we aren't that different, you and I, despite the paths we've taken. We have more in common than I ever imagined." The two of them might have fought different wars, but they both fought for the same thing, and they both carried the scars to prove it...the good counselor was just too busy trying to help everyone else with their wounds to tend to her own. From what Victoria just told her, she had spent just as much time playing in a war zone as Ransom had. Only her combat time wasn't spent in some third world country, she had found plenty of cruelty right here at home.

"Would you care to explain that to me?"

"Maybe, but not today." Ransom's eyes gleamed with secrets she obviously meant to keep. "Today we do something different. Today you learn how to use this."

Ransom pushed the plastic box back in between them.

"Ransom." Victoria's voice trembled a bit. Guns scared her. "I'm not sure I need a gun."

"Maybe not. I don't expect you to become an expert, but you should become familiar with it..."

Victoria held up her hands. "Yes, I know. Just in case, right?"

"You got it." Ransom's grin was fleeting. "But, seriously. This isn't a joke. You need to become comfortable with this weapon. If I don't think you can be safe with it, I won't push you about it, okay?"

Victoria stared down at the dull gray/black pistol. For something so small, it still looked deadly, and probably was. She shuddered and shifted her gaze back to Ransom's face. "I don't know how you're so comfortable around these things."

"Training, necessity." Ransom's expression was carefully neutral. "Respect for what it can do is important. It's designed to kill, Victoria. That's something you need to realize when you put it in your hand. Never point it at someone unless you're willing to pull the trigger. That's lesson number one."

"What's lesson two?" Victoria asked, feeling slightly short of breath. Maybe if she could push her heart back down where it belonged she wouldn't have to work so hard to breathe.

"Never give up your weapon. They're lying if they say they won't hurt you if you surrender."

"Okay." Victoria took a deep breath. "What now?"

"Now I'm going to teach you all about this particular weapon." Ransom picked up the .380 auto and pointed it towards the wall. A tiny red dot appeared in the center of a small painting hanging there. "Laser light. It's activated by your hand gripping the pistol. It lets you draw and aim in less than a second. At the distances you would need to shoot someone this is all you need to defend yourself. I'm talking maybe 8 to 15 feet at the most."

Ransom watched Victoria's reaction to her speech. She blanched instantly, turning a sickly green when Ransom mentioned shooting someone at close range.

"Problem?" Ransom asked, laying the pistol back down on the table. Victoria's eyes followed the path the gun took. She wasn't fascinated with the weapon; she just couldn't stop staring at it. *This won't do at all.*

"I don't think I could do it, shoot someone like that." Victoria's voice wavered.

"Not even to save your own life?" Ransom pressed her. "What about someone else? Someone you cared for?"

This was a cruel way to do it, but Ransom didn't have the time to coddle her. This was life or death, and if it came down to it, she needed to know that Victoria was prepared to defend herself.

"I don't know." Victoria's voice went up several octaves, she was close to panicking.

263

"Come with me for a minute." Ransom stood up and held out her hand. "We'll leave this here for now."

Victoria looked confused, which was just as well. Ransom ran her tongue along the sharp edge of her eye teeth to keep herself from grimacing. She hated playing this game.

"Sit, relax for a minute. I'll be right back." Ransom left Victoria sitting on the couch while she headed for her office.

The clink of ice on expensive crystal shook Victoria out of her fugue. Ransom stood above her, holding a glass of amber liquid out for her. "Here, take it."

Victoria didn't freak out until she realized that Ransom held a similar glass in her own hand. She didn't drink. She never drank hard liquor...that's what she claimed. So why now?

"Ransom? What's going on? What's wrong?"

Ransom took a sip of her cognac and signaled Victoria to do the same, noting how badly Victoria's hand trembled when she raised the glass. She didn't need to lay a hand on her to know her pulse was thumping away like a runaway train.

"Samuel called me today," Ransom said, choosing her opening line very carefully.

"When?" Fear flared in Victoria's eyes.

"Right before I joined you in the kitchen." Ransom put her glass down. She really didn't drink. The first sip still burned all the way down to her stomach. She didn't want the alcohol; she had poured a second glass so Victoria wouldn't feel odd drinking alone. That, and for some reason it comforted her. The reminder of that night in the bar was an isolated spot in time for her, neither past nor present. It stood alone, a moment of perfection she had clung to in her darkest hours.

"He didn't want to call me until the police were done with everything." Ransom smiled grimly. Samuel knew she would question him mercilessly about every detail and wisely waited until he had as much data as possible to give her before clueing her in on the day's events.

"Is he okay?"

"He's fine." Ransom watched Victoria sag in relief, then hit her with the rest of the story. "It seems that someone, more than likely your stalker, decided to visit your office early this morning and tear the place apart. Fortunately, it was well before the office was due to open so there were no clients there. Unfortunately, your assistant had come in early to get some extra work done and surprised him. He wasn't happy to find her there."

"Oh, my God! Bridget? What did he do to her?" Victoria's thoughts immediately ran to that poor PI in the hospital, barely out of the ICU and still unable to give any details on her attacker.

"She's bruised up a bit, but nothing's broken. He was looking for you and when she said you weren't there, he lost it."

Victoria stood up suddenly, almost spilling her drink on Ransom. "I've got to go...I need to make sure she's okay."

Ransom pulled her back down on the couch. "No. You don't. I don't know if this guy found what he was looking for, but now we know what he looks like. I need you to keep your head on straight and go back through your files. Find out if anyone matches his description. That information will help me protect you."

"But!" Victoria protested, still wild-eyed and half listening to what Ransom was saying.

"Meanwhile." Ransom inhaled deeply and let it out slowly. She had to be the calm one to balance Victoria's frenzied response. She raised her voice and repeated herself, more firmly this time. "Meanwhile, I have to ask you again. Can you see yourself using a gun to defend yourself, or someone you love?"

Ransom sat perfectly still, waiting for Victoria to process everything that had just happened. This would be the deciding moment. If Victoria couldn't find that part of herself, that hard core inside her soul that could pull the trigger on a human being, even one that deserved it, she never would.

She wasn't trying to force Victoria to say yes, she needed to know if there was a yes inside her. If there wasn't, she would put the .380 away and cling to the woman like Saran Wrap. That was just the way it would have to be.

***

*Closer, so much closer.*

# Chapter Twenty-Seven

A bright light flooded through the window and lit up the living room with a harsh glow that could never be mistaken for anything natural. It was just after sunset, which meant the security lights weren't even active until a few moments ago when Ransom could honestly say the last bit of daylight had left the southern sky.

Ransom rolled off the couch to land silently onto the thick rug insulating the wooden floor beneath her. She crouched there a second, resting on the balls of her feet, the fingertips of her right hand sinking into the thick weave. Her left hand found the 9mm hidden between the cushions, the grip finding her palm in a practiced movement as she drew the weapon from its hiding place.

"Get down," Ransom growled, grabbing Victoria's wrist and dragging her off the couch. Her glass fell to the floor and rolled under the sofa, filling the air with the sweet, burnt toffee flavor of good cognac. "Hush, wait."

Scanning the room and the hallway through the open door, she didn't notice anything out of the ordinary. Still, something had to have set off the motion detector— which meant something or someone was outside.

Looking back over her shoulder, Ransom spoke to Victoria in an urgent tone that held hard iron within it.

"Stay close, don't make a sound."

Ransom slipped through the house, choosing her steps carefully to avoid the creaks and groans that old wood was prone to protest with as she peered into the darkened rooms around her. She held her gun at the ready and stayed in the shadows as they went, checking to make sure that the doors were still locked and the windows were all still intact.

Her goal was the laundry room off of the kitchen. It was darkest there, on the opposite side of the house from where the security light had been triggered.

She stayed low, testing the doorknob to make sure the door was still locked, then peered cautiously out the window before falling back. As far as she could tell, no one was in the house.

She scuttled closer to Victoria.

"You're doing great. Now I need you to do one more thing." Ransom slipped open the catch to the hidden cellar. "Get inside the safe room. Close the door and slide the bar. Do not open it until I come back and tell you to. Do you understand?"

Victoria nodded vigorously, her movements jerky and awkward. The whites of her eyes gleamed in the shadows and she was breathing too fast. Then she was gone, a shadow fading inside the shadows behind the paneled door. Ransom waited until she heard the solid snick of the door seating itself in its frame, then the metallic hiss of the bar being dropped into place.

Cautiously opening the door, she avoided looking at the bright circle of light spreading away from the house so she wouldn't ruin her night vision. Stepping out onto the darkened porch, she stood perfectly still for a full minute; just listening. Nothing sounded out of the ordinary, *so what tripped the lights?* Taking a convoluted path out to the barn and the garage, she avoided tripping any of the other lights she had placed around the yard. Anyone else wandering into the yard would have tripped more than one light.

She ducked into the barn and stood stock still while her eyes adjusted. An odd scrambling sound followed by a high-pitched squeak spun her around, searching for the unexpected noise. A pair of shiny-black-button eyes peered out at her from the far corner of the barn, running along the edge of an old horse stall that hadn't been used for anything other than storage for decades. Tiny hand like paws grasped at the stalls edge, followed by another pair, until she found herself being observed by an entire family of very curious critters.

"Raccoons." Ransom let out a relieved chuckle. There were five of them, a momma and four half grown babies, and from the looks of them, all fat and sassy from stealing from her garbage bins. Ransom raised an eyebrow at the little thieves. "I wonder."

The security lights weren't set to go off if a small animal wandered by, but all of them together? It was very possible. Their combined mass might be sufficient to fool the system.

She took a different route back to the house, padding across the cool grass in almost pitch-black conditions. Raccoons might have set off the security lights, but she didn't relish the idea of being spotlighted in the middle of the yard either. As she zigzagged across the property, she noted a few weak spots where she could readjust the lights, something she would do tomorrow after Victoria's first real shooting lesson.

"Everything's okay," Ransom announced the second Victoria opened the cellar door.

A small hellion greeted her in return, subjecting her to something between the most erotic pat down she ever experienced and a rough attempt to seduce her. Ransom was trapped between the door, the steep stairs, and Victoria's body. All she could do was hold her arms away from the woman, keeping her gun out of the way while Victoria pulled her in so close, she could feel the distance between them between each breath.

"This cellar. You told me it was a safe room? No one can get in once the door is locked?" Victoria demanded in a rough voice. The yellow glow from the single bulb below them brought out a primitive amber light to her eyes that reminded Ransom of dark caves and glowing bodies dancing around a raging fire.

"Yes," Ransom managed to say. Victoria's hands on her body were sending delicious chills down her back that she was having trouble ignoring.

Victoria closed the space between them, kissing her gently at first, then more forcefully. When Victoria moaned into her mouth, the erotic sound sent reverberations through her body that set off sparks deep inside her. Ransom wasn't made of stone, no matter what she professed. She moaned and gave into the kiss, swearing to herself that it wouldn't go farther than that.

Victoria kissed her once more, nibbling lightly along her lower lip just enough to make Ransom shiver, then brought her lips close to her ear.

"Lock the door," she whispered, then disappeared back down the stairs.

"Christ," Ransom muttered. Her head fell back, resting against the unyielding wall behind her while she tried to catch her breath. Victoria felt so good in her arms and she moved so deliciously against her. The 9mm tapped out a rhythm against her left thigh, once, twice, thrice, then a pause before she counted out again. Her heart thudded in her chest, beating faster and harder from a single kiss than it had when she thought there was an intruder. She rubbed her forehead, chasing that thought away. Now wasn't the time to self-analyze what parts of her psyche were broken and how. The thrill running through her veins tasted sweet without the bitter dregs of fear or anticipation of combat to accompany it, which was all that mattered. She should thank Victoria someday for giving that back to her.

*Victoria.* She waited for her down below. Her fingers found the steel bar without shifting her gaze away from the stairs. It slid home, and she took her first step down into the cellar.

***

Victoria gazed up at Ransom as she popped one button at a time from Victoria's shirt. She couldn't move if she wanted too.

There had been no long speeches when Ransom joined her in the cellar. She had crossed the room, fierce and wild looking, her clothes still smelling of grass and woodsy things, the pistol in her hand something harsh and foreign that didn't belong there. She had put the weapon down on the table, very carefully, then reached out to touch Victoria's face. The kiss that followed made time stop, until the sound of that first button slipping from its cage set the clock ticking again.

"Ransom?" Victoria asked, surprised at how breathless her voice sounded. Ransom looked up from her lazy attempts to unbutton Victoria's shirt, her eyes dark and smoky looking. Nimble fingers popped the last button, leaving the silken fabric of her blouse free to slither open across her skin.

"This is what you wanted, yes?" A smile appeared, creasing the corner of her mouth and adding a devilish aspect to the hazy, heavy-lidded gaze that stole Victoria's breath and held her hostage.

"Yes," Victoria said, trembling beneath Ransom's touch. Ransom's movements were as smooth and slow as a snake charmer and just as hypnotic. She used her fingertips to trace lines across her skin that left a trail of fire in their wake. When those same fingers danced along her waistline, slipping along the fabric's edge without ever dipping below the surface, Victoria moaned out loud. The slow teasing was absolute torture.

There was no way the woman could maintain such restraint, not for long.

"Ransom, please?" Victoria found herself begging for a way to make the maddening woman lose some of that control and just take her. She wanted Ransom's strength against her, claiming her, not these gentle ministrations.

Ransom growled something in response to Victoria's plea. With a sudden, startling movement, Ransom pulled Victoria around, holding her tight around the middle while she pressed the length of her body against her backside.

Those searching fingertips, now not so gentle, found her breasts. She arched her back into the touch, eager for the contact between them. Somehow Ransom had unbuttoned Victoria's jeans without her realizing it. Her hand snaked beneath her already ruined panties to cup her sex with her palm. At the same time, teasing lips found that point at the back of Victoria's neck where the muscle curved down into her shoulder. She arched back, trusting Ransom to keep her balance as pleasure coursed along twin points of pleasure.

"Fuck, Ransom..." Victoria panted when Ransom parted her folds, dipping into the waiting wetness before sliding her fingers along the hard ridge hidden between swollen lips.

Finding her ready, Ransom slipped her fingers inside, feeling the silken muscles push against her sudden intrusion before grasping at her fingers and drawing her in deeper. Victoria arched her back, driving her fingers into her as she writhed against her. Pressing her palm against Victoria's mound to increase the pressure on her swollen clit, Ransom let the woman use her own movement to bring herself close to the edge. When Victoria cried out, her voice ragged and sharp around the edges in unspoken frustration, Ransom cried out with her. Fingers splayed wide against Victoria's stomach, she could feel every muscle as it contracted and rolled beneath her palm. She pushed past clamped down muscles that fought, then welcomed her fingers. Victoria's entire body tensed, then spasmed. Only Ransom's firm grip around her middle kept her standing as she rode out her orgasm, bucking into and against the fingers now riding her swollen clit.

Ransom watched Victoria's face intently as her orgasm took her. *God, she was a magnificent creature to watch as she let passion take her. Hell, she was magnificent to look at any time,* Ransom amended.

She smiled evilly when she pulled her hand up and out of Victoria's ruined jeans, enjoying the sudden gasp of pleasure when her fingertips accidentally slid across the sensitive bundle of nerves. Her own arousal felt slick and hot between her thighs and she had only one coherent thought running through her brain.

"You have too many clothes on," Victoria murmured, nuzzling her lips against Ransom's ear as she spoke, hoping she would get the hint.

"Too true," Ransom conceded, "But as you already noticed, there's no bed in here."

"You didn't need one, and neither will I."

Ransom shrugged and pulled off her flannel shirt, then laced her fingers along the bottom edge of her tank top and stopped. Victoria made an impatient noise in her throat and Ransom grinned at her. She was enjoying the slow tease, but was almost outmaneuvered by a small pink tongue darting out between Victoria's lips. Her tank slid up slowly, exposing her abdomen to Victoria's hungry gaze inch by inch. It was absolutely delicious torture for both of them.

She tossed the tank top next to her flannel and turned her attention to the next article of clothing.

"These too?" Ransom asked, popping the top button on her jeans.

"Oh, yes, especially those," Victoria said, licking her lips suggestively.

Ransom could hear her pulse thundering in her head and thrumming through her body as it sang in tune to her arousal. Nothing else existed around her except for hot skin, wet heat, and the promise of sweet release. She swayed beneath Victoria's touch, closing her eyes so that every kiss down her body was a surprise and every tentative lick made her thighs tremble in anticipation of the next.

Wound tight and so close to coming she could barely think, she dug her nails into the oak tasting table behind her, gripping the edge tight enough to make the wood creak. Her elbow struck something cold and hard. The 9mm skidded across the polished surface and stopped just outside of her reach. The deadly reminder of her place in the world sent a chill down her spine and generated an uninvited question.

*Would I have been aware enough, fast enough to stop an intruder if I had been so pre-occupied?*

Ransom growled in frustration. She was so close. Her gaze slid to the pistol again, then the darkened doorway above them.

*This cellar. You told me it was a safe room? No one can get in once the door is locked?* Victoria had asked her these questions for a reason. She knew Ransom needed to feel safe, too. Ransom took one last look at the 9mm. There was no need for it here, she could enjoy this and not worry that she was putting Victoria in danger.

"It's okay, sweetheart," Victoria whispered, her voice thick with emotion. "Just let it happen. I have you." She kissed Ransom's neck, then brushed the lightest of kisses across her lips. "Can you do that for me, for us?"

She teased along the pale curls at Ransom's thighs, just alongside her swollen clit, then retreating to lightly massage her outer lips. Ransom could feel everything she was doing, manipulating her own slick arousal against herself. The sensation was incredibly erotic, and it pushed her higher than she'd ever gone before without tumbling over the precipice.

"I will not ask where you learned how to do that," Ransom panted.

"Just as well, I wouldn't tell you," Victoria answered, her eyes blazing with a fierce joy. "I can tell you are close. Tell me what you want."

"I want," Ransom started to answer, then inhaled sharply. Victoria had changed tactics, choosing a direct assault that left Ransom momentarily speechless. "That was cruel."

"Mmm. Got your attention, didn't I?" Victoria purred in her ear. "You don't have to answer; I think I know what you want."

***

*The mental health field is a strange animal. You have the concept of sick people, then you have the concept of therapy to treat the sick people. What's therapy? Talking. That's it. The only difference between therapy and religion is the "Come to Jesus" moment, that's my opinion.*

*Now Psychiatrists? They just medicate the crap out of you. Doctors with fun drugs. That's an interesting way to go. If we can't fix you, we'll drug you till you're practically a zombie, or so screwed up in the head it doesn't matter. As long as you're not dangerous to society, who cares, right?*

*The question to ask, then, is...how easy is it to turn someone deemed not dangerous into something else? Treatment, goals, end results, all perfectly wonderful things-but totally dependent on intent and a moral code.*

*A little knowledge can be a dangerous thing. If you're a manipulative bitch, it can be deadly.*

# Chapter Twenty-Eight

"Breathe, concentrate on what you're doing. This is going to feel strange to you, and some of what I'm going to tell you will sound like it contradicts itself." Ransom stood just beside and behind Victoria. Every word was spoken calmly, with a patience that the overly nervous woman appreciated more than she would ever admit. "Now, just like we did earlier. Inhale, exhale...slowly. Good. Now squeeze the trigger."

The pop still startled Victoria, she blinked despite trying hard to stare down the target, wincing in expectation before the gun even fired.

"Okay, one more time. This time try to relax a little more. Remember, squeeze, don't pull the trigger. That's a sure way to miss your target."

"Got it. Don't hold your breath. Just use the natural pause between one breath and the next," Victoria finished Ransom's speech for her, or so she thought.

Ransom grinned at her. "Don't get cocky just yet, little lady. One more thing. Don't stand there staring at the target. Two things will happen. Your eyes will start to play tricks on you and your muscles will start to get fatigued. It won't seem like much, but believe me, it makes a difference. Just trust your instincts, the rest will follow."

Victoria nodded and returned her attention back to the human shaped target set up between two small hills behind the house. From the looks of things, Ransom had been using the area as a personal range since she arrived. There were other targets set up farther downrange, some over a 100 meters out and several set up near trees or other cover that made them more difficult to see. The pristine tan and black target Ransom had tacked up this morning for her was almost embarrassing in comparison. Both in the fact it still lacked any bullet size holes anywhere near the concentric circles representing a kill shot, and for the fact the target stood barely 16 feet away from them.

"I suck."

"It takes time," Ransom piped in immediately. "Don't worry, we have plenty of ammo."

"That's not what I'm worried about, but thanks a lot." Victoria made a face at Ransom, just in case she didn't notice the sarcasm.

"Focus, remember?" Ransom reminded her.

Victoria let her temper get the best of her. She was hot, tired and her ego wasn't just bruised after two hours of trying to get the hang of the small .380, it had taken a thorough pummeling. "I don't see you stepping in and showing me how it's supposed to be done..."

Ransom moved without warning, faster than Victoria could respond. In an instant she was right behind her, one hand snatching the .380 out of her hand, then spinning her around until she was facing the opposite direction. A blur of motion along her periphery coalesced into Ransom's left hand, holding her 9mm. Ten shots fired in succession, ten shots in less than 10 seconds, leaving

10 small holes in the center of her target that didn't even qualify as a connect the dot puzzle...each one touched the other like the outline of a fuzzy caterpillar crawling across the paper.

The 9mm disappeared again, and she bent down to pick up the .380, dropped the magazine, popped the slide before slapping the weapon back down on the small table next to them. Only then did she turn and look at Victoria with flat-green eyes that somehow made everything worse. "That's how a dick would do it. I'm not a dick. Please don't make me do that again."

That little demonstration took all the piss and vinegar out of Victoria and replaced it with something else. She went back to the table and tried again, loading the weapon with a resolute scowl that made Ransom smile, then sighted the small pistol downrange. This time she didn't flinch from the small pops, and while she didn't manage to Robin Hood any of Ransom's shots, she did hit the target each and every time. Ransom grinned behind Victoria's back. The good counselor had found her inner warrior.

"Very good. Let's stop for the day and head in," Ransom suggested, stepping in before Victoria could reload to shoot again. It was always best to end a day of training on a high note, and she couldn't think of a better time than now.

Victoria hesitated, then nodded. "You're right. I'm getting tired and I should keep going through my files. Also, Samuel had a question about one of my clients and I need to check a few things before I call him back."

"Things would go quicker if you'd let me help you, you know." Ransom made it sound like a joke, but part of her was serious. Victoria didn't think like she did. She wasn't looking for the things Ransom would look for. A fresh set of eyes would help.

"You know I can't do that."

"I know, I know." Ransom raked her fingers through her hair. "I just thought it might help hurry things along. I know you need to get back to your clients."

Victoria stopped dead in her tracks. She was learning a few things about Ransom Greathouse, and one of them was that she was a great deal more versed in manipulation than she let on. "Now you just wait a minute. I know exactly what you're trying to do and it won't work. I won't let you see those files no matter how much you tempt me."

She took off again, not waiting to see if Ransom was following her or not. The shocked expression on her face was enough to seal her guilt. Of course she would love some help, but she wouldn't break confidentiality to do it. Besides, there was no guarantee the answers are in there...it was just an exercise in futility meant to keep her from going crazy while she waited. *Meanwhile, my practice is slowly falling apart, and there's nothing I can do about it. This stalker couldn't have been crueler, taking me away from the people that come to me for help. Unless?*

She spun around with a question on her lips, only to realize that Ransom had indeed fallen behind. She was on the phone and she didn't look happy.

"Thanks, Buddy. I appreciate the heads up." If Ransom's expression could call the weather, they'd be running for cover from the thunder and lightning gathering.

"What's going on?"

"We've got a suspect." Ransom tucked her phone back in her pocket and rolled her neck. That was a sure sign she was irritated.

"I don't get it, this is good news, right? What happened? Who is it?" Victoria had a million questions.

"It is good news, I don't know who it is, and as for what happened?" Ransom took Victoria's hand and headed for the house at a ground eating clip.

"Someone showed up at Buddy's store, asking a whole lot of questions and making Buddy nervous. When he mentioned your name, Buddy, uh...well, he decided to help out a bit and make sure the man didn't leave until the Sheriff showed up."

"So, why are you so pissed off?"

"Because that was three hours ago." Ransom clenched her jaw so tight it popped. "We need to go see Roy and find out why he didn't bother calling us."

"I'm sure he has his reasons," Victoria offered. She was trying to be generous, but she couldn't quite pull it off. She still thought Roy was an asshole.

"We'll see," Ransom said, trying to curb her irritation. Whatever game Roy was playing, that was between the two of them, not Victoria. It was enough that she had to deal with a stalker. She squeezed her hand and smiled. "This is good news. Just think, it could all be over soon."

***

Ransom and Victoria were forced to cool their heels while Roy interviewed the suspect.

"Sorry, Bud, you aren't going anywhere. If my deputy here says you resisted arrest, then that's just what happened." Sheriff Jameson grinned at the greasy looking man they had taken into custody. "Now, I suggest you just sit down and relax until we get this all sorted out."

Before the Sheriff left, he looked back at the cuffed man. "Oh, and when you are ready to tell me what, or who, you were looking for on that itty-bitty back country road, I would be happy to hear that, too." His statement resulted in a gratifyingly shocked expression that left no doubt whatsoever that the man was up to mischief. How much of his "I don't know what you are talking about" routine was pure bullshit Roy still didn't know, but he'd sure try to find out before he had to release him.

"Is that him?" Ransom asked, impatient to find out what he knew about Victoria.

"It is, and before you ask, no you can't talk to him."

Ransom's head shot up, her eyes flashing angrily at the Sheriff. Roy just looked at her mildly and motioned towards the door. Ransom grimaced, her mood going from angry to royally pissed in one sentence. Ransom waited until the two of them were in the privacy of the Sheriff's

283

office, somehow managing to hold her tongue until the heavy wooden door was closed and the blinds were drawn.

"What the hell, Roy?" she thundered, not caring if her voice was sufficiently muffled by the thick glass between them and the rest of the station. She was pissed. "First, you don't call me when you arrest this guy, even though he was asking about Victoria, now you're not going to let me talk to him?"

Roy simply strolled over to his desk and pulled open a drawer. The muffled thunk of leather on wood was like a glove thrown down between them. Ransom looked down at the leather encased star sitting on the sheriff's desk. From the look on her face, it could have been a snake sitting there waiting to bite her.

"Now, Ransom," Roy continued in his mild tone, "if you want to interrogate this guy, you have to be legit, and that means being the power behind the badge." He gestured down at the silver-metal-star.

Ransom opened her mouth to disagree, the argument sharp against her tongue.

"No," Roy spoke more forcefully. "Ransom, I'm not budging on this. I've got nothing on this guy other than the fact he knows Victoria's name. That's pretty thin any way you look at it. If we don't get something more solid to link him to her case, I'm going to have to let him go eventually."

Ransom shoulders dropped. "There really is no way out of this, is there?" she asked, the defeat in her voice absolute.

For one short second, Roy felt sorry that Ransom was going to have to take the badge this way, but only for a second. He walked back around to Ransom, picking up the badge and placing it in the palm of her hand.

"I know you're hesitant, Ransom. But look at it this way. You get to interrogate the son-of-a-bitch in there, and you have the power and authority to protect Victoria—legally. This is a win-win situation. I know you don't see it this way now..."

He placed one gnarled hand on Ransom's shoulder, noting the iron hard strength there, and took pity on her. "Look, consider this a temporary appointment for now, eh? After Victoria is safe and sound, we will revisit this. If you don't want the job then, I won't force you."

Ransom stared down at the deputy badge and shuddered. That bit of silver represented everything she feared—taking responsibility for others, having their lives in her hands, the risk of failure. Ransom thought about that for a second, mentally grumbling over every detail, before coming to terms with the inevitable. The badge opened up resources she hadn't had before; she could always quit after all this was over.

"Fine, I'll do it. But just so you know, I'm still not happy about this."

Green eyes, just as pissed off and fiery as her father's had been, blazed beneath equally stern eyebrows. Roy chuckled at the younger version of his best friend. He would have been proud of his daughter, of what she had accomplished in her short life already...and what she would accomplish in the future.

"That is perfectly okay with me, Ransom...be pissed, if that's what helps you. Just remember, DEPUTY... you do work for me, so try turning that pissy attitude towards those who really deserve it." The Sheriff nodded in the general direction of the interrogation room. "Victoria's waiting for you out there. See if she recognizes this guy. Maybe you'll have better luck with him than I did, but as far as I'm concerned, he's nuttier than a squirrel turd."

"What do you mean?"

"You'll find out when you get in there." Roy sat down behind his desk. "Just try to get a name, anything. He won't tell us shit."

"What about ID, fingerprints?"

"Nope. No wallet, nothing, which is strange enough as it is. The man looks and smells like he hasn't taken a bath in a few days. He must have come by bus or hitchhiked in. That probably explains how he ended up out at Buddy's, there's a drop-off near there." Roy flung his pen down in disgust. "As for prints? The damn system is down. Server got fried during the last storm. We're still waiting for the technician to get us back up and running."

"This just keeps getting better and better." Ransom let herself and her sarcasm out the door with a sloppy salute to her new boss and one last parting shot. "You know; Victoria was right about one thing."

Roy looked up from his desk. "What's that?"

"You can be an asshole," she said, and then she slammed the door.

\*\*\*

Victoria stood up when Ransom walked into the room.

"What's going on, Ransom? No one's telling me anything..." her voice trailed off when she noticed the badge clipped to Ransom's belt, her gaze flicking past the shiny bit of metal to the 9mm now displayed openly on her hip. She sagged against the desk behind her. "Oh, no."

"Oh, yes." Ransom's entire demeanor had changed, every bit of her being screamed cop, and it wasn't just the badge.

"What happened in there?" Despite herself, Victoria had to admit that the transformation was impressive. Ransom must have been quite imposing in her military uniform.

"The Sheriff put an offer on the table that I couldn't refuse."

"He what?" Victoria exclaimed, turning back to stare at the closed door behind them. *What the hell game is he playing now?*

"It was either this," Ransom tapped the badge at her waist, "or he was going to lock me out of the investigation."

*That's it!* Hot anger blew through her veins and sent Victoria's blood pressure sky rocketing. "That's bullshit and you know it. I'm going to fix this now."

Victoria tore into Roy's office without bothering to knock.

"Can I help you, Ms. Carrillo?"

His tone, somewhere between bored and amused, infuriated her. She recklessly advanced farther into the office until she reached the only barrier between them. She leaned over his desk, slapping her palm down on the short stack of files there and sliding them away from his reach. She didn't want anything distracting him from what she had to say. "What the hell did you just do, use me as leverage to get Ransom to take that damn badge?"

"I used the case as leverage."

Roy leaned back in his chair to put some distance between them. The woman was barely five-two at the most, so looming wasn't exactly something she did well, but she was mad as hell. *Ransom has chosen a spitfire of a woman to fall in love with,* he thought, *life is going to be mighty interesting for these two.*

"I am the case."

"That's true, and that's also why she's wearing that badge right now." Roy wasn't above giving credit where credit was due. "She wouldn't have done it for anybody else. But you? She would do anything for you, you can see it in her eyes."

"That's rare, coming from you, especially after I just spent two weeks fixing what you screwed up the last time you 'talked' to her. You've got a lot of balls. Telling Ransom I was going to leave her was a shitty thing to do."

"Yeah, it was," Roy admitted.

Victoria staggered back a few steps, shocked out of her angry rant by Roy's unexpected admission. She stopped reacting and started thinking, hard, about what was going on between Roy and Ransom. She gazed around the office before saying one more word to the man.

"Ransom's father was the Sheriff before you, wasn't he?" she asked, stopping in front of a large plaque she had noticed before but hadn't paid much attention to. The standard government photo, replete with patriotic flags in the background, didn't look any different from the dozen or so other photos plastered along the main hallway, not until she took a closer look at the youngish face glaring back at her. She had seen that fierce, hawkish gaze before...the first time Ransom greeted them at the gate.

"Yes."

Victoria spun around. Caught off-guard, Roy gave himself away. A fleeting shadow of some deep emotion crossed his face before he could chase it away. Sorrow, guilt? "I think you and I need to have a long talk. You aren't being an ass to Ransom just for kicks, there's something else going on that you haven't told her. Why?"

# Chapter Twenty-Nine

There was more drama going on behind the scenes in this small town than one of those cheesy day time soap operas. It was all giving Victoria a headache.

She left Roy's office with a lot more to think about.

"Hey, can I talk to you for a minute?" Victoria asked Ransom.

"Sure, but I really need you to tell me if you recognize this guy." Ransom looked over Victoria's shoulder, but Roy was nowhere to be seen. Something wasn't quite right, Victoria was way too calm after her little chat with the Sheriff. "Let's go outside, I could use some fresh air."

At the least, they'd have some privacy if Victoria needed to let off a little steam. God knows she'd left that office more than one time ready to beat the snot out of her training dummy.

Once they reached the parking lot, she expected Victoria to go off on a tirade about Roy, not get hissed at like an angry cat.

"What the hell are you pissed off at me for?"

"You haven't told Roy about your PTSD, have you?" Victoria kept her voice low, but her eyes blazed. She wasn't just pissed, she was furious.

"No, I didn't. It's none of his damn business. Besides, the VA gave me a clean bill of health two years ago."

"Excuse my French, but screw the VA. They're good people, but if they're anything like the rest of our governmental agencies right now, they are overworked and all too eager to send people on their way out the door. Especially if that person knows exactly what to say and not say." The weighted look she gave Ransom left no doubt who she was talking about.

"Why are you doing this now?" Ransom growled. "Because Roy cornered me and made me his Deputy? That's stupid, it's a done deal, whether I like it or not."

"Oh? And if I marched in there and told him that you weren't ready for that badge, what would happen then?"

In a voice as cold as ice, she put an end to Victoria's empty threats. "I warned you from the beginning. Do not try and analyze me. March in there if you want, say what you want to Roy, I will deny everything categorically."

Ransom took a step back, from Victoria and from her anger. "Why are you doing this now? I don't get it. Everything was fine between us. Now we got some guy sitting in a holding cell and all of a sudden you're back to questioning my freaking state of mental health."

"I'm not, I mean, that wasn't my intention," Victoria cried out after Ransom's retreating back. "I just thought..."

"Just thought what?" Ransom asked, poised at the door, ready to go in and do her job with or without Victoria.

"I just thought that if Roy knew, he wouldn't push you so hard. I know you only did it for me, not because you wanted to," Victoria admitted. She knew taking that badge from Roy was the last thing Ransom wanted for herself. "I thought, maybe, if I told him it wasn't a good idea, he'd listen to me rather than keep on with this ridiculous promise to your father."

Ransom closed the door and returned to Victoria's side. "What promise?"

"He promised your father that you'd follow in his footsteps."

"Roy's been pushing me to join the department so I can take over as Sheriff when he retires?"

"That's about it," Victoria said. "He told me that's all you ever talked about, before...well, you know. Before."

Ransom closed her eyes and took a deep breath. Fool ass man. "I know. Before I came home busted up and scarred."

"He showed me your application, the copy of your degree. I didn't know you had a Bachelor's in Criminal Justice." Victoria laid a gentle hand on Ransom's shoulder. She could feel the scars Ransom mentioned hidden beneath her shirt, hard ridges of tissue that would never heal smoothly after being burned so thoroughly. "He's been holding onto that badge for a long time."

"It was an old dream, Victoria. A youthful one. My father was my hero. All shiny and full of purpose. I didn't want to disappoint him, so I did exactly what he did at my age...I joined the service for the experience even though he didn't want me to. Going out into the real world opened my eyes. I realized my father's dream for me was never going to happen."

"Why?"

"You said it yourself, Victoria. Johnsonville is a tiny little podunk town. We're out in the middle of nowhere. Being called a liberal is about the worst insult you could hurl at someone. You've met Mrs. Johannsen, that's how they treat people like us around here."

"Then why stay?"

"Because I don't give a shit what they think." Ransom smiled evilly. "And I enjoy being a thorn in their side far too much to leave my home. They don't know what to do with me. On one side of the coin, I'm their latest and greatest war hero, someone they're supposed to feel pride over. But when you get right down to it, I'm still Sheriff Greathouse's lesbian daughter, the one they talk about on Sunday when Pastor Jones really gets rocking at the pulpit about sin."

"Jesus, Ransom, I knew this town had its share of drama, but wow."

"Oh, don't be surprised. There's nothing to do in towns this size but gossip, which is why I kept you up at the farm as much as possible. By now, half the town probably knows I'm wearing this badge, the other half knows there's a beautiful woman with me, and they're all sharing what they know with each other." Ransom grimaced. The cat was literally, out of the bag. "I truly hope this is our guy, because if it isn't...I can't guarantee they won't find you here after today."

"I won't say anything to Roy." Victoria's heart skipped a beat when Ransom mentioned the stalker, fueled by a surge of adrenaline urging her to run from danger. She wondered how long the fear response would last after all this was over, or if it would ever go away. "I don't know what I was thinking."

Ransom pulled Victoria into her arms, not giving a damn if everybody within sight of them saw her do it. "You didn't want to see me forced into doing something I didn't want to do, and you tried to use what you knew to help me out of it. Your heart was in the right place, and I love you for it."

A quick kiss was all she got before Ransom returned to the business at hand. "Now, are you ready to get a good look at this guy? We've wasted enough time already. I want to go home."

"God, yes." Victoria practically raced Ransom to the door. Worry free, uninterrupted sex outside of a locked safe room was at stake here. That, and so much more.

***

"Well?" They stood outside the interrogation room, watching the man on the other side of the one-way mirror pace back and forth nervously.

A smallish, unkept man that could use a few more meals in him before he could even qualify as skinny, he didn't appear the least bit dangerous, but Ransom knew from experience how deceiving looks could be. One of the deadliest men she ever had the pleasure of meeting was a diminutive Senior Chief who always had a joke handy. He also just happened to be a highly decorated SEAL team instructor. You didn't earn that position because you had a pleasing personality.

"No. He doesn't look familiar." Victoria rubbed her eyes, trying to force her brain to cooperate. She was afraid of making a mistake. "At least, I don't think so, I don't know."

"He's a nervous little man, isn't he?" Ransom observed. It wasn't just the constant movement. He needed to touch something continually, scratching his head, smoothing his hair...then moving to his face before giving up and moving to something in the air in front of him. His lips moved in time with his hand movements, it looked like he was doing math on an invisible chalkboard. "Why are his hands shaking so bad?"

"Probably coming down off something." Roy joined them, a fresh cup of coffee in hand.

"Hello? Hello?" The disheveled man ran towards the glass and stared into it, disturbingly close to Victoria's face. She blanched and stepped back a pace.

"Jesus, that's creepy."

"Can I leave now? I still have to find her. She said I have to find her and apologize to her. It's important." The man started weeping, actually weeping as if his soul was on fire, and slid to the floor. "I didn't mean to scare her, I love her. I would never hurt her, never. I need her to know that."

"What is he talking about? It sounds vaguely like something from a 12 step program."

"Hell if I know." Roy took a sip of his coffee and grimaced. "Needs sugar."

"Screw it, I'm going in and talking with him." It didn't take long for Ransom to regret that decision. The man did smell as bad as he looked, and now she was locked in a room with him and some hellacious halitosis that had some time to build up since he was brought in earlier that day.

"Who are you?" Ransom demanded, her voice cracking like a whip in the small room. The weasel started to sweat more, his eyes rolling around the room so that the whites showed.

"No one, I'm no one." He licked his lips, scraping an equally dry tongue across chapped, flaking skin. Ransom winced, but didn't look away. *Gross.*

*Okay, let's try this again.*

"Okay, Chappy, how about this. Why are you looking for Victoria Carrillo?"

Victoria's name barely made it past her lips before Chappy hooted and jumped up, starting his finger math again. The rhythmic movement seemed to help him concentrate, but he had to be encouraged to talk at the same time.

"We were talking about Victoria?"

"Victoria, yes. That's the one. I need to find her. Do you know where she is? I lost her and I've been looking...and I..." He stopped, his expression going sly. He stood up straight and tugged at his clothes to make himself appear more presentable. He looked at her with a haughty expression far exceeding his dress, and addressed her in a very clear voice that didn't sound a bit like his prior rantings. "I'm not speaking another word. I believe I get a phone call and a lawyer?"

Roy waited for Ransom to join them outside the interrogation room. "I told you he was nuttier than a squirrel turd," he said, sounding overly pleased with himself.

"What do you think, Victoria? Could this guy be your stalker?" Ransom turned to their resident expert.

"It depends; he's obviously compromised right now. I'd have to know what his baseline is. There's a good chance he's off his medications and that's why he's acting this way."

"That's good enough for me," Ransom said.

"But not good enough for a conviction," Roy added. "We need solid evidence to link him to your case. I'll talk to the judge, let him know what's happening and then see what I can get done this weekend. He needs a psych evaluation and that gives me a good reason to hold him."

Ransom rolled her shoulders, feeling the tension building there. It would have to do for now. At least the man was in a cage and not running amok.

"Go home Ransom. Take care of your lady." Roy slapped her arm before ambling down the hall. "I'll call you if I hear anything."

# Chapter Thirty

"I've got some news for you."

Ransom landed on the couch energetically enough to bounce Victoria, taking the short route over the back rather than walking around.

"You're in a good mood." Victoria looked up from the book she was reading. It was so nice to just sit and relax for once. She had been enjoying it, and so had Ransom. With the stalker locked up, it was just the two of them, and she had to admit, just sitting and enjoying each other's company was wonderful. *I could definitely get used to this,* she thought, feeling a momentary sadness. This place was becoming a second home to her, mostly because of Ransom, but she was also falling in love with the house, the woods around it...even though she hadn't had a good latte in weeks and she missed the Thai Take-out Palace down the street from her house terribly.

"Yes I am. Here, I brought you a cold one." Ransom handed her a tinted bottle, while she kept its twin for herself.

"Beer? Since when do you drink beer?"

"Mm. We're celebrating so I brought out the good stuff." Ransom clanked her bottle against Victoria's and took a swig, then squinted at her while she swallowed. "The best micro-brewed root beer you can find in the state. Non-alcoholic, of course."

"Goof." Victoria turned her bottle around until she could read the label.

"Me? Never. I am the epitome of seriousness." Ransom managed to solemnly swear she wasn't acting goofy while still being a goof. That was true skill there.

"Normally I would agree with you, until you brought me root beer." Victoria chuckled, delighted to see Ransom's playful side coming out. The last time she remembered drinking root beer there was ice cream involved and she hadn't graduated from high school yet. She took a careful sip, expecting a mouthful of caramel flavored bubbles, but was delightfully surprised by the bite and undertones she tasted. "Wow, that's different."

"See? You have to trust me." Ransom grinned and took another swig from her bottle, then rearranged herself on the couch, tucking one leg under her and leaning back against the side cushion. "So, back to my news. We're one step closer to proving this guy is your stalker. Roy was able to get our John Doe's mugshot uploaded. Your assistant, Bridget? She positively identified him as the one who broke into the office. Even if we can't pin the stalking on him we still have him for that, and since he assaulted her, it's not just a simple breaking and entering. He's facing a shitload of other charges when they get him back home."

"That's great. I mean...other than Bridget getting hurt, at least he'll get the help he needs." Victoria nervously started peeling the damp label off her bottle. The man was not well, he needed therapy, not jail time. "Have they had any luck finding out who he is yet?

"Oh, yeah. About that." Ransom scratched her forehead. There was something seriously off about the entire case, she just couldn't put her finger on it. "The minute a lawyer showed up, our guy was all over the place. Tossing out names left and right, demanding to see his family, to be released, threatening to sue everyone who was anyone in the county for holding him. A real nut job, right?" Ransom realized what she said and bit her lip. "Oops, sorry Victoria. I know that's not what I should call him."

"It's okay, Ransom, just go on." Victoria waved Ransom's concern away. It wasn't like she hadn't heard worse coming out of the mouths of people who should know better. Those people she would correct but not Ransom. Ransom wasn't trying to be cruel on purpose, and she was trying. That made all the difference.

"Okay, so Roy looked him up. We thought it was odd someone like that didn't have a record. Even with the system back up and running, we didn't get a single hit on his prints...then we found out why."

Ransom rummaged around in her jeans and pulled out a folded up piece of paper. "Mr. Matthew Thomas Theodosis, the Third, no less. Seems he has a rich daddy who wanted to keep it quiet that his pride and joy wasn't such a prize. He's been in and out of institutions for the last few years, but it was all done privately. No court orders, no arrest warrants, and no prison time."

"So, how did he end up here and looking like that?" Victoria asked, mentally pulling up the image of the dirty, disheveled man that had been glaring at her through the

300

one-way mirror. Blue-gray eyes so pale they looked washed out against the broken capillaries branching across his cheeks and nose like a hundred red tinged rivulets flowing beneath paper thin skin. *Matthew Thomas Theodosis? Matt Thomas?*

Her face went blank. She blinked, very slowly and raised her eyes to meet Ransom's. "Oh, my God. Ransom. I know him. I know who he is."

The way she said "him" made it sound like a bad thing. Alarmed, Ransom scooted closer to Victoria and took her hands. They were ice cold. "You know Matthew? How?"

"Matt, I knew him as Matt Thomas." Victoria clutched Ransom's hands. Afraid that if she let them go, she'd lose her way or her courage. Either way, she wouldn't be able to finish her story, and Ransom needed to hear it.

"Matt was going through the same study program I was. He seemed nice enough at first, but over time things kept happening that started to disturb me. Subtle things that sounded stupid when I tried to tell one of my instructors about him. They chalked it up to 'student over diagnosis syndrome'...you know, where you start to see symptoms in every mundane behavior?" Victoria's eyes widened and she shuddered. "But it wasn't that, Ransom. He was creepy. He started following me around, checking up on what I was doing, who I was hanging out with. Even after I told him that I wasn't interested in him one bit, he insisted that we had a thing. I told him I was a lesbian. He scoffed it off and started digging up fringe studies

301

supporting his beliefs that homosexuality wasn't part of the natural spectrum of human sexuality."

"What happened?" Ransom asked.

"He became increasingly paranoid over the last semester. His grades started slipping and he started complaining to the instructor's that it was my fault...that I was keeping him from studying either because I was ignoring him or because I was distracting him. He could never decide. The man was totally obsessed with me by the end of the semester. I was afraid to go out at night because he would somehow show up wherever I was. The movies, dinner, it didn't matter. He'd just show up."

"Then what happened?" Ransom was almost afraid to ask. Behaviors like that had a tendency to escalate, then turn deadly.

"We were supposed to start our internships in the fall. I couldn't imagine him working with real clients and I finally decided enough was enough. I went to the dean and lodged a formal complaint against him. Matt, of course, denied everything. They almost believed him over me. It was terrible. As it was, I lost my internship with a great facility and had to scramble to find a replacement location. He got to them, somehow. God knows what he told them. He could sound quite convincing and sane when he wanted to."

Ransom nodded. She could see that happening after watching him flip so suddenly. The smooth, cultured voice, the arrogant way he looked down his nose at her...he certainly knew how to play the snotty little rich boy. *Or maybe, buried beneath all that mental illness, that's the real Matthew Thomas Theodosis, the Third.*

"That's really frightening, Victoria. What made them finally believe you?"

"That's the thing, I'm not sure they ever did." Victoria swallowed against the memory driven nausea and forced herself to continue. "The biggest insult wasn't how long it took the school to act, it was the fact that my complaints had nothing to do with his removal. It was his academic status. Remember what I said about those papers? I think he was losing it and his altered mental status was showing up in his work. That was what sent him home, not my complaints."

"He must have found you again and decided he wasn't done with you yet." Ransom felt cold anger return to the pit of her stomach when she thought about what might have happened to Victoria. It was hard for her to reconcile her desire to punish the man that tormented Victoria so much with the one she talked to. He was sick, that was true, but at the heart of that sickness, there was still that twisted sense of entitlement that she hated so much.

"Maybe," Victoria said, sounding troubled. "But that takes me back to my last question. What happened to him after they kicked him out of school?"

"His parents tucked him away in a comfortable little place that kept him medicated and happy, that's what happened," Ransom muttered. "Of course, it was all voluntary on his part so I guess he decided he had enough one day. He signed himself out and disappeared, much to his family's dismay. My best guess? He's been living on the street or staying at one of the homeless shelters downtown."

Victoria took a deep, cleansing breath and let it all out. "Well, it's all over now. We can finally relax and get on with our lives. I cannot tell you how happy that makes me."

It was Ransom's turn to feel nervous. All that fear and trepidation that Victoria had been feeling somehow transmitted itself to her through their joined hands and it made her feel shaky. She smiled and nodded, but her heart wasn't in it as much as she wanted it to be. "What are you going to do now? I mean, now that he's been caught?"

"First thing tomorrow, I'm going to have Samuel drop me off at home and make sure my house is still in one piece. I don't live in a bad neighborhood, but a vacant house in the city is sure to attract attention. My rose garden is probably a mess, and I need to make sure nothing is rotting in my refrigerator." Victoria made a face, anticipating the mess she was expecting to find. "Samuel's a good guy, but I doubt he thinks about stuff like weeds and expired milk. Then I need to go into the office and see what's left of my practice."

*And talk to Samuel about a few things,* Victoria thought to herself. *People like Mrs. Johannsen shouldn't have to rely on charity donations like that to survive. Something has failed miserably here and I have a feeling Samuel might have a few ideas how we could help.*

"Tomorrow?" Ransom asked, unable to keep the disappointment out of her voice.

Of course Victoria would be raring to get back. This stalker situation had already cost her weeks out of her life, and like she said, it had already affected her practice. Asking her to stay would be greedy and selfish.

"I'm going to head out tomorrow, not because I'm in a hurry to leave, but because the sooner I leave the sooner I can come home to you." Victoria exhaled slowly. She was banking a lot of what she was saying on assumptions. "We're only a few hours apart. As soon as I get everything settled, I'd like to come back. If that's okay with you?"

The uncertainty in Victoria's voice quieted Ransom's doubts about where they were headed. She hated that part of herself that told her she wasn't worth it, that her emotional baggage was too much for anyone to want to deal with. At least she had moved past the ugly voice inside her head that swore Victoria's interest in her was motivated by some perverse need to fix someone she thought was broken.

"Okay? That's more than okay." Ransom wanted to jump up and hug the woman sitting there so calmly discussing their future...the woman who just saved her from having to swallow her pride and ask if she was planning on coming back. "When will you be back?"

Victoria chuckled. "I haven't even left yet!"

"I know, I know. I'll try to curb my enthusiasm." Ransom felt something shift in the air between them. It was reflected in the way Victoria looked at her, and in the way her lips shaped themselves around her next sentence.

"Not too much, I hope, and not just yet."

Victoria uncoiled from her spot on the couch, that was the only way to describe the slow and sinuous movement as she made her way to Ransom's corner. All of a sudden, Ransom found herself straddled by a very intense woman gazing down at her with a smile on her lips that spelled trouble and a look in her eyes that told her it was the kind that could get them both arrested in some states.

"I believe that you and I have unfinished business to attend to. If I have to leave, I want to make sure you remember exactly what you'll be missing while I'm gone."

Victoria leaned down and nuzzled Ransom's neck, kissing the sensitive flesh there before bringing her lips close to her ear. "I think you and I need to go to bed, where you can tell me again how much you love me. Unless you prefer the confines of the safe room?"

The teasing voice sent Ransom's pulse skyrocketing. She flashed hot and cold, goosebumps rising wherever Victoria's breath brushed across her skin. She became painfully aware of how open and exposed Victoria's position made her. Straddled open legged across her lap, she was pressed against the seam of her jeans, close enough for Ransom to feel just how hot she was. Lust jumped like a flame in Victoria's eyes just a second before a wicked smile curved her lips into a delicate bow. She moved against Ransom, just the slightest bit of movement, but it sent a wave of arousal coursing through her body. Her hips jerked in response, forcing Victoria to grab on to

Ransom's shoulders for support. The low moan that followed was sweet in Ransom's ears.

"The bed will do just fine," Ransom growled, rapidly losing the ability to think past what Victoria was doing to her body.

"Are you sure?" Victoria reared back, the evil glint still shining brightly in her eyes. "The safe room is right down the hall, no stairs to run up."

"If you don't get up those stairs, you won't have to worry about the damn safe room. You won't make it off the couch."

Victoria must have taken Ransom's warning at face value. She was gone in a flash with Ransom not far behind her. All of that training had served her well. She managed to sprint up the stairs and make it to the bedroom door before Ransom caught up with her.

"Got you," Ransom crowed, pulling Victoria towards the bed. She wasn't above claiming her prize.

"I let you win," Victoria threw back, not willing to give Ransom the victory that easily.

"We'll see who calls mercy first."

Victoria wasn't sure if that was a threat or a promise, but it didn't matter. She had a feeling she was going to win either way.

# Chapter Thirty-One

Ransom managed to get Victoria into the bedroom only to find her bed already occupied.

"Shoo, Whitman." She waved her hands at the haughty feline, as if that would be sufficient incentive for him to move from his comfortable spot. He gave her a baleful, blinkless stare that would have turned into a standoff if Victoria hadn't scooped him up and tossed him out into the hallway. Closing the door before he could voice an opinion over such an insulting form of transport, she giggled at the look on Ransom's face.

"What? So I don't like an audience."

"You are so not a cat person. Will you at least feed him while I'm gone?"

"He knows how to hunt, Victoria. He's getting fat."

"So, let him." Victoria ran her palm down Ransom's face. "Please, for me. I don't want him wandering away while I'm gone."

"Fine," Ransom growled. This was not what she wanted to be talking about right now and she knew exactly how to get Victoria back on track. She pulled off her shirt and tossed it in the corner, then waited to see what she would do.

"Um, yeah." Victoria licked her lips. "You could have warned me that you weren't wearing a bra."

"Why?" Ransom back stepped towards the bed, her hand resting along her beltline. She undid the top button on her jeans, then looked up at Victoria. From the hungry expression on her face, she was pretty certain Victoria had forgotten all about the little ginger cat. "I'm not wearing any underwear either, does that help?"

"Yes," Victoria answered roughly, her voice betraying her. "Yes, it does."

It only took a few moments for Victoria to catch up to Ransom, and not long at all before they found the bed.

Ransom pinned Victoria beneath her, playfully using her superior strength to first hold her down, then raise herself up on her elbows. Her thigh slid between them, pressing against her center, finding enough moisture there to begin a slow, careful rhythm that drove Victoria wild. She raised her knee, evening the playing field when Ransom gasped and shifted angles. Victoria realized she had an advantage, Ransom couldn't touch her but her hands were free to wander as they may...and let them wander she did.

She found Ransom's nipples first. Victoria would have preferred using her mouth, but Ransom was a greedy woman. She was intent on ravaging her lips, stealing her breath with soul searing kisses that ended in gasps. Victoria abandoned the obvious to run her fingers along lean muscles, tracing the lines of her hips until she managed to push just enough to roll both of them on their sides. From there it was an easy trick to lay Ransom flat on the bed. Too easy, by far, but she would pretend she had won that skirmish.

Ransom certainly seemed eager to see how far she was willing to go. She remained silent, but her eyes glowed with desire, hungry and powerful.

"Magnificent," Victoria murmured, following a winding path with her lips that would take her to her ultimate goal. Moving down Ransom's lean body meant losing the heated connection between them, but her need to taste the other woman was overwhelming. Pushing Ransom's legs wider with her body, she settled herself between Ransom's thighs. Eager lips found Ransom's clit, slick and hard and almost too sensitive for her tongue. That she was so close already...it made her shiver in anticipation. She wanted to slow down, to hold back and make it last longer, but Ransom made a low noise in her throat, a throaty growl that demanded she continue.

"Don't stop. Finish me."

She listened to that voice, and she didn't stop. She held on tightly, wrapping her arms around slim hips that bucked and thrust violently against her as Ransom came undone.

"Fuck!" Ransom yelled, her back arching until her upper body came off the bed, her biceps flexing as she strained against the sheets beneath her.

Victoria refused to give up her prize just yet, curling her tongue and lapping at the sweet essence, delving as deeply as she could reach with each long swipe. It was only when Ransom locked rock hard thighs around her head in a desperate attempt to end the torturous aftershocks that she stilled her treacherous tongue.

She crawled up Ransom's body, retracing her path along skin that glowed with a soft sheen of perspiration, intent on kissing those lips with the taste of her passion still upon them.

That was how Victoria ended up with a leg on each side of Ransom's hips, an overly pleased grin plastered to her face and nothing between them, only damp curls and hot sex and the smell of passion. Her grin widened, remembering the sounds Ransom made when she came, the strength she possessed when she bucked against her, her back arching beautifully into that perfect form only good sex could create. She should have remembered, then, how fit the other woman was when Ransom's lips curved into an inviting smile that masked her true intentions.

"Come up here," Ransom commanded, pulling the smaller woman up as easily as she had thrown her down on the training mat down in the basement. Victoria found herself straddling Ransom's head, a pair of wandering hands sliding down her back until they found her ass. Mischievous green eyes looked up at her from between her thighs as she licked her lips in anticipation.

"Hold on," Ransom suggested, her lips curving into an evil grin one short second before grasping her hips and pulling her down. Before she could ask why, a sharp tongue slipped between her thighs, spreading already swollen lips to lap along her center.

The sudden movement compromised her balance. She reached out, grasping at anything. Her fingertips scrabbled against the headboard, then found the rounded edge of the heavy wooden rail along the top. Her fingers

311

convulsed around the rail, nails digging into the dark finish.

Where Victoria's approach to sex was all about logic and progression, Ransom worked on instinct, her tongue running wild until she found the right rhythm and pressure to quickly send Victoria over the edge.

She felt a flash of unwanted embarrassment at finishing so quickly, followed by a short lived and entirely irrational sense of being cheated. Her forehead found the headboard rail. She could barely feel her legs, and what she could move felt as floppy as rubber bands.

Before Victoria could recover, Ransom slipped out from under her and twisted around, covering her with her own body. One hand shot out to capture hers, so that they were both gripping the headboard together. Victoria was still kneeling, facing the headboard, and now she couldn't move, not with Ransom's fingers laced across hers.

Ransom pulled her upright, supporting her in a close embrace while bared lips found her shoulder, her warm body pressed tightly against her backside.

"Can you support yourself now?" Ransom whispered.

"Yes."

"Good. Don't let go."

Victoria shivered in anticipation when she felt Ransom's free hand caress along her back, slowly tracing a pattern along her spine, tickling along her ribs until she skimmed dull nails across her ass teasingly. An insistent thigh pushed her knees farther apart, opening her to further exploration. Long fingers slid along sensitive flesh, making Victoria moan and buck against the inquisitive digits. Those long fingers dipped inside her, only to abandon her needy flesh to spread the copious moisture everywhere. The lazy circling continued until the moment Victoria thought she would scream from frustration. Ransom made a sound, deep in her throat. She wasn't immune to this teasing play, and Victoria knew she could end this game if she just asked her to.

"Ah, Ransom. Please. Don't tease anymore." She begged for release from the ache sitting deep in her belly, the need that only Ransom could fill.

Ransom took her from behind. Unable to move freely, her hand captured in Ransom's along the top of the headboard, she was totally at the other woman's mercy. Her desire was an unquenched storm beating against the inside of her skull. It wrapped itself around her spine, electrifying nerves until her entire body tingled with unclaimed potential, and Ransom was her lightning rod.

"God, you feel good," Victoria cried out, feeling that potential start to spin out of control.

Ransom's rhythm faltered for just a moment, slowing the inevitable rise in passion before sending it into overdrive when Ransom twisted her fingers inside her, searching for that one sweet spot that would send her over the edge.

Her breasts heaved as she tried to breathe past the waiting orgasm, her movements becoming desperate as the illusive spark failed to ignite until Ransom released her hand. She reared up, able to push back against each powerful thrust. Her pulse pounded in her temples and between her legs as ecstasy flooded her veins, blinding her to the world around her. She screamed aloud and clamped down on Ransom's fingers, riding her orgasm to completion. Her fingers spasmed around the headboard, digging her nails into the heavy wood until she could feel the finish give way beneath the blunt tips.

Exhausted, the two women collapsed onto the mattress, a throbbing puddle of limbs held together by breathless laughter.

"I think that will do it," Ransom finally said, reaching behind her to pull one of the sheets over them.

"I think so." Victoria glanced down at her hands. Surprised to find her manicure still intact, she wondered if the headboard had fared as well as her nails. She supposed she could find out if she was willing to move, but Ransom's chest made too good of a pillow, one she wasn't willing to abandon to satisfy her warped curiosity.

She cuddled in closer, content to listen to Ransom's heart beat for a while.

"Ransom?"

"Hmm?" Ransom asked drowsily. She hadn't quite fallen asleep, but she was definitely partway there.

"I'm going to miss you," Victoria admitted, trying to fight the melancholy mood coming over her. Ransom's hand found hers, and their fingers locked together in a very different way. It was sweet and mellow and it made her want to stay just like this forever.

Ransom raised her head, propping it up on an elbow. "What's wrong?"

"A week ago I was wondering if this scary, crazy stalker thing was ever going to end. Every day I was here was another day away from my practice, my home, my friends, everything. The only thing that made it all worthwhile was having you here with me. Now that it's all over, it feels weird going back home."

Ransom understood what she was saying, probably more than most. "I get that. These last few weeks were traumatic, terrifying even. That sort of stress stays with you, and when it goes away, you feel lost."

She had felt that way the minute her unit landed back in the states. Deployments were a huge ball of shit all rolled up in a one-year increment. Terrifying one day, mind-numbingly boring the next. Too hot, too cold, humid, dry...full of bugs and bad food, but you had your unit...your family to keep you going.

The minute you walked off that plane, you were expected to leave all of that behind. Being home meant returning to civilization, with all the neat, happy civilized ways of handling things. Normal, mundane things. Dull things. Nothing felt real because nothing carried that sharp edge you had gotten used to. Victoria had just lost that sharp edge and was noticing its absence. Her world had just become less colorful by becoming more comfortable and that was what was bothering her.

Victoria looked up at her. "Are you the therapist now?"

"Nope, I just know what it feels like to be addicted to the thrill of danger. It makes everything else in life pale in comparison."

"Everything?" Victoria purposefully ran her gaze down the length of Ransom's body.

"Mm. Almost everything." Ransom kissed Victoria's forehead. They could talk about this all night but what she needed was time, not talk. "I'd love to lie here all afternoon, but I've got things to do still."

"I know, me too," Victoria said. She needed to call Samuel and arrange for him to come pick her up. It was a Sunday so the only thing she might be interrupting was a round of tennis at the gym, and he could live without that.

She and Samuel had a lot to talk about and the long drive would be a perfect time for them to discuss her client hours. All she needed to do was drop one day from her schedule and she could easily run a Tuesday, Thursday, Saturday practice. That would make commuting to Johnsonville possible. She wouldn't have to choose between her work and Ransom. She could have both. It wouldn't be easy, but it would be doable.

"And dinner?" Ransom's pitiful starving waif expression was absolutely adorable and completely contrived, but it worked.

"And dinner," Victoria agreed.

# Chapter Thirty-Two

"Good morning, Sunshine!"

Victoria opened one bleary eye to find Ransom standing next to the bed, fully clothed and ready to start the day. She groaned and rolled over, blindly searching for the covers and tossing them back over her head. "You are way too peppy this morning."

"And you've slept in way too late."

Victoria gave up and rolled back over. "It's Sunday. Why are you dressed like that?"

"Roy called. I have to go into the office and start filling out paperwork. He's serious about me learning the job and as he put it 'what better time than now?' since we have to get your stalker transferred this week."

"That sucks," Victoria muttered around a huge yawn. "And it's not my fault I'm tired. You're the one who kept me up late."

"All the better to remember me by, my dear." Ransom leaned down and kissed her forehead. "Now hop up like a bunny and get dressed or you'll miss breakfast."

Victoria perked up a bit at the mention of food. "Breakfast? You made food?"

"Yup. Coffee and pop-tarts. The breakfast of champions." Ransom chuckled. "I even gave up the cinnamon one's for you, and those are my favorite."

"Infant," Victoria teased. Ransom was too perky, probably already hopped up on caffeine and sugar by the looks of it. "You can have the pop-tarts. I'll stick with the coffee."

"Suit yourself." Ransom shrugged and tucked the deputy's badge in her belt. The 9mm had found a new home in a shiny black leather holster on her left hip.

"That looks nice," Victoria had to admit.

Ransom looked down at herself and scoffed. "Don't get used to it. I hear that Roy already called in an order for my uniform shirt. Too bad I can't quit today."

"What do you mean?"

Ransom sat down on the bed next to Victoria. "You know that just because we caught this guy that it's not over yet? We've still got a long way to go to prove he's the one that's been stalking you, and then it has to go through the court system. Roy really roped me in this time. I won't give up this badge until I know this guy is behind one set of bars or another, but it could take months...years even, before this is over for good."

Ransom hated being the one to give Victoria the bad news. She had been so excited to get back to her life yesterday that Ransom had let it slide. Hell, she had ridden that happy train right alongside her, but today was another day. Today Victoria was planning on leaving, and that meant she was going to be too far away from her to be of any use. *At least Samuel will be around. He's good in a pinch. Not as good as me, but at least he's another set of eyes watching out for her.*

"Oh." Victoria's cheerful little bubble didn't pop completely, but it did deflate a bit. "I didn't even think about that. Should I call and cancel my trip home?"

"No. I think we'll be okay. Just do me one favor? Keep the .380 close to you and stay aware of your surroundings. If anything, and I mean anything, happens that makes you feel the least bit hinky...you haul out of there and call me."

"Isn't that taking things a bit far? I mean, everything fits. Do you really think I'm still in danger?"

"No." Ransom frowned and shifted her feet. "I don't think so. Maybe I'm being paranoid. It's hard for me to turn it off."

"I understand. And if it will make you feel better, I'll be extra careful."

"Good."

***

Ransom left soon after that, with a firm promise from Victoria that she would call her the minute Samuel showed up. "Don't leave until I get back. I haven't seen Samuel in a while either, it would be nice to pick on the old man for a few before you all leave."

The solo Jeep ride into town felt strange after having Victoria riding shotgun the last few weeks but this was her last chance to look at the case files before she left. *There was something*...Ransom rubbed the back of her neck, trying to get rid of the prickling sensation crawling up her spine. Matthew Theodosis was the perfect stalker. Everything about him, his history, his growing obsession with Victoria, everything...it all matched. So why was it bothering her so much?

*It was too easy.*

Once she got to the Sheriff's office and started pouring over the files, her sense that something was very wrong with the whole thing just kept growing. Two cups of coffee and two hours later, her eyes started to blur with the effort to find some hidden message she just knew they missed. "Ach, time to take a break."

Ransom went in search of more coffee and ran straight into Roy. She barely managed to keep either of them from wearing the hot liquid. As strong as it was, it would probably eat right through her shoes and start on the floor wax, mutate into some alien creature and murder them all before Church let out at noon.

"Shit, Roy, what the hell are you doing here?" Usually they had minimal staff on Sunday, someone to man the switchboard and an officer to handle any other calls.

"We have a prisoner, remember? Have to rotate officers through 24/7 until we get him moved." Roy sounded grumpy. He must have drawn a short straw, trying to play fair with his officers and volunteering his Sunday morning so they could have more time with their families. That was one of the things she did like about him. "What about you? Why are you here?"

"I wanted to look at some files while it was quiet."

Roy raised his eyebrows at her and sat himself down at the edge of the desk she had taken over. "You mean Victoria's stalker in there? Why?"

*Great, now I'm not ever going to get rid of him.* Ransom groaned, putting her coffee on the desk and plopping back down in her seat. "I don't really know. Something's just bothering me about the whole thing."

"Again, why?" Roy wasn't about to let up. "You have good instincts, Ransom. Don't ignore them. If you think there's something we're missing, keep looking until you find it. We have this guy until tomorrow morning. Try to find whatever you're looking for before then."

*Yeah, but Victoria will be gone by then. That's not fast enough.* Ransom sighed and flipped opened another plain manila folder. The glossies Samuel had given her slid out. Photos from the stalker. Well framed out, semi-professional looking black and whites. The kind you could produce in a home lab. A few smaller photos fell out. These were from the PD. Color shots of the black rose left at Victoria's house after Samuel had spirited her away. This one they had found in her bed. She leaned forward to get a closer look. The same deep black/red velveteen petals and dark green leaves. They made the blood-red nail polish painted neatly along the tip of each thorn all the more garish in contrast.

Ransom rubbed her eyes and tried not to let her frustration get the best of her. It didn't help that there was someone sitting in a cell not 40 feet away from her that probably had all of the answers she needed and she couldn't get them out of him.

Her cell phone started ringing.

*Victoria.* Her call should have been a welcome distraction, but it also represented the last turn of the hourglass. Ransom glanced up at the clock on the wall. It was only 10:30.

*Shit. He's early.* Her timeline had been tight enough as it was, now it was practically non-existent.

"Hey." Ransom picked up the phone on the second ring.

"Hi," Victoria answered back. She sounded out of breath, or excited about something. "Guess what!"

"I have no idea." Ransom shook her head. *What was going on out there?*

"Samuel had car trouble so he sent Bridget to pick me up."

*Bridget?* Ransom leaned back in her chair. "That's your assistant from work, right?"

"Yes, I had wanted to talk to Samuel on the way back, but that can wait until tomorrow."

*I wanted to talk to him, too.* Ransom could practically hear Victoria smiling over the phone. "You said something about lunch. Will Roy let you go so you can come home? I'd love it if you two could meet."

"Hi, Ransom!" An equally breathless, girlish voice made its way through the phone to her. The two of them sounded like they were having a grand old time.

"Bridget says hi," Victoria said.

"I heard," Ransom drawled. *How could I have not heard?*

"So, about lunch?" Victoria asked again.

"I think I should be able to get out of here by then," Ransom sighed.

There was no escape. It was either go, or miss saying goodbye to Victoria.

"You know what. Maybe you can help me out. Wait a minute." She shuffled through the files until she found what she needed. "This guy, Matthew. He's on some pretty powerful Antipsychotic drugs. When they brought him in they thought he was coming down off of something or withdrawing. Could his medications be causing some of the behaviors we witnessed?"

"They could be. The agitation and restlessness, certainly."

"What about the hand tremors?" Ransom pulled out another form. Matthew's signature was a painful scrawl that scribbled across half of the paper. She'd seen 2nd graders with better handwriting skills.

"Dyskinesia? Certainly, why?"

"Just making sure I understand everything I'm reading here." Ransom frowned at the mess on her desk, her gaze falling on the rose once again. *What kind of sick fucker sends black roses?* "Look, I'll get this done and head up in a few, okay?"

"Okay. Hey, Bridget wants to know if you could stop on the way up and buy a case of Pepsi and some fresh hamburger for lunch? I didn't defrost anything."

"Sure." Ransom scribbled down her request on a yellow sticky and stuffed it in her chest pocket. "Is that it?"

"I love you."

"I love you, too."

"Aww, isn't that sweet?"

"Fuck off, Roy."

"Hey, is that any way to talk to your boss?" Roy peeled himself away from the wall he had been holding up.

"It's a way, maybe not the right way, but it's a way," Ransom grumbled, tossing her pen down on her desk.

"I take it you found something odd in the file?"

Ransom rubbed her face, trying to get some feeling back into it after sitting still for so long. "I don't know. I want to say I'm just being paranoid, I really do. But look at this."

She slid the photo of the rose over to Roy.

"Okay, so?"

"I have one just like it up at the house. Each thorn painted bright red just like in the photo there. Meticulously painted, Roy. Not a single spill anywhere. That guy in there? He can't even sign his name. How the fuck did he do this?"

"Good question." Roy looked down at the photo again. "What's it painted with?"

"It's hard. I thought it looked like nail polish. Victoria wears a similar color." Ransom jumped up. "Oh, fuck!"

"What?"

"Where's the damn report on the break in? The one at Samuel's office?"

She found it, then tore through it looking for one specific notation. "What the hell? Didn't they check for fingerprints?"

"Of course they did. There weren't any." Roy was starting to get concerned. Ransom was way too agitated about a simple fingerprint report. "That's not so unusual. Thieves often wear gloves when they break into places."

"Yeah? Only this guy isn't a thief. He's a freaking nutcase that can't stop touching himself let alone everything else around him."

"What are you saying? That he wasn't the one who broke into the office? We have an eyewitness placing him there."

"Yeah, we do." Ransom felt her blood go cold. Her mind raced through a dozen possibilities, from best to worst-case scenarios. It could still be a mistake on her part, it didn't have to mean what she thought it meant.

*But there's one sure way to find out.*

"I need to make a phone call." Ransom closed her eyes, took a deep breath, and found that calm inside herself that let her forget her fear. There was nothing left but cold anger and determination. *For her sake, please let me be wrong.*

"Samuel, I need to know why you sent Bridget to pick up Victoria."

"I did no such thing." Samuel managed to sound offended and anxious at the same time. "I was actually just getting ready to leave."

"So, you're not having car problems?"

"What? Hold on." A muffled curse followed close behind a louder, clearer one.

"Shit. I am now. What's going on? Why is Bridget there? Better yet, how did Bridget know where Victoria was?"

"Those are all good questions, Sammy," Ransom snarled. "I'll ask her when I get the chance."

*If the woman stays alive long enough to tell me how she orchestrated this whole thing,* Ransom added, wisely keeping that thought to herself.

"Son of a bitch." She wished she had called Samuel on the office phone, slamming that down on the receiver would have felt so good. Hanging up a cell phone just didn't have the same impact. "I have to go."

"Now hold on, Ransom." Roy caught her mid-stride, pulling her back by the arm before she made it two steps. He pretended to ignore the fact that her free hand went straight for the 9mm at her waist, although his bladder wasn't quite as brave as the rest of him. "You can't just go off half-cocked like this anymore. You have that badge. There's rules."

Ransom looked down at Roy's hand, then slowly raised her head. Eyes the color of chipped emeralds and colder than frost stared him down. "Let me go, Roy. You can have the badge. I never wanted it, anyway. But, unless you plan on arresting me, I'm leaving now. Sure, you might make it up there in time. You'll do your best like you always do, but if that woman hurts Victoria..." Ransom left the rest of her threat unspoken. They glared at each other for far too long. Ransom felt every second counting off in drops of blood. She relaxed her stance, just an iota, and removed her hand from her gun. "Don't you see? It has to be me. She's expecting me. Victoria's girlfriend. Not the entire Sheriff's department coming down on her. All you'll do is create a hostage situation. Let me do this, my way."

Roy dropped his hand. "Fine. I'll give you a ten-minute head start, then I'm coming in behind you. I'll even come in running silent."

"No," Ransom said, surprising Roy with her response. "Give me twenty minutes, run hot up to the lower gates...then slow it to a crawl. Give me a couple of extra minutes."

A little extra pressure was always exciting. Like agitating a bottle of champagne, you never knew when the cork might pop.

Ransom left Roy standing in the middle of the Sheriff's office. He listened for the Jeep, expecting to hear tires peeling out of the parking lot, but there was nothing. That showed a level of self-control that most people would never achieve. *Maybe Buddy, but that was it,* he thought, heading for his office to get a few things before following behind her.

# Chapter Thirty-Three

Erica Ford wanted to puke, listening to Victoria coo over Ransom like a lovesick dove. *How sickly sweet these two are. I just can't stand it.*

"Is she bringing the food?" she asked, slipping back into Bridget mode an instant before Victoria turned around to face her. She hated the vacuous woman, all the way down to her clothes and the way she spoke...but she was useful. Everyone trusted Bridget, they thought she was a wonderful person. Perky even. Perky was annoying. Would they still love Bridget if she walked and talked like Erica? She doubted it.

"Yes, she said she'd get here as soon as possible." Victoria beamed at her protégé. "I still can't believe that you're here. It's so good to see a friendly face after being gone for so long!"

"I know. I've missed our lunch dates. I feel like I have been floundering through my classes without your help." Bridget smiled and suffered through the second enthusiastic hug of the morning. "But I have to admit I'm a little jealous. From the sound of things, it wasn't all horrible. At least this guy, what's his name?"

"Matthew."

"Matthew. Yes. At least he didn't find you here." Bridget sniffed and brushed her hair back behind her ear, exposing the colorful bruise gracing her right temple. Victoria's eyes widened. The horrified expression on her face was exactly what she was looking for, as was the stuttered apology Victoria kept stumbling over. Bridget bit her lip and turned her face away a little. Would Victoria think the gleam in her eye was an attempt to hold back tears? Let her. She was trying not to smile at how easy it was to manipulate the woman. She changed tactics, narrowing her eyes and gazing slyly at Victoria. "And Ransom, I assume she's sexy as hell if you went after her during all of this. Downright irresistible, I'd have to say."

The insinuation was clear. Victoria went from apologetic to self-conscious in one hot second. "Bridget!"

"What? Do you think you could just disappear off the face off the earth for a 'family emergency' and not tell me the truth without paying for it? I'm supposed to be your friend, and you lied to me."

Just the right amount of righteous anger and pouting made Bridget sound like she was teasing. Victoria didn't even hear the threat couched in the friendly banter between them. Bridget shook her head and smiled forgivingly. "It's okay. Forget I said that. You were in danger and didn't know who to trust, I get that."

"I do trust you, Bridget." Victoria still felt guilty about keeping her in the dark. "I wanted to tell you, believe me. I could have used your sense of humor more than once the last few weeks."

*I'm sure you could have.* Bridget realized she was tapping her fingernails against the armchair fabric. She was bored, but it wouldn't do to let Victoria know that. "Me too. It's been hell at work without you."

She took a deep breath and threw up her hands, tossing away her frustration like so much imaginary confetti. "But let's not talk about work and school. Tell me all about you and Ransom. You know I was teasing you earlier. But really, what's she like?"

"She's amazing, and you're right. She is hot." Victoria chuckled at Bridget's all too accurate assessment. "You know, I think I mentioned her to you before, a long time ago."

"How? I thought you two just met?"

"That's the thing. We didn't. Do you remember that night we went out for drinks after your finals?" Victoria made a face. Tequila was evil, and she hadn't been able to drink the stuff since that night. "We were daring each other to reveal our deepest, darkest secrets, and I told you about that wild weekend I spent with a woman..."

"The one who was in the Navy?" Bridget asked. "She was getting shipped out the next day, wasn't she?"

"Yes."

"Wait, a minute. Ransom was that woman? The woman you were so hot to trot about all those years ago?" Bridget was rarely surprised by anything, in fact, she made it a point to always be one step ahead of everyone else around her. Perhaps that was why she didn't watch what she said next as carefully as she ought to have. "And now she's a Deputy here in town, with the Sheriff's department."

"Yes," Victoria said, then furrowed her brows at the other woman. She didn't remember mentioning Ransom's new job. "How did you know that?"

"Oh, I think I saw the name on one of the reports, you know, when they wanted me to identify the person who broke into the office."

"Yes, let's talk about that, why don't we?" Ransom's voice came out of nowhere.

Victoria spun around. Ransom was standing just a few feet away from her. Somehow she had made it into the house, through the kitchen and into the living room without alerting either of them to her presence. "What? Ransom what are you doing? It's just Bridget." She half stood up, then sat back down. Her heart in her throat, confused and frightened, she watched Ransom step closer, her 9mm trained on the other woman.

"Ransom, please, put the gun down."

"Victoria, get out of the way." Ransom's voice was cold as ice, but the look in her eyes was pure death. "Nice to finally meet you, Bridget. Now. Victoria asked you a question that I would very much like to hear the answer to. How did you know I was working with the Sheriff's department?"

"I told you, I saw it..."

"Nah. You can do better than that. I just talked to Samuel. He didn't send you here this morning, which means you have another agenda going on. Talk."

"Fine," Bridget snarled. "I saw you two, together, at the station. It was a right nice argument you were having too, until it got all lovey-dovey again. I just wish I was close enough to hear what it was all about. At least that little snit you were having let me follow you up to the house here. Which, by the way...nice place."

"It's not mine."

"Oh, I know that. Samuel's got his own little box of secrets tucked away, doesn't he? Private Investigator's and hired gun's on the payroll. Doesn't it make you wonder what he's been up to in his spare time? I could tell you." A feral grin lit up her face.

"Don't listen to her," Ransom growled, keeping her attention firmly on the woman who, up until today, was someone that Victoria trusted unconditionally.

"What is she talking about?" Victoria asked.

"Nothing, she's just trying to get into your head." Ransom shifted her position to get a clearer shot. She needed Victoria out of the danger zone now.

"Please, Victoria. Just get behind me. All you need to know is that Matthew wasn't acting alone. He had help. Her help."

"That's just ridiculous. Why would she do that?"

"Because she's the freaking stalker, Victoria. That's why." Ransom watched Bridget's face closely, looking for some kind of tell from the other woman to prove her right. A muscle jumped at the corner of her eye and something closer to hate than surprise flashed through her eyes.

"I wasn't 'helping' anybody. Matthew was just a sorry, sad-ass-sack-of-shit that I thought would be fun to bring into play for a while. Poor little rich boy who played Alice for too many years...until all those pills he loved so much made him crazy. Tell me, Victoria. How long did it take you to recognize him? He didn't look that bad when I convinced him to leave his posh little rehab clinic. You're the one who told me how fixated he was on you in school.

I enjoyed breaking him, then sending him after you, all ready to cry at your feet and beg for forgiveness. It's too bad you caught him first, I really wanted to know what would have happened when he realized you barely remembered him. He was quite volatile emotionally." Bridget smiled at them, a slow, creeping smile that transformed her into a completely different person.

Without warning, she lunged forward. Victoria gasped and took a step back to avoid her. Arms wind milling, her foot tangled in the coffee table leg, Victoria fell backwards.

Ransom launched into action. She lowered her weapon so she could catch Victoria. Pulling her up and around, she dragged Victoria away from the other woman, then swung her weapon in an easy arc to zero back on her target. *Fuck.* A pistol, very similar to the one she had gifted Victoria, appeared in Bridget's hand seemingly out of nowhere.

"Drop it," she commanded, but Bridget just laughed at her.

"Why don't you just drop yours?"

"You know I won't do that." Ransom's gaze never left the other woman's face.

"Jesus, Ransom. I'm so sorry." Victoria trembled against her. Ransom had a sneaking suspicion she was getting a good look at the real Bridget, the one hiding behind a very carefully constructed mask. "What are you doing, Bridget? This isn't you."

"You're right, it isn't. My name isn't Bridget." She shrugged and gestured with the pistol. "Well, technically, it is...but things change, don't they?"

The woman was starting to ramble. Ransom took Victoria's hand, hoping to take advantage of her confusion. "Go, get to a safe place. This is my fight now."

"No!" The pistol went off, leaving a wound in the couch, exposing white stuffing that could have been somebody's innards. "You aren't going anywhere."

Ransom exhaled. The 9mm was a fixed point in space—the site was just a formality. She knew if she squeezed the trigger, a red rose would blossom like a third eye in the center of Bridget's forehead. Her finger itched to do it, to just finish this tiresome tirade, but she held fast, determined to do things by the book. She would try it Roy's way...at least until she could honestly say it didn't work.

"Bridget!" Victoria screamed in terror. "Stop this."

"It's Erica," she snapped. "Stop calling me Bridget, I hate being Bridget."

*She said she hated being Bridget, not being called Bridget.*

"Okay, Erica." Ransom made sure to use the name she wanted to be called by. "What do you think this is all going to accomplish? You have to realize this isn't going to end well."

"And whose fault is that? Yours," Erica screeched. "You could have just shown up with the damn Pepsi and burgers. We could have had a nice lunch, and we would have been on our way. You could have kissed your girlfriend goodbye one last time, and kept on living your boring little life out here, but no! You had to play super cop and figure everything out just in time to save the girl. But you aren't going to save the girl, are you?"

"Four."

"What?"

"I didn't play anything. It wasn't all that hard to figure out the clues you left behind." Ransom made sure to toss an extra dose of sarcasm in, let it drip all over her next sentence. "Let me guess? You tore up Samuel's office yourself, then took a couple whacks across the face with a door frame to make it look real? That's how you finally found us."

"Very good, Deputy. Only I went the extra step. The asshole who thought he could do this to me for fun is laying on a slab in the morgue. No loss to society, so don't worry too much. Just another pimp who thought I'd be easy meat." Erica smirked, remembering how much the man cried once he realized his mistake. "He was wrong."

Victoria felt Ransom stiffen next to her.

"Three," the number was uttered just above a whisper. Victoria looked up at Ransom, a question in her eyes. A quick shake of her head, so subtle it could have been explained away as a tic, told her not to say anything.

"That's impressive. I guess we could stand here all day and compare kills, but I think I've already disturbed your timeline. Why don't we just cut to the chase? What's your endgame here?"

"You don't want to know why I've done this?" Erica looked genuinely surprised. "You aren't the least bit curious?"

"No." Ransom managed to sound bored. "Frankly, it doesn't matter to me why someone decides to terrorize and kill people. All that matters to me is that you consciously chose to do it."

"Just like that, huh?" Erica sneered, then turned her attention back to Victoria. "And what about you? Where do you fall in this? Is it nature or nurture? Or a little of both, hmm? What about the shitty childhood excuse? You should know all about that, Victoria, since you did such a good job at making sure my childhood was a fucked up mess."

"You're Erica B," Victoria whispered. "But your last name wasn't Ford, it was Timmons." Erica looked so different now, nothing like the gangly teenager she had met so many years ago.

"My adopted name," Erica corrected her. "There's a cute trick, if you know how to do it. Getting adopted as a child gives you a new birth certificate, did you know that? But if you keep all your original documentation? It's like the adoption never happened. Like it should have never happened."

"That's not my fault, Erica. I didn't have anything to do with your adoption, only your stepfather's arrest a few years later."

"Yes," Erica bellowed, "and do you know what happened after that? My mother blamed me for everything. We lost our house, she lost her way...and I was put in the system. One shitty foster parent after another. It was hell. All because you people didn't get it right the first time and then you screwed me over the second time."

"So why come after me now, after all these years. I don't understand?"

"Of course you don't," Erica sighed, the gun wavered in her hand before she brought it back up again. "Everyone else involved is gone. I've taken care of them. But it's not over yet. It won't be over until everyone involved is dead and gone and I can rest."

"I don't even hate you, not really. You tried, even though you finally gave up and left, you were one that did try for a while." Tears started falling down Erica's face. "I saved you for last because you weren't the worst, and now all my plans are ruined."

"Two."

Ransom's arm was getting tired. The 9mm was a fine weapon, but it was heavy, and Erica was working on madness and fueled by her emotions. Fatigue would get to her soon enough, and then she would be forced to choose. From what she'd been saying, Ransom didn't think she'd just give up and drop her weapon. The girl needed help, not a bullet, but she wasn't sure if she hadn't lost that chance a long time ago when she decided to become judge, jury and executioner.

"You killed all those people."

"They deserved it." Erica pushed her jaw out, stubbornly refusing to take any responsibility for her actions.

"Including your mother?"

"She was a coward. She killed herself. Slowly...with drugs and booze. I don't mourn her passing."

"I don't believe that," Victoria said, finally finding her voice. "I don't think you believe that either. Guilt killed your mother, not DSS and certainly not you. She chose to marry that man, knowing what kind of monster she was bringing into your home. She hid his history from us so we'd approve your adoption, then kept hiding his crimes until the police caught him. He was the evil in your house, Bridg...er, Erica, not us."

She took a deep breath and pressed on, despite being more terrified than she'd ever been in her entire life. "What you're doing now. It's no different. It's suicide. You're using us to kill yourself."

"No, I'm not."

"Yes, you are and I will tell you why. Ransom will not let you hurt me. She will not let you leave here and she will certainly not let you walk away, not after what you've done."

"I could just shoot her," Erica said.

"Are you that good of a shot?" Ransom asked. "I am."

Ransom's cool response made Victoria shiver.

"One."

"Why do you keep counting down?" Erica screamed.

"Because you have one minute to decide what happens between us and then I'm done," Ransom said, very calmly. "The cavalry is on the way and once they show up, I can't help you anymore."

The faint sound of sirens made it to her ears. She was sure that in Erica's state of mind they sounded like all the hounds of hell baying after her. Ten heartbeats later and they grew even louder. There was no mistaking it, they were coming in closer by the second.

"Choose," Ransom said, loosening her grip on the 9mm one finger at a time before her hand went completely numb. Her shoulder was screaming. It was either end this now or lose control of her gun hand.

"I'm not going to prison, and I'm not going to end up in some mental facility so people can talk at me all day." Erica started shaking her head back and forth. Her knuckles whitened, and the gun started to waver, then slip towards Victoria's chest. "No way. That's worse than hell."

Ransom licked her lips. There was no way out of this. "Then I don't have a choice."

Ransom shoved her, hard, a loud bang following close behind. The pistols report deafened Victoria, then left a residual ringing in her ears that made it hard for her to hear. Through the claxon sound, someone screamed, then started hurling curses at the universe. Victoria shook her head to clear it, then regretted her decision immediately. The world was still tilted off its access and for some reason she couldn't find her footing in it yet. She looked around her and found Ransom kneeling on the floor, her gun back in its holster and Erica? She was lying on the ground, writhing around in pain.

"You asshole, you shot me."

"I did. I told you I would." Ransom didn't understand why the woman was fussing so much.

"You should have killed me. You told me you were a good shot. You fucking missed. I'm still alive," Erica hissed.

For all her concern about whether she was going to live or die over her wound, she kept her hand clamped over the bullet hole in her right shoulder.

Dark-red blood oozed out from between her fingers, but nothing spurted and none of it was bright red. She pulled out her cuffs. Roy would be there soon, but you could never be too careful.

"I am a good shot. If I'd wanted you dead, you'd be dead. If I'd wanted you maimed, you'd be maimed, but you aren't. You might have a little problem with that arm for a while, but you aren't going to bleed out." Ransom grinned up at Victoria even though she was addressing the woman bleeding on Samuel's living room rug. "I'm sorry to say it, but you're going to have to put up with getting talked at every day for a good long while."

"Are you okay?" This time she was asking Victoria.

"I'm fine," Victoria said, surprised to find that she meant it. She took in the entire scene. The woman she thought she knew, cuffed and bleeding on the floor. Their friendship had been nothing but a ruse. Erica's request for mentorship was nothing more than a carefully cultivated plan so she could get close to her. The sense of betrayal should have been overwhelming, but right now she just felt numb.

Her gaze flicked to Ransom, searching for any signs of stress. She had blood on her plain white shirt. That was to be expected after messing with Erica, but she kept staring at it, her brain trying to process what her eyes were telling her. The blood was slowly blossoming into a bright-red flower along the edge of Ransom's shirt, just below her right arm.

"Um, Ransom?" Victoria felt her heart skip a beat before it began to race out of control. "I think you've been shot."

# Chapter Thirty-Four

"I'm fine, Samuel. Really." Ransom sighed and let her head fall against the back of the couch. Staring at the ceiling was better than watching the two of them stare at her. "I am not going to go to the hospital, not for a scratch."

"The woman shot you, you should at least get it checked out," Samuel grumbled.

Ransom rolled her head forward. She was tired and her side hurt like a bitch, and those two wanted to give her the second degree over a flesh wound. "It's just a graze. It's not even bleeding anymore."

Victoria winced at the harsh tone Ransom used with her friend. "He's only worried about you, Ransom."

Ransom sighed and rolled her shoulders. They still ached after holding one position for so long, and she hoped nobody expected much more from her than finding her bed and falling into it, preferably staying there until next week. "I know he is, and that's why I'm not chewing him out for it."

She turned her attention back towards Samuel. "By the way, how the hell did you get here so quick? My math is telling me you should still be an hour out, at least...and that's if you left the minute I hung up. I thought your car was jacked up."

"It was. Bridget did a good job on my BMW." Samuel leaned forward and rubbed his hands together. His forehead wrinkled, like it always did when he was nervous. A weak smile replaced his scowl. "Good thing she didn't know about Betty."

"Betty? You pulled out your little pocket rocket and put her on the road?" Ransom was so shocked she sat straight up, a move she immediately regretted. Pain lanced across her side and something hot and wet trickled down along the edge of the bandage the Paramedics had taped on. She grunted and fell back against the cushions, then had to put up with several minutes of fussing by both Samuel and Victoria until she could convince the two of them that she was fine.

"Who's Betty?" Victoria asked.

"An old 1960 Porsche Speedster he's been restoring for like 20 years. He never takes it out of the garage, ever." Ransom smirked at Samuel. "You had to be doing, what, at least a hundred to get here this fast. How'd you avoid getting pulled over?"

"Luck?" Samuel asked, not even sure himself how he managed to do it. "I didn't even get a chance to enjoy my first ride out on the open road with her. I was so focused on getting here, I just jumped in and took off."

"Bullshit," Ransom called Samuel on his lie. "Admit it, you were having a James Bond moment the entire drive in."

He grinned and ducked his head. "Maybe. She's a sweet ride. But just to be clear, I was more worried about the two of you."

Victoria stood up. As much as she was enjoying the conversation, Ransom needed to get some rest, and she needed to have that heart to heart with Samuel.

*And honestly, I could use a change in scenery.* The cushion no one wanted to sit against still sprouted stuffing and no matter how much she tried to pretend otherwise, the dark stain working its way through the rug next to the coffee table was still blood. The urge to throw open every window in the room, just to get rid of the faint odor of gun powder and smoke, grew with every passing moment.

"Samuel, why don't we let Ransom get some rest," Victoria suggested.

Ransom yawned and stretched out on the couch. "I'm good right here. Whatever you guys need to talk about, just take it into the kitchen."

Samuel snorted, then vacated his chair. If Victoria thought she was being subtle, she was doing a terrible job of it. "I could use some coffee."

Ransom's eyes were already closed. She just waved them away without bothering to even look. "Go."

Victoria took Ransom's suggestion and headed for the kitchen. She also took her own suggestion and opened a couple of windows, then took a couple of deep breaths to clear her lungs.

"I can't believe she's taking a nap in there after what happened," Victoria said, unable to shake herself free from the events of the last few hours. "It's mildly disturbing."

"It's Ransom," Samuel simply said.

"That's true." Victoria turned on the coffee pot and sat down. Everything she had been holding in around Ransom just started spilling out until she was shaking and tears began to fall. "My God, Samuel. I can't believe it. Bridget or I guess Erica. I feel like a horrible failure. How could I work with this woman, day after day? Mentor her, be her friend, and all the while she was doing this? She so much as admitted to killing God knows how many other people. How did I not see her for what she was? My clients, you...how many people were at risk while this viper sat in our office and pretended to be something she wasn't?"

"She fooled me too, Victoria," Samuel said. "I was duped just as much as you were."

"And Ransom." Victoria looked away, her gaze automatically turning towards the other woman like a compass finding true north. "I listened to Erica, Samuel. Just long enough to doubt Ransom. It gave Erica the chance to pull her weapon. I could have gotten her killed."

"But you didn't."

"No, I didn't. But she did get hurt." Victoria took a deep breath, then decided it would just be easier to jump right in and say it. "I've had a lot of time to think about things these last few weeks. This isn't going to be easy for me, so please let me get it all out before you say anything."

"Today really hit home for me. It's not just about me, or my practice anymore. It's about a woman I met a long time ago and never thought I'd see again. When I realized that Ransom had been shot today, the only thing I could think about was how unfair life was. I already lost her once, Samuel, and I almost lost her again today. I can't go through that, not for a third time."

"What do you want to do?"

"I know what I need to do," Victoria admitted. "I'm just scared to death to do it. I've already started over once, doing it again? That's terrifying. Erica did accomplish one thing on her list. She screwed up my practice royally. I'm sure that was part of the fun for her. Now that it's done, I'm not sure if I want it back. Ransom needs me here, and from what I've seen and heard, the people here need me, too."

Samuel cleared his throat and steepled his fingers beneath his chin. "So, what you're telling me is you want to stay."

"Yes."

"And what do you need from me?"

"Absorb the rest of my clients. I'll help any way I can with the transition."

"And?" Samuel held her gaze and waited for her to finish.

"Tell me what I need to do for Ransom. I know this place is yours. I won't do anything that will jeopardize her home here. She still needs this job, and her sanctuary away from the world. It was generous of you to let me stay here while we dealt with the stalker situation but…"

Samuel held up his hand, forestalling any additional worry on Victoria's part. "Don't concern yourself. You're welcome for as long as Ransom wants to be caretaker here. In fact, I think I might have a solution that might solve your other problem as well. A little bird told me about Mrs. Johannsen's situation the other day. Frankly, I'm disappointed. I'm tired of the town council begging me for donations every year for their pet projects, only to discover that they are ignoring the town's neediest citizens. I think it's about time to put those funds to better use and start up a new program-one designed to help people just like Mrs. Johannsen. Do you know anyone that might be interested in something like that?"

Samuel grinned at the look on Victoria's face. "I thought so. We don't have to hash out the details right now. Go and take care of her. I'll take care of all the details, both here and back home. Meanwhile. I'm going to head out. Betty might have come out for her first jaunt since the 80's but I'll be damned if I'm going to let her out after dark. If I leave now, I'll make it home before sundown."

Ransom woke up the second they walked back into the room. "Is it dinner time yet?"

"Not my job, Ransom. I've got to run. You take care of yourself and don't give Victoria too much grief," Samuel said before bending down and giving her a quick hug so she didn't have to get up from the couch. "Victoria, we will talk more later this week...after everything has settled down."

"Later Sam," Ransom said, then scooted her hips over a little so Victoria could fit on the couch with her. The smooth growl of the antique Porsche made her smile. At the speed he was going, it would take him ten minutes to make it to the blacktop. "Poor Betty. He's going to be a nervous wreck by the time he gets home. I hope she doesn't get a ding or scratch anywhere. It might just devastate him to the point where he'll need therapy."

Victoria chuckled. "Now that's funny."

Ransom pulled herself up a little so she wasn't trying to talk to Victoria while she was laid flat out. She grimaced when the wound edges pulled against the bandage, then winced when Victoria accidentally brushed against her side with her elbow. "So, Samuel's gone. Erica's in jail where she belongs and all's well with the world again. I guess the big question is, when are you leaving?"

"Never, if that's okay with you?"

"What about your practice and your life in the City?"

"I figured out a few things today. It took me three years to get you back and just a second to almost lose you again. That tends to make a woman think about her priorities."

"It wasn't that close." Ransom downplayed her injury like it was nothing, but it could have been much, much worse. Victoria knew that. A couple of inches to the left and Ransom wouldn't be able to so easily wave away how much danger she had put herself in.

"Close enough." Victoria took Ransom's hand and squeezed it. It wasn't worth arguing over, not when there was so many other things to talk about. "I refuse to waste my time any longer. I'm not willing to compromise, or do this part time. I'm ready to jump in, feet first, without worrying about how deep the lake is. I want to be with you. I want to help all the people here that really need it, even if it means living in this little podunk town with a stubborn ass Sheriff and the best pizza in three counties. I've fallen in love with you, this place, the forest around us, everything."

"Wow, that's quite a speech," Ransom murmured, captivated at how impassioned Victoria became when she talked about her plans for the future. Her face lit up, glowing with an inner fire that Ransom recognized. Victoria had found something in her life worth fighting for, and it filled her with purpose. That was a rare thing, and Ransom wasn't about to do anything to snuff out that fragile flame.

"I hope you don't mind, because I'm afraid you're quite stuck with me," Victoria added, suddenly shy after speaking so boldly.

Ransom found her first genuine smile that day. She reached out and stroked Victoria's cheek, relishing how she moved into the caress. "Who's stuck with whom could be our first real argument, or, you could just kiss me and be done with it."

"Mm. The best way to ever end an argument."

Ransom closed her eyes and found peace in her heart. She had come home from the war looking for nothing more than a place of sanctuary, to be left alone to lick her wounds and deal with her life as it had been dealt to her. Her debts would haunt her forever, without any chance at redemption. She never expected to be freed from her past, until someone from her past walked back into her life and made her face her greatest fear. She had proven she could be responsible for someone again. She didn't fail in her mission... and in the end, she also managed to get the girl. It was a good way to end a story. There was just one loose end that needed tying up.

"Victoria?" Ransom kissed her one more time. "I think I'm ready to read those letters now."

# If you enjoyed this novel, please check out more offerings by Rhavensfyre.

Follow on Facebook @ Characters of Rhavensfyre

www.rhavensfyre.com

twitter@rhavensfyre

# Works by Rhavensfyre

## LIFE IS NOT A COUNTRY SONG

This romantic novella is book one of Chase and Rowan's adventures.

Rowan St. John is on her way back home with an empty horse trailer and down a driver.

Chase Meadows had it all, until she came home one day to find her lover in bed with another woman. Now she's left with nothing but her truck, her horse and a definite need to find a new start. California was about as far away from North Carolina and the past as she could go. All she had to do was get there with her pregnant mare, Smoothy—the only thing she had left in her name that she would never give up.

When Rowan St. John responds to her ad for a last minute horse transport, she thought she had finally gotten a break. A deal is struck that benefits both women, more than they ever expected.

## LOVE IS NOT A ROMANCE NOVEL

This romantic novella is book two of Chase and Rowan's adventures and the sequel to Life is Not a Country Song.

Chase and Rowan are given some time to learn more about each other when the last leg of their trip is delayed.

Rowan sees it as a way to show Chase everything the Southwest has to offer, including her, while Chase is more worried about earning her keep and making sure one special little colt is strong enough to travel. Trust and understanding are tested, and some internal demons are laid to rest against the backdrop of sun-kissed mesas and tall pines.

Both spiritual and sensual, the ladies discover that some journeys aren't measured by how many miles you travel, but by how far you are willing to take your heart.

## LIFE, LOVE, AND LOYALTY

This lesbian romance is the third in the popular Chase and Rowan Series. After a few detours along the way, Chase and Rowan have finally made it to California and are settling into their lives at the Flying S ranch. An urgent call sends them back on the road again when wildfires get close enough to threaten an old college friend's farm. Without a second thought, Rowan agrees to help evacuate her friend's horses, and from there on nothing goes as planned.

Rowan and Chase find themselves in a volatile situation that places them both in danger.

## A CHRISTMAS PROPOSAL:
## A CHASE AND ROWAN NOVELETTE

Chase and Rowan have been through a lot together but this Christmas will be their first. Plans change and Chase is still learning a lot about family, but when it comes to Rowan, she has a steep learning curve. This romantic novelette is exactly what it says, all you have to do is read till the end to find out if it's a yes or no. Of course, getting there is the best part of the story.

## TIE DYE AND FLANNEL

Dr.Stacie Phillips' comfortable, pragmatic life is about to be turned upside down. Dr. Phillips is a young Veterinarian caught up in her carefully constructed life, trying to protect her family, her new career, and most of all-her heart. Her best friend, Josie, only wants what is best for her, and if that means meddling in affairs of the heart she will do it. Josie has her own reasons for wanting Stacie to be happy, and the last thing she wants is Stacie putting off her life to help Josie deal with hers.

Stacie meets Maria, a free-spirited herbalist from Arizona, when her goddaughter Rowan literally runs into her at a farmer's market. Unfortunately, Rowan's mother, Josie finds out about the chance encounter and things start to spiral out of Stacie's control.

## LADYSMITH

There is a saying among the old ones, "If you dream of a mare, a MacLeod is sure to be near." Rohanna MacLeod grew up listening to her grandmother's stories of her family and the old country, the myths and legends of the Fae becoming dearer to her with each loss in her young life. True to her family name, Rohanna carries the MacLeod gift with horses. With single minded determination, she denies herself everything else that life offers in order to keep what is hers, to keep and preserve the family farm from an abusive stepmother she abhors.

Everything changes when she runs into trouble on the way to a horse show. A chance offer and a plain business card sends her to the Ladysmith, a farrier and blacksmith with a mysterious past.

Alexandria Strider is drawn into Rohanna's world. Caught between new bonds and old oaths, Alex holds the key to Rohanna's past and an unrealized destiny, if she can find the strength to do what is necessary.

## SABRE

During the Civil War, hundreds of women cut their hair and donned the uniform of the common soldier on both sides. History tells us they did it to follow their husbands and brothers to war, rather than stay behind to uncertain destiny. A few, though, found their freedom beneath the heavy wool uniform and shorn hair.

These are the few that are not spoken of, the ones who desired no husband and found liberation behind the blue or the gray. Meet JC. Resigned to a solitary life, an unexpected gift changes everything for this Union soldier.

## STEPPING OUT

Enter Micah and Olivia's world from Switching Gears and enjoy a tale of a night out on the town that was so deliciously naughty it was too hot to keep hidden away. Join Micah as she takes a walk through her past, leathers and all, for a night she soon won't forget. What can we say? Some fantasies can't be put to sleep until they are put to bed.

## THE POTTER'S WHEEL

Would you dare love a Goddess?
The Potter's Wheel is a lesbian erotic romance. A short tale of epic love, both lost and found, and the undeniable passion between two unique and otherworldly women.

## THE MISADVENTURES OF TWO RELUCTANT ZOMBIE HUNTERS: ZOMBIES AT THE CON

No one expects the zombie apocalypse...not even those who make a living pretending it exists. When a troupe of Zombie Hunters find themselves in the midst of a real zombie apocalypse they have to find a way to escape. After all, there aren't any real weapons allowed at the Con...and only wits and ingenuity will keep them alive long enough to make it home.

## REST AND RELAXATION

Prescribed some R & R, overworked executive Allyse DeLeon heads for the country, where she meets quirky loner and farm owner, Dani Saxon. Dani. Allyse finds herself attracted to this unique and solitary woman, and soon finds out her heart is in more danger there than it ever was back home.

## SWITCHING GEARS

A year after Micah Connolly walked out of Olivia Holden's life, Olivia spots her on the streets of New York, giving her a much needed second chance.

The problem?

Micah isn't the quiet intern Olivia remembers. She's darker, edgier, and carrying around a secret blacker than the leathers she wears. Olivia thought she preferred being the one in charge, until this new Micah shows her another path.

Intense, sensual and transformative, this novel isn't your standard romance. Secrets have to be told, and the risk is great…but if Olivia and Micah can find their way, the rewards will be well worth it.